EVERYTHING YOU ARE

BRITTNEY LAUREN

Author's Note

Everything You Are is a work of fiction and while it's a romance first and foremost there are some serious elements that I'd like to make note of before you take a trip back into Fairvale.

Mentions of military related PTSD, childhood neglect, alcoholism, some on page violence (not between main characters), explicit language, prior abusive relationship.

Resources for help can be found at the end of the book.

If any of these could be a trigger for you this may not be the book for you and that's okay.

Xo - Brittney

For anyone that's ever felt like a second choice.
And for Richard, for always putting me first.

He showed me his scars, and in return he let me pretend that I had none.
- Circe, Madeline Miller

The Playlist

1. "The Prophecy" - Taylor Swift

2. "What I See" - CJ Fam, Song House

3. "Feel Like This" - Ingrid Andress

4. "Rain" - Sleep Token

5. "Feathered Indians" - Tyler Childers

6. "Risk" - Gracie Abrams

7. "Begin Again" - Taylor Swift

8. "I Could Fall In Love" - Selena

9. "You Should Probably Leave" - Chris Stapleton

10. "Kaleidoscope" - Chapell Roan

11. "Now That I found Her" - GIO DARA

12. "sun to me" - mgk

13. "Cover Me Up" - Morgan Wallen

14. "Beginning Middle End" - Leah Noble

Listen on Spotify

ONE

Abby

THE WORLD WAS MORE than the tangible parts we saw on the surface. Or at least that's what I liked to believe. Horoscopes, manifesting, the power of crystals, all of it sounded about right to me. Soulmates—absolutely; curses—the jury was still out on that one. You name it, I'd probably fallen down an internet rabbit hole and decided it was truth. But curses, that one I wasn't quite sure about, yet. Honestly, who knew how any of it worked or if it was real, but if it was, then I think I may be cursed.

Okay, cursed was a bit dramatic, even for me, but lately, I had been waking up more frequently only to lay in bed and wonder where I went wrong. At what point in my life did I mess up that this lonely version of my life was the one I was forced to endure?

I liked to think that I was a good person, or at least I thought I was a good person. I'd never done anything horribly wrong in my life. Maybe an occasional little white lie here and there. But who hadn't? There was nothing about my past that I would shrink away from. There were no skeletons that could be drug out of my closet and hung up to scare me into submission.

All in all, I was a basic, maybe a little boring, suburban woman. I was a product of my environment if anything, and maybe not the greatest environment, but I managed to live by the most simple rule: what you put into the universe, you got out of the universe.

But still, every once in a while, I wondered if maybe I was cursed. Maybe the universe did hate me. That had to be the only reason for my current situation.

It seemed that no matter how hard I tried, nothing changed. No amount of self help books, meditation, or journaling helped. It didn't matter how many crystals I bought and put throughout my house or in my car or in my purse. I was always overlooked in the love category.

It shouldn't be this hard. In fact, love shouldn't be hard at all. Otherwise, what would be the point?

Growing up, my sister had an unyielding devotion to movies with fairytale endings. Princesses who found their prince, the simple farm girl who found true love in an unlikely person, or, a personal favorite of mine, two people who had nothing but disdain for one another only to realize they couldn't possibly live without the other. In the end, they all found their person. The movies made it out to be so simple, and yet I found myself in a record number of failed relationships over three decades of life. All the while, my sister has found not one, but two people who've truly loved her.

How was that fair?

It wasn't, and no matter how many times I'd been told that life's not fair, I still expected it to be because while she's out living her second perfect love story, I'd been staring at a piece of salad caught between some guys front teeth for far too fucking long. And I didn't even want to be here in the first place.

"Abby?" the man across from me, whose name I seriously could not remember, asked.

"I'm so sorry I got distracted. What did you say?" I plastered on my fakest smile and peered at him over the flickering candlelight. Maybe he would think he distracted me and take it as a compliment. The cocky smile he returned told me that I was right.

Riverside House did a good job at pretending to be a nice restaurant, but I should've known better when he asked to meet here for dinner after only a few hours of texting back and forth. No self respecting man took a woman out to Riverside House on a first date unless he had no brain. It was the only actual restaurant in Fairvale, which made it the restaurant you took someone you put little thought into.

But I was hungry, and he offered.

At least he looked like his profile picture. Muddy brown hair that was perfectly coifed and a fake shy smile with pearly white teeth that were almost endearing. Almost. "I was asking if you ever thought about going to law school?" His voice was smooth, as if he asked the same questions hundreds of times and it was just another thing to check off a list.

It was everyone's first question when they figured out I was a paralegal. Like it wasn't a perfectly acceptable career choice to be a paralegal. They always assumed it was a stepping stone to something bigger. Every time I heard it, I wanted to retort with, "If all the paralegals in the country became lawyers, nothing would get done."

But I didn't. At least not this time.

"Why would I?" I asked. His arm stilled with his next bite halfway to his mouth before he lifted one shoulder lazily in response.

I offered him a thin smile. "No, law school's never interested me." My voice was teetering on the side of annoyance masked by sweetness. I made a mental note to change my dating profile so we didn't match again by mistake. Or maybe I needed to delete it all together. It never worked out the way I wanted anyway, and dating was starting to feel like a chore.

He hummed a response. A dumb sort of noise that made it seemed like they agreed but really it made you feel as if they're questioning all of your life choices before cutting into his steak. My fork twirled around the pasta lazily. At this point, I didn't even care if I looked bored.

My whole life, I wanted to be in love. It was the ultimate goal, before I even knew what it was to love someone outside my family. I came close a few times, or at least it felt like I did. There were men who swept me off my feet and men who declared loudly and publicly that I was the love of their life and I fell for it, every single time. Once I spent a semester abroad during college because I was convinced my great love story would happen overseas.

Spoiler.

It didn't.

Every relationship was how I thought it should be until it wasn't and they ended in disaster, blew up in my face. I could never explain it, but something was always missing.

No Name finished his meal without so much as another word and I counted down the seconds until the server dropped off the check. At least his hand darted out to pick it up before we did the awkward dance of chivalry versus a modern dating skit of who pays the bill.

"It was really great getting to know you, Abby," he said while slipping the plastic card into the bill holder.

Was it though?

"Yes, I had a great time as well." I didn't know how much longer I could pretend.

My back pressed into the wooden chair as I turned to peer out the bay windows that overlooked Orange Grove River. Dusk was settling beyond the horizon and soft pink tuffs of cotton candy clouds sat in the sky reminding me one of my favorite seasons was almost in reach, and soon I would be eating my weight in empty calories at the county fair.

The scrape of his chair pulled me back to the restaurant. He stood, sweeping his suit jacket off the chairback and slung it over his shoulder on one finger. Of course, he didn't even bother changing. He came straight from work. Another strike against him, and I was convinced I knew exactly what was coming next.

We pushed the heavy oak doors open and I praised past-Abby for agreeing to meet him at the restaurant instead of driving together. My keys clinked together as I pulled them from my purse.

"You know it's still early and I don't live far from here."

"No."

He startled at my sudden response.

I sighed, a bored, wistful sort of noise that I was sure he would confuse with an attitude.

"What?" His head cocked to the side.

"No, thank you. I won't be coming over to your house."

He scoffed. "Then what was the point?"

There it was. The enviable tit for tat, or in this case, a meal for sex.

I couldn't even hold in the laugh as it bubbled up in my throat. It didn't warrant a response, so I turned on my heel and headed to my car instead.

I turned my ignition over as I dialed Carina and put her on speaker. She answered on the third ring.

"What a dud," I said with more spite than was really needed, and turned out of the parking lot to begin the short drive home.

"I'm sorry, sorella." The softness of her voice was an instant comfort. Carina was who I turned to first when I needed any sort of comfort. I loved my sister and she would be there for me in a second if I needed anything, but there was something about being called sister by someone you didn't share blood with. I turned my wheel to the left and entered into my neighborhood.

Cookie cutter houses whirled by with manicured lawns and kids still playing in the front yard in the late summer dusk. Deep green trees filled the skyline in a way that I could only describe as home. I traveled a bit in my early twenties and was always surprised that not every city was filled with as many trees as Fairvale. I think that was why I liked it here so much, I never felt open or exposed.

Dead air waves coursed through the car. We sat together in silence until a voice floated in from Carina's side. I couldn't quite make out what was being said, but it was definitely male. She harshly shushed the mystery person.

"Who are you with?" I questioned quickly, although I already knew the answer, even if she refused to admit it.

She shushed the background speaker once more. "No one important." A bark of laughter echoed from her end that she ignored.

"Okay, Carina. You keep telling yourself that." I laughed.

A few houses later, mine came into view. I left the engine running after I pulled in and kept her on the phone a bit longer. Being alone was the farthest thing from my mind.

"Maybe I should take a break." I practically whispered into the emptiness of my car. "From dating." I didn't know whether she was waiting for me to elaborate, but I continued anyway. "I don't think there's anyone out there for me, Carina."

"Oh, amore," she murmured.

I didn't talk like this. Ever. I was the person you turned to when you needed to hear the positive side of an issue.

"You will find someone when it's your time, not a second sooner. Until then, sei la mia anima gemelli." *You are my soulmate.* I smiled at the words she taught me and my sister shortly after the death of my sister's husband. As long as we had each other, we would never be alone.

But I needed more.

I wanted more.

Didn't I deserve more?

This was unraveling into a pity party that would be hard to crawl out of if I let it go on any longer so I said a quick goodbye and hung up. I thought a nice, simple date would be what I needed to turn this bad day—who was I kidding? A bad week, a bad year even—into a silver lining. But instead, I was left feeling like my heart was clenching in my chest.

The night was still warm as the last bit of sun clung to the horizon; my date might not have been the break I was looking for but I knew there was one thing that would tip the scales my way.

I sat with my keys in hand for a second longer and allowed my eyes to flick towards the time and then to the rearview mirror. It was only a matter of time before he would pull open the garage door. I counted my heartbeats and like clockwork, and thirty loud thumps later, the heavy metal door rattled open. Seconds bled into each other as I watched him walk back and forth from his workbench to the rack of tools on the opposite side. I was too far, but I could picture the way his shirt would stretch over his chest and arms as he worked. Or the way the ends of his dark hair curled where they poked out from under his baseball cap in complete disarray. And I was sure that he would be muttering under his , complaining about whatever he was working on.

One glimpse. That was all I wanted. A second to look, to pretend a little, and then I would go inside.

It was stupid the way I watched him, it made zero sense. I could easily go over and talk to him. We weren't friends but we were far from strangers. We were some weird in between that always left me wanting more. An in-between type of relationship where for the past five years, he's helped me fix up my house on the occasional weekend but rarely did we interact during the week.

None of that stopped me from sitting in my driveway waiting for even the smallest glimpse of him, because on days where it seemed like I would never find someone, I liked to imagine what it would be like to belong to Kaiser Price.

After one last look, I pushed the car door open and climbed out. I walked the short pathway between my lawn that was in desperate need of mowing up to my front door, slipped the key into the lock, and turned the handle. But stepping inside, I took one last glance and, like always, my heart fluttered when I noticed him already looking at me. My hand lifted to wave brightly, but I was only met with his usual curt nod.

I disappeared into my home and into my own sinking thoughts. I never got what I wanted. Maybe it was time for me to give up on my wishful thinking that I was meant for someone and there was someone meant for me.

TWO

Abby

THE FAUCET IN MY kitchen continued with its insentient *drip, drip, drip* and was fraying my nerves. I tried every fix imaginable since I bought this house five years ago, but nothing worked. Nothing stopped the drip. Or at least nothing short of replacing the whole thing, and that was not a task I wanted to dive into yet.

When I bought my home, I knew it needed work. It was livable, but dated. Old shag carpet covered every inch of flooring, and I mean every inch, even the bathroom, which was a fact I tried to forget about. Ceiling fans that rattled anytime you clicked up from the first speed and wallpaper, that took much longer to scrape off than it should have, papered walls it never should have been on. There wasn't a single corner of this house that said Abby Faulkner lived here and it took a while for it to feel like home. I changed things over the years, mainly the floor and the wall color, spruced it up with a lot of decor and antique thrifted furniture, but it would be a long time before everything was the way I envisioned. And that was fine. I was here for the long haul, and honestly, you couldn't pay me to move all of my junk again.

The main issue with buying a fixer upper was there was only so much a video and a DIY blog could teach a person who had never fixed a thing in her life. My sister Lennon was the first to tell me how much work it was going to be, but did I listen? Absolutely not, and you wouldn't find me running out to tell her she was right any time soon.

Instead, the first week in the house, I drove myself to the nearest home improvement store, bought every power tool I thought I would need and made best friends with the workers that way I would always have someone to answer the millions of questions I had.

But sometimes, when the improvement store was closed, or I found myself in a pinch for info, I had the next best thing right across the street.

I crouched down, bringing the cake I had plated eye level and spun it slowly, searching for any break in the frosting or lopsided-ness that needed to be fixed. One final spin of the spatula around the frosting on top for good measure, and it was almost perfect. I took a step back, licking rouge frosting off my fingers before tossing the utensil into the sink. It landed with a clatter in the small puddle that appeared daily because of that damn leak.

One day, I'd re-do the kitchen, but not today; all I knew was I needed a quick fix for the current leak.

My hands reached behind my back and tugged the tie free of my flour covered apron before I slipped my head out of the straps and placed it on the hook beside my refrigerator. I pulled the old yellow cabinet doors open and shuffled around a few forgotten appliances before finding the plastic cake carrier. Only wincing once when the cake slipped out of my hand and bumped into the side of the lid, and even though I caught it before making a complete mess, there was now a missing patch of frosting on the side.

I wasn't a talented baker, or even a decent one, that much was obvious but when you realize you have nothing to show for your life except that you're good at your job, it's sort of a wake-up call. Or at least for me it was and that revelation happened about eight months ago, right after the explosive demise of my last relationship. Besides work, I had nothing to show for my life. I didn't even have hobbies. Most of the time I found myself with more free time than I knew what to do with and the realization I have nothing of substance to offer the world. Maybe that's why I threw myself into relationships. If I occupied my time with a person, there was no time left to think about who I was on my own. Which was fine by me. I learned to put myself on the back burner a long time ago.

I wasn't great at anything or even good, except maybe my job, but who wanted to be remembered for only their work once they were gone? Carina, maybe—but she was always different, and now it was almost endearing how much time and effort she devoted to work and not at all concerning in the way I found it to be when I first met her.

The lid of the cake holder snapped into place before I picked it up and turned to leave the kitchen. As I passed the mirror, I paused to stare at my reflection before leaving. My hair was a little on the flat side and the curls that were fresh this morning for work were limp and almost non-existent. Some days I wished for my sister's curls, the kind that never needed a tool to achieve, but seeing her in the morning when they were often too wild to tame was enough for me to be thankful for what I had. With head cocked to the side, I thought for a moment about changing, but decided against it. The dark blue silk blouse wasn't that wrinkly and was a pretty color against my chestnut colored hair.

It would have to do, and he never looked past my face, anyway.

Within a minute, I was knocking against Kaiser's front door. My toes wiggled in my flats as I waited for him to answer. I did this more often than I needed to, and I was nervous every time. Even if I knew by now that he would agree, there was still an inkling of fear that I would have a door slammed in my face.

The door swung open, and like clockwork, I forgot to breathe for a second. Kaiser Price was as tall as he was broad, his entire frame easily taking up so much space in the doorway that I couldn't see past him. His face was half hidden by a dark beard that was, by my count, a few days past his normal shave schedule, and I hated myself for even knowing that.

Even more so for the excitement that laid in the pit of my stomach knowing he would trim it down soon and that was always my favorite look on him.

"Hi, Kaiser," I beamed and hoped it looked at authentic as I felt. The last thing I wanted was for him to think I was using him, even if that kind of was what I'd been doing.

"Abby," he stated, and as usual, with no infliction, nothing to give way to what was passing through his head. His eyes flicked down to the case in my hands. "What do you need now?" He leaned on to the door frame with one shoulder and crossed his arms across his chest. His very large, muscular arms, across his equally large and muscular chest, stretching the fabric of the plain tee he was wearing.

What did I come here for?

I wished I could say his voice carried a playful tone, but it didn't. It was chilly and lacked any of the warmth I put into my own. But he never turned me away, so I guess that's why I kept coming back.

How did that saying go?

A glutton for punishment?

He hadn't moved from his spot, like he was already bored with the conversation that hadn't even started. Butterflies kicked up in my stomach and I wanted to rip off their wings. I shouldn't feel like this over him, over anyone. Not after the disaster that was my last relationship, but my feelings for Kaiser had been complicated since the day I met him and almost impossible to shut off. Instead, I kept them in a lockbox that was only held closed with a tattered piece of thread.

Kaiser was always a bit chilly though, so it was hard to tell if it was me that did it to him or him in general. I told myself it was part of his charm. Nothing seemed important to him, and he made sure you knew that. He leaned on doors, talked without emotion and anytime I thought he might crack the tiniest of smiles, his mouth refused to turn upwards. As if his body physically refused, or it had forgotten what it was like to be happy altogether.

The only time he would light up was when he was working.

"Nothing major, I promise, but the faucet is leaking again. I tried the tape thing you did last time, but it didn't work." It was about the third time of me persuading him to help me that he broke down and insisted on showing me an in-depth tutorial of what do to when it leaked. It went a little over my head, so there was a chance I was the problem and I was sure he'd tell me as soon as he took a look at it.

"You need a new sink." It was a matter-of-fact statement. No fuss to his words.

He kept his eyes on me, never straying from my face. I melted under his gaze and it wasn't the first time either. Every. Single. Time. I always felt like I had his undivided attention whenever we spoke. Even if the conversations were short-lived and mostly one sided on my part.

I shifted on my feet, moving the case from one hand to the other. "I know, I know, but I don't have the time to re-do the kitchen and I couldn't decide on what I want so I don't want to. Not until I have to."

He rolled his eyes and if I blinked, I would've missed the way that his lips tried to pull up in a smirk before they flattened into a thin line again. Before I forgot, I held up my bargaining chip. "It's another cake, and I thought maybe you could—" He cut me off as he quickly removed the case from my hand.

"I can come by tomorrow."

It had been like this for a while, maybe since I moved in. It started with simple requests, like if he had a screwdriver I could borrow or what the difference was between sanded and not sanded grout and if one was better than the other. It didn't take me long to realize he was as adept as a handyman as I was at knowing what crystals had the best properties for better sleep. The baked goods were a new part of our relationship and all a part of my master plan to get to know myself better. I had no idea if they helped soften him up, but he returned every container empty, so I was sure it wasn't hurting.

His hand hovered over the door, ready to close it. "I'll be up early, so come over whenever and don't forget to try the cake. I want to know how I did this time." The words were quick before he could close the door. His response was a small grunt of acknowledgement and a tight nod before the door shut and I turned on my heel and started back home.

On the surface, Kaiser was a hard shell of a man. All cool toned and level headed, quick to lock down any ounce of emotion that threatened to surface. But underneath all of that, I knew that there's a softer version of him, and every once in a while I caught glimpses of it, but I wanted more. He was an enigma that I wanted to crack wide open. I only needed to find the right tool.

THREE

Kaiser

The solitude of Main Street under the first light of sun was my daily ritual and one of the only things I looked forward to. I never set out to be a small business owner but now that I was years deep in the career, I couldn't image doing anything else. Mornings in my shop, in the heart of Fairvale, were the only time I could get back to myself. When there was only an occasional person on the street in a hurry to get the to the office building at the opposite end of the street. Before customers strolled in and pulled my focus away from a project I was working on to ask questions. And before I was drained of all my energy from dealing with whatever headache the day brought.

When I started out with woodworking, and still lived with my mother, my nightmares woke me well before my alarm or the sun. No matter what I tried, wrestling myself back to sleep never worked. Instead, I would creep into the garage and take on the project I was using to hone my skills. The smell of pine and the methodical back-and-forth movement of sanding helped, if only for the time being. In the end, the nightmares always returned, but I cultivated an entire career off the skills the early morning wake-up calls left me with.

Over the years, I worked to control the nightmares, but rising with the sun stuck.

Wood working gave me a lifeline. I was a teenager who was turning his mother prematurely grey with every decision I made. I was in and out of class during high school, barely bothering to show up half the time, and woodshop was an elective I never wanted to take, but ended up in anyway. The teacher saw something in me. Maybe it was talent, or maybe it was the defiance he knew I was using as a mask, but either way, I was soon under his wing and back on track to graduate. A single class in high school that I barely put any thought into became my livelihood once I was home for good after my stint in the Army.

I had about an hour until I needed to flip the open sign and I'd been running through emails after putting them off all week. All it did was drag me down when I realized that less and less were about commissioning pieces and more about payments that were due. The shop had been in a steady decline for the past six months and I have no idea how to turn it around. I couldn't lose the shop, I'd rather sell my house and live in the back office than close.

I wasn't in any real danger, at least not currently, of closing the doors or anything, but if it kept going this way, I wouldn't be able to justify keeping my apprentice Randy or Kaity. And the last thing I wanted to do was have to get rid of Kaity—she was the only buffer I had between me and actually talking to customers, and as much as she loved to push my buttons, if I didn't have to give her up, I wouldn't.

My only saving grace for the headache forming behind my eyes was that it was Friday. I had the weekend free and plans to spend it alone on the lake, bright and early. Unless something came up unexpectedly.

By the time my truck rumbled into my driveway, the headache that formed after lunch was a full-blown migraine, throbbing behind both eyes and blurred my vision as the sun went down. All I wanted was to sit on my couch and do nothing until I was hungry enough to move, and when you have no one in your life, that was easy to do.

I had exactly one friend who blew into town maybe every few months and my mother who lived close but knew I preferred to keep to myself. I didn't even have a dog. So when I walked into my empty home, stillness washed over me.

My boots struck the floor in a heavy cadence before I fell back onto the couch. My fingers made quick work of the laces and as I was pulling the last boot string loose a knock echoed out into my house. It was past seven and there was only one person it could be. I toed off my boots and placed them under my coffee table.

A brief smile played at my lips as I walked to the door and there was a glimmer of hope that she could be right outside. It wouldn't be the first time she's appeared on my porch at the end of the day and God I hoped she never stopped showing up when she needed help. I swung open the door and almost sighed with relief. The sight of her as effective as medication for the pulsing pain in my head.

Abigail Faulkner stood on my porch, the setting sun almost blinding behind her, as if her sunny personality couldn't bear to stay inside of her. Her shirt was almost the same shade as her dark blue eyes and in this light her hair was so red it almost looked like it was on fire.

Easily my favorite version of her.

Until she smiled and said my name. As the syllables left her mouth, her dimples appeared on each cheek, and I was quickly reminded that every version of her was my favorite.

"Abby."

It's all I had in me; her name, that was it. All my energy went directly into not getting distracted by the delicate curve of her neck blending into her shoulder. Or the black slacks that hugged her from her hips down through her thighs before flaring out around her calf. I stared directly at her face, like a focus point you choose when you didn't want to get dizzy.

Maybe I took one look, but that was beside the point.

The large plastic container knocked against her knee, which could only mean one thing. "What do you need now?"

"Nothing major, I promise, but the faucet is leaking again. I tried the tape thing you did last time, but it didn't work." A mental image of Abby fighting with her faucet popped into my head and I was sad I missed it.

Abby was all sunshine and suits for her law firm job or whatever it was she actually did. Not the type of woman who tackled projects on her own or one to get her hands dirty. Besides the minor projects we did together occasionally, she didn't know the tail end of the wrench from the vice.

"You need a new sink." I had been telling her this, religiously, since she moved in five years ago, but she keeps putting it off. It didn't matter that I offered to do all the labor for her. She always had an excuse.

Her eyes darted around from my face down my chest before flicking to the side like she stopped herself from going further. "I know, I know, but I don't have the time to re-do the kitchen and I can't decide on what I want so I don't want to. Not until I have to."

I rolled my eyes and sucked back the urge to laugh.

"It's another cake, and I hoped that maybe you could—" I plucked the case from her hand.

"I can come by tomorrow." That was rude, I knew it was, but I could never seem to find the right way to behave around her, so I ended up in my default mode of being an ass. I was glad it never seemed to stop her from smiling at me. She told me to come by in the morning, and I gave her a quick nod before closing the door.

Abby occupied my thoughts almost day and night from the first time I met her. Even to this day, I could never put my finger on what it was about her that kept me hanging on to every word of hers, even though there were a thousand reasons for me not to. She was too young. Too cheerful, kind, positive, trusting. Practically everything I wasn't, but I couldn't get her out of my head. Instead, I kept myself available for her and treated it like a burden, hoping one day she'd take the hint and cast me aside because God knows I didn't posses the strength to do it myself.

I popped open the case and was confronted by a chocolate cake that was missing frosting on one side. I huffed out the remaining air in my chest. This was going to be bad. She started baking a few months ago, and it was only slowly starting to get better and I knew by now to try things out of her sight.

The cake mocked me from the counter.

I'd been to war, multiple times, so in fact, getting ready to taste one of Abby's desserts was a little like getting ready for a mission. My palms pressed into the counter as I squared my shoulders, preparing myself for the first bite.

To plainly put it, I didn't want to try it. They'd been getting better, but not enough, and even though she couldn't see me, I had a deep-seated need to please her. And I knew this would make her happy.

My reluctant lips met the fork, and for a moment I was pleasantly surprised, but then I realized the frosting was probably from a can; only canned frosting could taste that perfect. The cake itself, though, tasted as if she'd mixed in a box of crayons. I choked down the first and only bite, then scraped the full cake into the garbage.

I wasn't going to the lake tomorrow, and that was okay, but I wouldn't risk spending the day sick. Not when I got to spend the morning doing my next favorite thing.

FOUR

Abby

WHEN I TOLD KAISER to come over whenever, I should have known that it would be at the crack of dawn. Maybe not that early, but it was early enough that I was still in my pajamas with my hair piled high on top of my head when he knocked on the door. A yawn forced its way out before I was able to turn it into a smile.

"Good morning," I said, my voice cracking from last night's sleep. Kaiser stepped in, brushing past me and straight into the kitchen. He knew the drill at this point, it was practically routine. The smell of clean wafted in with him, with a hint of pine that never seemed to leave his skin. I breathed him in like a wake up call and only then was I ready to take on the day.

His tool box clattered to the ground in front of the sink and he wasted zero time reaching under my sink where I now knew the shut-off valve for the water was located. We'd done this before, to the point I probably could do it myself, but it was much more fun this way. Even if by the end I knew I was going to endure some sort of lecture about how it was time to replace the whole thing, and I should think about my bill with the amount of water the sink leaks. It was the same every time, and I was sure he knew I was going to tell him I'd think about it, only to wait another six months for the problem to resurface and ask for his help.

It's a never-ending circle of my design that kept pulling us together, and I think that's what I liked about it.

"This shouldn't take long," he said, "maybe twenty minutes and then I'll be out of here."

In and out, as always. He never lingered, never hovered for small talk. He came in, did the work, and then he left.

I often wondered why he kept coming back. Was he a really good neighbor and that's all? Did he feel some sort of good samaritan call to help the poor, incompetent woman across the street? These are the things I think every time I ask him. But when he was here, in my home, I could feel it was more than that. I didn't know what it was, but one day I wanted to figure it out.

The smell of coffee permeated the air as he pulled the handle off the faucet. I grabbed two mugs from the open shelf above my makeshift coffee station on the opposite wall of the sink. It was my favorite part of the house and one of the first spaces I turned into my own when I moved in. I hated mornings, but this little corner of my home was one of the few reasons I got up in the morning.

Kaiser muttered under his breath while he slid the valve from the handle as I walked behind him to open up the refrigerator for the much needed coffee creamer. His eyes flicked over to me as I shut the door with my hip. It was fast, a quick up and down. I would have missed it if I wasn't already staring back at him and I was reminded that I was still in my pajamas.

I was a connoisseur of many, many things. Horoscopes, crystals, gold jewelry, movies where the world was ending by some natural disaster and pajama sets. Last night's set was deep blue with yellow constellations dotted everywhere. The shorts were a little on the short side and the top button had been missing since I bought it, but it was my favorite and it was still too hot during the night to sleep in anything more.

It was also my house and I would wear what I wanted.

My morning routine continued. First, I poured coffee into the mug, followed by three pumps of vanilla, then topped it off with the creamer. Normally I'd froth it up, but I gave up my favorite part because I could still feel his eyes on me every other second.

I added coffee to the other mug and walked it over to him. Setting it on the counter, I watched him replace the cause of all my issues. "I don't know what you got in your water," he grumbled as the new O-ring was securely in place.

I smiled behind my mug. "We have the same water," I reminded him.

He simply grunted in a reply.

The coffee warmed my chest as I took a sip and watched him work. I wished I knew what Kaiser did to fill his weekends, besides giving up time to help me or the endless hours he spent at his shop on Main Street. I knew from seeing fishing poles in his truck bed some late afternoons that he spent some time at the river or possibly a lake. But I wanted to know what were the little things he did to occupy his time. What did he do for fun? Did he even know how to have fun?

The faucet handle was placed back on. He turned the handle back and forth a few times, testing it. It shut off and turned on as it should, with no extra water in between.

He wiped his hand on the front of his jeans, water prints darkening the fabric. "That should hold you over, but you really should—"

"I know, I know."

I slid the coffee a little closer to him. Maybe this time he'd linger.

"Thanks," he grumbled as he picked up the mug and took a sip.

"I wasn't sure what you take in your coffee, but I have practically everything," I volunteered the information as I gestured to the corner behind me. "Use whatever you want." A look of disgust crossed his face.

"No, thanks, I drink coffee, not hot flavored pastries."

"What?" I snorted out a laugh.

"Coffee should taste like coffee." That's all I got from him, but he was so passionate about it, that it was hard not to continue laughing.

There wasn't a label for what Kaiser and I were. Neighbors, obviously, but there wasn't a name for the weird in-between place we stood. A space where I didn't know how he takes his coffee or what he did on the weekends to past the time, but I knew he mumbled to himself when he was working or that his eyes would turn from blue to green depending on what he was wearing. There was also the faint memory that reminded me I also knew what it felt like to be wrapped in his arms. A memory that had been haunting me for years and each day that passed it grew dimmer and I hated that, it only reminded me I spent too much time fixated on a man I didn't really know.

"You people and the need to ruin a good thing," he muttered as he shook his head. His brown curls shaking slightly under the ball cap that with his store logo.

"And who is you people?"

"Your generation, millennials, or whatever you're called. Always fucking up a good thing." A boisterous sort of noise expelled past my lips, startling him. I pressed my fingers to my lips to keep from snickering further. Kaiser was funny without meaning to be, which made it that much more endearing.

"You're, what, ten years older than me? I'm pretty sure we're the same generation, which makes you a millennial as well, you know."

"Don't remind me." He rolled his eyes before taking another sip. He stayed propped up by the counter, silence weaved in and out of us while the sun made its way higher in the morning sky. When he turned back, a look rolled over his face that made my heart stop. It wasn't the first time that had happened either.

"Eleven years," he eventually stated.

Kaiser always looked as if everything in the world bothered him, like happiness was a far off dream and he had been stuffing his feelings into the recess of his soul to be forgotten. But every once in a while, he softened. I could never tell what did it to him, but I liked to think it was me. That there was something about our time together that melted his icy exterior ever so slightly.

As fast as it appeared, the look vanished, and I was once again left in the chill of his demeanor. Whatever it was, I was thinking maybe I only imagined it.

"Oh, did you get a chance to try the cake?" I set my cup down and eagerly waited for his reply.

His face went to stone, not even a flicker of emotion. My heart dropped, it sucked, I knew it. Empty silence passed between us before he finally answered. "It was good."

"Really?" My voice shot up multiple octaves.

"Yeah, you're getting pretty good."

I beamed under the praise. I knew it wasn't the recipe I had been looking for, but at least they were getting better over all.

"Thank you, and thanks for coming over. I hope I didn't ruin any plans," I murmured. My voice was oddly gentle and suddenly self conscious. He picked up his toolbox and we walked the few steps to the front door in silence.

"Anytime." That was his normal response, one I'd come to expect. "You only have to ask," he added. Cornflower blue eyes softened slightly, giving me a glimpse of the man underneath the hard exterior. Then I blinked and it was gone. He was walking away, and I was left with whiplash.

My life would be easier if I ever found myself with a man like Kaiser, or with Kaiser himself. Yet somehow I always found myself with the wrong person, giving everything I had to them only to have it thrown back in my face. A shiver ran down my spine at the thought of the last relationship I clawed my way out of barely a year ago, though other times, it seemed like it was only yesterday.

I promised myself, never again would I put myself in a position that would cause me to lose the parts of me I loved most. That my next relationship would be my last, the next man would be my husband. Until then, I would do what made me happy, find new hobbies to fill my time, learn things I'd always thought about but never got around to doing...

Who knew how long it would take, but I was worth the wait. It took me a while to figure that out. How could I expect someone else to treat me like a first choice if I didn't treat myself like one?

FIVE

Kaiser

CANCELING MY WHOLE DAY to help Abby for twenty minutes was the most ridiculous thing I could have done, but I seemed to have little control over my feelings or simple brain power when I was around her. I doubted she even knew the power she held over me. It would have be easier if I could tell her, but every time I thought I'd found the strength the words slipped from my head and seemed impossible to form. As if my brain slid into the driver seat kicking out my heart, reminding me that distance was for the best. I was unlovable, that much I knew. It didn't matter that it had been almost twenty years since my last relationship, When someone told you that you weren't worth loving, it tended to stick with you.

I placed my tool bag back into the garage, with more attitude than needed, and contemplated grabbing my keys. Wildflower Lake wasn't that far, I could still make out and have more than enough hours to sit and do nothing. It's where I went to think and not think, it's where I went to just *be*. It would probably be for the best, I would get a chance to clear my head of the clouds that started to take over the second I saw her earlier.

Instead, I hovered in the garage staring at my fishing pole. *I should go.*

But I didn't.

Giving up, I slid into my truck and turned the ignition over and wound my way around the neighborhood until I pulled out to the main road to follow it to Main Street. I might regret not going out to fish, but I would never regret extra hours in my shop.

I was what my store manager liked to call, a workaholic. My shop saw more of me than my home most of the time and if I had more friends they would say the same thing. In general I tended to forgo most human interactions in order to work and when I did have free time, I spent it up at the lake—alone.

My hand trialed down the logo etched into the glass doors that lead into Price & Company. It had been decades since I started my own business but I still felt a swell of pride every time I opened the doors into my brick and mortar shop. The smell of pine hit my senses and I was sure there was nothing better in the world, I would bottle up the smell if I could. Small specks of sawdust floated through the air as I walked through the front, past an oak dining room set I built two years ago and has yet to sell, and a pair of mahogany rocking chairs I finished a few months ago. Every piece of furniture that filled my store was a labor of blood, sweat, and I guess sometimes love. If it could be made out of wood, odds are,

I'd probably done it and it's available in my store. Cutting boards to kitchen tables, outdoor benches, to the small pens I keep at the register. All painstakingly handmade by me.

A few customers were loitering around, picking up different cutting boards or leaning in for a closer look at a rocking chair I had made last year but still hadn't sold. A woman browsed the front end of the store near the window where we displayed items made by local makers that I had on consignment. Honestly, I couldn't tell you what was even available there, Kaity handled that small nook of the store. I presumed it was mainly filled with trinket-like things, or stuff you'd find at craft fairs. Which was how I got my start, I guess it was a way to pay it forward.

A couple stood between a pair of dining room tables on the left hand side of the store as I trailed toward the back. Katiy's long pink hair was a stark contrast to the natural feel of the rest of the store. Her hands animated whatever she was pitching them, in wild motions. She showed up about a year ago with a resume in hand that had nothing but fast food work listed and talked her way on to my payroll but I was grateful for her. She took to schmoozing the customers into buy the bigger pieces of furniture like a pro and made it so I didn't have to. She also did it a lot better than I ever could, but I kept that fact to myself.

Our eyes caught briefly as I passed by, and confusion swept across her face before she waved and went right back to her conversation without so much as missing a beat.

I popped into the side area where my actual shop was and found Randy dragging a stain soaked rag across a custom mantel piece. It was one of the first I let him complete start to finish after much back and forth. His head ticked up at the sound of my footsteps.

"Hey, Boss," he chimed with a smile. Too cheery, always too cheery, but that's what I got employing some fresh faced kid barely out of high school. Between him and Kaity, I was constantly chastising myself for employing a couple of kids. My head ticked upwards in my usual greeting.

They're aware that I was a man of few words and even fewer emotions, and I was well aware of the fact that it wasn't not winning me any congeniality awards. Which was fine, my preferences laid with activities that provided me the most solitude, for the simple fact that's where I was most comfortable. Where I didn't have to worry that I might say the wrong thing. Not because I was saying anything that would offend anyone but my mouth didn't always articulate what I want it to mean, and it was embarrassing. To the point I would rather say nothing at all, which led to me not getting close to anyone.

I lived alone, I had one friend who I saw maybe every six months and was probably due for a visit, and if I had it my way I would work alone. But I learned early on I couldn't run my store on my own, no matter how hard I tried, and at least now I had nights and most weekends off to not be around people, so it was an easy trade.

"Run into any issues yet?"

He stared at the wood for a moment, then back at me with a look of fear in his eyes.

"I... uh," he stuttered over the simple answer. "Weren't you going to be out today?" I could tell immediately why he asked. There was shit everywhere. Pieces of cut wood were scattered across the floor, multiple open cans of stain in various colors like he couldn't decide which to use and every tool I owned seemed to be littered across the workbench. This was a workshop but I hated the chaos of a mess while working and he knew it, but appeared to not hold the same sentiment. His eyes darted around the mess. "Im going to clean up I swear."

"I'm not checking in on you, it's fine." It wasn't fine, my blood pressure was rising simply from being in the same room.

"O-okay," he answered timidly. I left him to his finish up and headed to my office across the hall.

The weathered leather seat groaned under my weight as I fell into it. I pulled the hat from my head and tossed it aside and threaded my fingers through my hair. I didn't actually have anything to do, the only custom piece request I received for the month was with Randy, but I couldn't talk myself into leaving for the lake.

It was a weird feeling, I never thought there would be a day with nothing to actually work on. This was my dream, so why was I feeling more and more restless with every day that passed? I jiggled my mouse until my computer whirled to life. There was only a few emails but one subject line had me leaning in for a closer look. I double clicked my mouse to open it. It's almost time, it read, for the craft competition at this year's Fall Festival. I scrolled through to read the rest of the details even though I already knew them.

The Fall Festival was nearly as old as this town; it was held for one weekend in the middle of October and brought in more revenue for the town in those two days than any other event they put on during the rest of year combined.

Fairvale started as a farming town, and with a farming town came blacksmiths, woodworkers, carpentry shops—the works. It's said the fair started out as a competition between the workers on who could sell the most items during the summer and they'd pull their sales around October to declare the winner. They did this for decades until the trades faded out and the town was built up. In its place, an actual fair popped up and to honor Fairvale's beginning, a craft competition open for anyone to enter.

The first year I opened my business, I entered in a dining room table to help get my name out in the town. Not only did it work and bring business into my store in droves but I won. I kept the lovely trophy behind the counter on a shelf as a reminder. Although, all it did was collect dust.

Maybe another win is what I needed to help boost my sales. It had been ten years since I last entered, it couldn't hurt, that's for sure. I printed off the form and filled out all the info they needed quickly before I had the thought to back out. There was a small entry fee that I had ready in my wallet. Without another word to Randy or Kaity I walked out of the shop and headed toward the middle of Main Street where Town Hall was located. Which was really only a small room sandwiched between a fine jewelry store and bike shop.

I breezed in through the doors and spotted the entry box on the counter immediately. My hand only hesitated for a moment before I dropped the application and cash into the small cardboard box that looked more like a second grade valentine card box than anything else. The clerk wished me good luck as I dropped in my entry and I left swiftly after.

The late summer sun was beating down on the asphalt when I walked back outside and I imagined this was what it would feel like stepping into an oven. Despite the heat, families leisurely strolled up and down each sidewalk, dipping into different stores to browse, some walking out of the restaurant that served breakfast on the weekend only. Late August was brutal, the heat nearly unbearable, but it meant we were so close to cooler weather. Except that meant I had about a month and a half to, not only design a project, but execute it, whatever it ended up being.

Winning the competition wasn't the highest point on my list. What I needed was to come up with a design unique enough to catch people's attention. But not too unique that nobody would want it in their home.

Simple.

This project was needed so there was no time left to think about her.

Abigail Faulkner was my deepest fantasy come to life. On the nights sleep didn't evade me, she slipped into my dreams and made me hate the mornings. With her pale skin and pink lips, hair that shined like copper in the sun, and eyes that were bluer than the deepest parts of the ocean. Quick wit and a sarcastic outlook of life under her sunshine persona.

And those fucking dimples.

She was also a kind of a nightmare to have for a neighbor but I liked it. But I was no good for her, or anyone, if my own thoughts were to be believed and for the most part I did. This project would give me one more hiding place, that wasn't my shop or the lake. The next six weeks would be a piece of cake, I would keep to myself, work on my entry for the fair and not think about the object of base desires. If Abby needed anything, she would have to wait.

SIX

Abby

MY SISTER GLOWED FROM the inside out. And I hated it. Not in a hated her type of way, but in a 'I hate how lonely I am' type of way. And I hated that I hated it. I was full of warring feelings and I didn't know what I wanted anymore.

Lennon and my new brother-in-law, Theo, got back from their honeymoon after spending two weeks traveling across Europe. It seemed like they were on a plane every other month zipping around state to state or even country to country for Theo's job and yet they chose to spend their honeymoon doing the same thing. You would think they would get enough of old buildings, castles and boring historical sites that would drive me, or any regular person, to tears during their regular travels for his work. If it were my honeymoon, I'd spend it somewhere where the water was always warm or somewhere I could sit in the beauty of nature and just be.

Not learning, that's all I knew.

I leaned onto the kitchen island with my head propped in my hands and watched the happy couple tell Carina about their time in Italy, only halfway paying attention.

"Did you get to go to the one I told you about?" Carina asked while she stirred the large pot of sauce. The aroma of the acidic tomatoes and rich garlic wafted through the kitchen causing my stomach to lurch with hunger.

"Yes, Buonconsiglio Castle!" Theo exclaimed. His eyes brightened like only a history nerd would and Carina looked almost as excited as he did for once. On a normal day, she was right with me trying to convince Lennon that looking at old buildings was boring, but apparently this wasn't one of those days. She nodded along while Theo told her about the walls or windows. I really didn't know, and this left me feeling very much like an outsider.

"That's close to where my parents grew up. I thought you'd like it. I'd been saying how I want to make time to go back there, but I haven't made it yet," she replied.

"Were you born there and then immigrated with your parents?" he asked.

She brought the spoon up to her mouth for a quick taste. "No, my mother was pregnant with me when they moved. I was born here." She added a quick pinch of a few more spices before tasting it again. Theo nodded before his eyes searched for my sister. When they landed on her, there was a physical change in his body. He relaxed, knowing she was close. It was an interesting thing to watch from the outside, and my heart ached a bit more.

No one was happier for my sister and Theo than me, and no one rooted louder for them to be together. What I didn't expect was the sickening feeling that began slugging through my veins since their wedding. I cried buckets of tears on that day, but I was feeling the beginning stages of what might be jealousy.

I blamed it on my failed relationship that burned down and left its scorch marks deep in my flesh.

They married quickly after their engagement, both too much in a rush to be tied to each other to wait and plan something lavish. It was a small and quick ceremony at the courthouse with a dinner at Carina's parents' restaurant. Despite the size, it was romantic and their love for each other spilled out onto everyone who attended. Of course, my crying throughout surprised no one, and mostly it was because I was happy, but many other reasons surfaced that night.

I missed my brother-in-law, who died unexpectedly four years ago, and I struggled with knowing if he were here Lennon wouldn't be getting married again and it was a complex I barely knew how to handle. The amount of love that coursed between my sister and her new husband was overwhelming, and I longed for someone to look at me even a fraction of the way Theo looked at her.

I was also angry that Carina and I were all she had on her side. I hated that our mother lived mere minutes away from us and yet could no longer be a part of lives because of her own actions. I hated that should I ever be lucky enough to marry one day that it would likely be the same. It didn't matter how much I wished it were different. There was nothing for either of us to do.

Even thinking of it caused an uncomfortable feeling to slink up my spine. I shuddered and tried to refocus on the dinner being cooked and the family I had in front of me.

Normally Carina and I would go back and forth poking fun of the happy couple, but she'd been different lately. She wouldn't admit to anything, but my gut said it was the changes at work and the new, or I guess, old faces that have popped up. She wouldn't talk about it, but it's been leaving me feeling even more alone than normal.

"Abby." Someone called my name, and I rapidly blinked to bring my focus back only to find three sets of eyes on me.

"How's your list going?" my sister asked. She saw that I was checked out and was worried, but didn't want to bring attention to it. Typical. The mother in the form of an oldest sister in her was showing.

"The list, yeah, it's going good. Great," I rambled, pushing away from the marble island while they still watched me. "I'll go set the table." Anything to get me out of where that conversation was going.

The list was riddled with issues, and I'd been kicking myself for ever mentioning it to them. First, I didn't even know what to call it. It was a bucket list at its core, but that felt too juvenile. It was more of a list of random things I always wanted to learn but never made time for, since I was always too busy with finding a person to spend my life with. Then the biggest hurdle was I didn't know how I was going to learn or do anything that I put on it. I'd had it for months, and I hadn't scratched anything off.

It was a silly thing to start, but at the time, I needed something to distract myself.

I dated a lot, and that was fine. Mostly. I liked meeting new people, but what I looked forward to the most was the beginning sparks of a relationship. When learning everything about them was exciting. When each touch and embrace seemed to light my skin on fire. Then last year it blew up in my face, leaving me scorched and heartbroken.

Liam was perfect, until he wasn't. The start of our relationship was no different from any of my other ones, but it was better. He did all the right things, said all the right things. I was floating on cloud nine each day we spent together. I was in a haze of budding love. When the change happened, it was so fast that I barely registered the shift in him and how he treated me until it was almost too late.

The break up was messy. It pulled me into a dark space, where I spiraled, thinking once again everything I wanted was slipping through my fingers. The worst part was that I never even told anyone about it because I wasn't the type to let a bad situation get me down. That's what my friends always told me, so when I needed help, I didn't reach for anyone. Instead, I folded in on myself and swore off men completely. I was finally going to focus on me and doing the things I wanted to do instead of always trying to please the next person.

Carina and Lennon barked out in laughter when I told them about my list, and my stomach heated with embarrassment. I didn't even know what I was calling it. List of random things I always wanted to learn but never made time for was too convoluted, bucket list seemed too middle school, but I had no other name for it so bucket list was what I sprawled across the top of the paper when I began to write it out.

They had so many questions about what spurred this all on, and I tripped over my answers, trying to come up with anything but the truth.

"I don't know, myself, not really. There are simple things that I wanted to do, learn, or see but never made any effort to because I focused all my energy on finding a person to spend my life with. It's stupid. You think it's stupid." I backtracked quickly over my admission.

They both promised it wasn't, that they were excited for me. They asked what was on it, but I couldn't bring myself to tell them. It all seemed too trivial at that point.

I was placing the last of the silverware onto the table when Carina came up beside me. "Are you sure you're okay?" I studied her for a second. Her light colored brows sported a small line in the middle of them as she looked back at me. Her pale green eyes pinged between mine, waiting for me to give her some sort of sign that would never come.

"Of course," I said, full of fake happiness, and she bought it because Abby Faulkner was always happy.

The dinner passed in a blur as I poked at my food while mentally counting down the minutes for an appropriate time to leave that wouldn't upset anyone, but when that time came, no one even batted an eye. Lennon and Theo were too wrapped up in each other, and Carina's head was entirely somewhere else.

My life was stagnant in a way that seemed almost impossible to get out of. There was no excitement or passion or even genuine joy at this point. I only had myself and I was the one in charge of creating a life worth living, but I found that harder to remember each day that passed. I needed something more. Whatever it was.

Headlights cut off after pulling into my driveway. I climbed out of the car and walked along the path toward my front door, not really in a hurry to walk into an empty house.

My hand reached out with my key when I faced the front door, ready to slide it into the lock, only it was already open. Adrenaline spiked through my system. It started at the base of my skull and zipped down my spine. The fear coiled across my arms and into my legs, freezing me for a moment.

The door was open, but I wasn't the one to leave it that way.

My heart hammered, and I did the only thing I could think of.

I turned and ran.

SEVEN

Abby

"KAISER!" MY VOICE WENT hoarse at the first scratch of his name as my fist hit against his door with such force over and over that I was sure my knuckles would split and bloody the wood. Tears spilled down my cheeks and I didn't even remember starting to cry but there was no stopping it. Someone had been in my house.

"Kaiser, please open up," I begged through the tears. When the door pulled open I tripped over the threshold as I scrambled to get in, falling into his arms.

"What the fu—" The word died in his mouth the moment he registered it was me. Ribbons of hard muscle tensed under my grasp as his arms held me up but made no move to pull them from my waist. As I looked up at him, I braced myself to find anger burning in his eyes, but instead his gaze was stilled and for an instant there was a flicker of wistfulness in the blue orbs looking back at me.

We stood pressed against each other, embracing the moment as if he was meant to hold me and I was made to fit in his arms. The panic that coursed through my body lessened as his fingers sank into the soft flesh over the thin shirt I was wearing. For a second I forgot what I was here for.

"What happened?" he demanded, and I tried to pull away, my hands pushed at his body to take a step back, but I was locked in his arms. We were so close it was intoxicating. His hands only added to the flurry of electricity pinpricking across my skin as they began to move over my body. "Are you hurt?" He checked over me until his hands came to a stop at my face, brushing the strands of hair away from my forehead and taking my cheeks between his palms.

I was having emotional whiplash. Panic morphed into calm as the rough skin of his finger tips grounded me to the moment. It would have been a lie to say that I never imagined this before, but my dreams never felt as good.

Why was I here again?

"Abby." His voice demanded again, finally dropping his hands from my body to flick the light on. I was plunged violently back into reality causing embarrassment to flood my veins.

"I came home and my door was open," I started to explain but suddenly felt like a silly child talking about monsters hiding in a closet. Maybe I imagined it? I never pushed the door open. Maybe I was the one who forgot to shut it when I left early this afternoon. Maybe there wasn't anything wrong at all and it was all in my head. We still hadn't moved from each other, the heat of his body seeping into mine made everything that much more hazy.

"Abigail."

My name, my full name. He'd never called me that before. I looked up at him again. His eyes were pale blue in this light. They often changed from blue to green depending on what he was wearing but this was one of my favorites of his.

I wasn't thinking when I ran, I didn't call 911 or jump back in my car to go back to my sister's. I ran here, to him, without a second thought. There was some underlying meaning to that, I was sure, but there was no time to think about that now.

"I think someone broke in and I was too scared to look." My throat worked to get the words out. "Will you...or I mean, if you're not busy." I felt stupid. Stupid, stupid, stupid. No one broke into my home, I started convincing myself. He didn't want me here, I must've looked unhinged. But a knot in my gut told me that I wasn't wrong. "Can you check for me?" I finally shuddered out.

There was a flash of something across his face.

"*Please,*" I added since I was unsure if it was a look of annoyance.

"Stay here." It was a rough command, but a command nonetheless. I blinked and he was out his front door, with quick long strides carrying him toward my house.

I'd never been one to follow the rules and I didn't like being told what to do, so I followed him, naturally. I walked into my home seconds after he did but I wished I hadn't. For once in my life I wished I listened when someone told me what to do.

Glass crunched under my foot and Kaiser abruptly faced me. "Didn't I tell you to stay at my house?" He growled. He stalked to my side, putting himself in between me and the rest of my house, muttering something under his breath that sounded a lot like 'she never listens'.

"Yeah, but this is my home, I wasn't going to wait around to see what was going on."

It was my turn to feel annoyed.

He stood up taller, if that was possible, putting his full height on display to look down at me. Fire had ignited in his eyes. "And what if there was someone here waiting to hurt you or whoever was the first to walk in?" He looked at me like a person scolding a child.

"You're here, aren't you? Would you let them?"

He opened his mouth, but quickly closed it. Seconds passed before he spoke again.

"Keep close to me and don't wander until I clear every room, you hear me?"

I nodded and we started a slow walk down the hallway to the back rooms. In each one he placed my back on a wall while he methodically swept through them, checking every corner and closet with such precision I wondered for a moment how or why he knew to do all of it.

Kaiser was serious about not letting me move from the wall, and within a few minutes my house had been swept through and he was finished. The house was empty but what was left was almost worse. The urge to sink to my knees in defeat pressed on my shoulders. If it weren't for the shards of glass littering the floor and pools of water seeping out from my kitchen I would be a curled up sobbing on the ground.

Everything was destroyed. Everything I had worked so hard to bring my vision of a home to life was in pieces. My mantle had been swiped clean, broken candlesticks and their holders were found lying across the room. My coffee table, which I saved for months to buy from Kaiser's shop, was flipped on its side with two broken legs. Chairs were tipped over, my beautiful wooden frames were knocked from the wall and in pieces on the floor. Holes in the wall, the sliding glass door that led to the backyard had a large spiderweb crack in it, as if someone lost their temper and threw something at it.

Chaos was the only word I had to describe it.

And the kitchen. That was pure bad luck. It didn't look like anything was broken but the sink finally gave way from all the patches over the years. Water spilled from under the sink in a steady stream, pooling over the tile. Water moved through the grout like an aqueduct soaking everything in its path.

I brushed past Kaiser where he stood like a statue in the middle of the dining room with anger rolling off of him in steady waves. They could almost be seen rippling over his clothes and in the space around us, and I needed to get away. It was only making me antsy.

"We should call the police," he stated, finally breaking the silence.

"I-I—" I stuttered. I wanted to say no, that the police would get here, trample through my already violated home, and have nothing to offer me. But what else could I do?

I nodded. "Okay." It was a whisper of a word when I finally agreed.

I let him make the call. My voice would only fail me.

The wait for an officer was excruciating and by the time they arrived my eyes were twice their size from the tears that never left and my throat was burning. I spent the hour it took them to respond, walking through the wreckage, crying and by the end I was only angry.

Fairvale was safe, as safe as any town could be. I would say the of place where you didn't lock your front doors but that was stupid—you should lock your front door no matter where you lived, but I knew that I wouldn't think twice if I forgot to. There was virtually no crime, some neighbor squabbles here and there, but nothing like this. Nothing that made me want to pack up and leave without looking back.

The first officer was tall and lanky, he introduced himself as Officer Nolan even though we both knew everyone called him Matty. We went to school together for all thirteen years, we weren't friends but we grew up in circles that often intertwined. If he was surprised to see me he made no mention of it and that was fine by me.

I gave my statement and ignored his skeptical eyes. "And you are sure you locked the door before you left?" he questioned for the fourth time in twice as many minutes.

"Yes," I snapped.

Kaiser came around the corner at the sound of my raised voice, sharp eyes flicking between me and Matty. Annoyance that I somehow could have caused this by leaving the door unlocked was getting to me and I could only wave Kaiser off.

I turned back to Matty. "And do you know of anyone who would want to do this to you?" he asked with a pen posed on a small notebook.

That was the question I was turning over and over in my head. I didn't have enemies, this wasn't a bad revenge movie.

But I had an answer.

Liam and I broke up almost a year ago at this point, it ended in a screaming match in the very room we were standing in. I yelled about how controlling he was becoming, that I was feeling suffocated by him. I screamed until I was hoarse. My last words to him still bounced around in my head.

"Liam, we are no good for each other and we both know it. It's best that we go our separate ways now before either of us ends up doing something we regret." I told him through clenched teeth. He stumbled back like I smacked him and had the nerve to look shocked by my words. I remember moving past him from the kitchen to the living room. "It's not working and I think you need to leave." My words were as clear as water, leaving him little room to use against me. That was when the first sound of breaking glass came, then the tinkling of the shattered pieces hitting my hardwood floor. I whipped around as a vase whirled past my head, shattering on the wall behind me, joining the broken mess on the floor.

"After everything I've done for you, you think you can cast me aside?" Liam had snarled.

I have a temper, it was a flaw I was acutely aware of and one I work hard to keep under wraps but as he stood in front of me with his nose a fraction away from mine I snapped. "Done for me... What have you ever done for me besides make my life a nightmare?" There was a tremor in my voice and I prayed he couldn't hear but it didn't stop me from spewing everything I was thinking.

"You are the worst type of person there is. You manipulated my love for you and twisted it up until it was something ugly. All for what? Because you wanted to, because you can? I would have given you anything you wanted but that wasn't good enough for you, was it? You had to take from me, but I will not allow you to treat me like this any longer." My chest was heaving by the end of my declaration and it didn't matter that my hands wouldn't stop shaking, I was finally speaking up for myself.

As I stood in front of Matty, trying to come up with something to say, all I could think of was the last time Liam sauntered toward me like a lion with eyes set on its prey. The way he whined, "Please don't do this," as he flipped his charm back on, but I was no longer a defenseless gazelle. "I'm sorry I didn't mean to lash out. I've been stressed with the changes at work and I snapped, okay? We can work through this." His hard voice failed to match his tender words.

"You make it impossible for me to love you." I remember yelling with as much conviction as I could muster when all I wanted was for this man to get out of my house so I could break down in private. "And the worst fucking part of this whole thing, Liam, is I would have spent my life begging for scraps of your affection had you learned when enough was enough." The words leaked into the air, tainting everything around us with my honesty at that time.

He left soon after, but not after promising it would be the biggest mistake of my life. But that was so long ago, there's no way he would have been stewing over our break up for this long, only to lash out once he was almost gone from my mind.

He wouldn't go this far.

Right?

No one would do all of this because they were rejected.

Right?

So his name stayed lodged in my throat when the officer asked the question again. Instead I swallowed it down and shook my head no.

He finished up the canvas of my home and left a copy of the report with his contact information saying he'd be in touch but to call if anything else came up or I had any further information for their investigation.

I was left standing in the living room, my arms wrapped around my body, keeping myself from falling apart. What were a few more broken pieces on the floor anyways. Kaiser approached as if I'd scurry away if I heard him. When our eyes met, all I wanted was to be wrapped in his arms again as much as I knew I shouldn't. But he was here and that was enough.

"Kaiser, what am I going to do?"

EIGHT

Abby

Silence swirled around us and the steady drip of water from that fucking faucet. Every towel I owned was on the kitchen floor and in the entry way soaking up the mess. Luckily Kaiser had the mind to turn the water off, staving the flow before the cops showed up. I was useless and that feeling continued to sink in.

This was almost as humiliating as it was depressing.

I felt uneasy in my home and that was a feeling I never thought existed. It was gross and itchy and for a moment it seemed as if I would never be safe again. The longer we stood there, the more I contemplated if I wanted Kaiser gone or for him to never leave my side.

He still hadn't answered me, asking what I was supposed to do in this aftermath. I left him standing and walked into the living room, I couldn't look at the soaked towels any longer. I bent down, scooping up fragments of a broken crystal I had kept near a potted plant in the window.

The tears started again, they ran down my face hot and angry. Without thinking, I turned abruptly and threw the rocks against the wall and let out a strangled scream. They shattered on impact and fell to the ground making only more of mess for me to clean up.

"What was the point!?" I yelled, "Who does this?" I gestured around. "And why me?" Another sob escaped. I buried my head into my hands and collapsed to my knees and remained there with my eyes squeezed shut until I felt him near me. Close enough to touch, but it never came.

When I finally pulled myself together, I opened my eyes to find him crouched at my level, elbows on his knees simply waiting for me. We stared at each other in an uncomfortable display of vulnerability before he finally, dragged his hand down the length of his face before stopping to scratch at his close cropped beard. He was wrestling between two sides of something like he didn't know which would win.

"You can't stay here in this mess."

I nodded.

That much was obvious, and I was dreading the call I would make to either Lennon or Carina because either one was bound to be a lecture or full of questions that I didn't want to hear. I would have to call out of work for a day, maybe two so I could clean up. Or maybe I could clean everything up tonight and not have to tell anyone else about a thing. Kaiser and I could act like none of this ever happened, it wouldn't be the first time we've pretended that a night between us never occurred. Maybe I was being dramatic, not totally out of the realm of possibility for me. Maybe this only looked like a giant mess and none of this was really as bad as it was.

But the longer I stood in the midst of the destruction the more the tears burned my eyes. I was going to have to call Lennon, I finally admitted to myself after a few more beats of silence between Kaiser and I. She would welcome me with open arms in a way that only an older sister could and I would lapse into feeling that I would always be her burden.

"Why don't you come and stay at my house for a little while and we can work on putting everything back together," he announced causing my thoughts to screech to a halt.

Looking at him was my only response. Stay with him? Surely I didn't hear that right. Something bubbled up in my chest, and not the simple fluttering I sometimes got in the pit of my stomach when I was around him. It was more like panic rattling the cages of my insides. Maybe I was going into cardiac arrest and these were going to be my last moments.

A flurry of feelings skated through my veins at lightening speed. Panic mostly, or at least it's the most recognizable one. Anger definitely was making its red hot presence known but underneath that was a slow wave of calmness that allowed me to finally draw in a deep breath. Although once I did, the anxiety ramped up again. I was a snow globe of emotions that someone wouldn't stop shaking.

Kaiser and I limited our time together to daylight hours where the sun was so bright that any feelings for him kept themselves nicely tucked into the darkest parts of my heart. We didn't hang out at each other's house, or share meals. We spent some weekends in close interaction as he pretended to be annoyed by every question I had, about whatever project I asked for help on. Mornings where I brought him whatever I baked the night before because I needed to soften him up to borrow another tool. But once the sun disappeared, so did we from each others' lives.

I didn't know what he's like at night. I didn't even know what his house was like inside.

My hands wiped roughly at the half dried tears under my eyes.

"Or I park my ass in front of your door day and night and wait for whoever it was to show back up. Your choice."

A half-hearted laugh bubbled up out of my chest before I answered. "I can't stay with you."

"What if this person comes back, Abby? I don't want you here alone. Let me help you. Please?" The words were tentative, but the plea was thunderous.

After I first moved in, there was a brief moment, one night, where I thought maybe we could be something, but nothing ever came of it. I thought about that night often. More often than I cared to ever admit out loud, and I wondered if it ever crossed his mind, too. After that, he always seemed to keep me at an arm's length, so to me, that meant he did and maybe wished it never happened. But I knew what I felt and that's what I'd been hanging on to all these years.

Staying with him in his house would jeopardize all the work I'd put in to keep my feelings for him locked away. Lennon would take me in. It would be second nature but she would pry at the situation, and having her find out why Liam and I broke up wasn't something I wanted to happen. I could've called Carina, but she'd been distancing herself lately. She had been more secretive with her free time and what she'd been doing outside of work, and I couldn't handle any amount of rejection from her.

"You shouldn't stay here." He reached his hand out and took mine, pulling me up onto my feet. "Let me help you."

My gut was telling me this was no random break in. Fear started to fester inside of me the moment I noticed the door. It was a familiar feeling, one controlled by a monster and his name was Liam. If he had enough rage to destroy my home, it would have only been a matter of time for him to turn and unleash whatever anger was still inside of him onto me. I was a sitting duck in my own home with no way to protect myself.

I took a final look around. "Okay." The feeble word barely heard by my own ears.

I had spent my thirty four years of life always looking on the bright side because I believed happiness shouldn't be hard to come by. Eight months with Liam and that was all it took to lock me away in the dark, I thought I pulled myself out once I left him but I was wrong.

He was taunting me, I could feel it. He was mad that I left him in the darkness that he created and he wanted to pull me back. But as Kaiser held out his hand and offered me a place in his home, the light appeared at the end of a dark tunnel.

NINE

Kaiser

Abby stepped into my home like a baby deer with shaking legs and small calculated steps. She had never really been in my home, there was never a reason for her to be, all the projects we worked on were on her house, so why would we ever be here? Not that I hadn't spent most of our time together thinking about what it would be like if I had it in me to ask her over for dinner or to see what she did during the week.

Neighbors didn't develop feelings, neighbors didn't fall in love, and neighbors certainly didn't end up hurt once they found out I might be incapable of being anything other than the cold, detached man that I am. It was easier to convince myself I was nothing more than a helpful neighbor to her. So that's what I did. Week in and week out, I bit my tongue, kept my eyes off the soft curves of her body and listed in my head all the reasons I would never be enough for Abigail Faulkner.

Ridged was a common word that's used to describe me, as if preferring order over chaos was a bad thing. But as her head swiveled back and forth as she peered above the box in her hand I was suddenly self conscious of what she was seeing. Her eyes roamed the walls, taking in the lack of decor, the beige paint and overall lack of warmth. Or at least that's what I assumed. It's home, but not homey. I liked for everything to have a place, anything extra was a hassle. There were no excess pillows on my bed or on the couch. I had exactly four plates, four cups, four bowls, and that's only because they came in a set; otherwise, I'd probably only have one of each. There were no pictures or art on the wall. When I came home from work, my boots went in the same spot near the fireplace without fail.

We didn't know exactly how long she would stay until we were able to wade through the damage that was left behind. I made her walk back to my house with me to grab some boxes to pack and then walk back at my side, I wasn't willing to leave her. Not even for a second. Was it overbearing? Yes. Did I care? Fuck no. She was too important.

When we got back, I told her to pack whatever she might want or need for at least a week and we could go from there. She was hesitant, protesting that a week was far too long for her to be in my space, that a day maybe two was all she needed.

Even thinking about her being here alone sent a wave of panic through me. What if whoever did this came back? What if they were watching her, waiting for her to start the clean up only to ambush her when she was distracted. I would never forgive myself if something happened to her over there that I could've easily prevented by having her close to me.

In the end I won and she agreed to a week. One week was all she would impose on me, or at least that's what she said. If I was a braver man, I would have told her that no amount of time with her would be enough and that she could never be a burden, even if she tried. None of that came out though, instead I carried whatever items she deemed important enough to bring over.

With two of her boxes balanced in my arms I attempted to maneuver past her when the top one teetered a little too far to the right. The entryway wasn't made for meandering, especially when I was trying my best not to touch her in the process. We've been here for roughly four seconds and I was already on high alert of where my body was in proximity to hers.

Her eyes widened as I regained my balance right before its contents spilled out across the floor. "Be careful, will you. Precious cargo," she chastised before taking a few steps forward and coming to a halt in the middle of the main hallway, unsure where to go next.

"It feels like you have rocks in here." The boxes shifted in my hands again and I tried to keep my balance under the weight as I reached for the first door on the left.

A wicked smile crossed her face.

I groaned. "Abby, are these boxes full of your rocks?"

That earned me a glare. "They are not rocks, Kaiser. They're crystals, they serve a purpose," she quipped, as she often did, because I refused to call them what they are, "and only one is full of them."

One of the first projects I helped Abby with was fixing rain gutters. A storm blew through about a month after she moved in, wind whipped across the town taking everything not nailed down, including the old gutters her house had. After the wind, rain poured for two days straight and a small lake formed in her front entry way where the gutter was busted and left barely hanging onto the eave. We were sweeping out the water before working when a black glassy looking rock came into view. I picked up and turned it around in my hand, it was nothing like I had ever seen lying around before, with its long ridges, but it was a rock nonetheless. My hand pulled back to toss it into the yard when she yelled out. She lectured me for almost twenty minutes that she had put the stone outside of the house on purpose. That the storm must have moved it from the corner of the porch she left it in.

Protection crystal, she called it; it was the same kind that was always tied around her neck.

The more projects I helped out with, and the further I was able to venture into her house, the more rocks I found. Small, clear, oval stones in various corners of rooms or on windowsills. More shiny black stones, like the one I found on the porch, or stone that reminded me a tigers eye or even rainbows on fire.

They were everywhere.

There was one in particular I found while replacing a vent in her office at home. It was dark blue, and sparkled as if a million stars were captured inside. It was like holding a piece of the night and not any regular night, but the kind of sky I stared at when I spent nights out at Wildflower Lake.

With no light pollution, millions of stars dotted the sky, farther than the eye could see and more than the brain could comprehend. And with the Milky Way swirling itself into the mix, the sky wasn't black, but the deepest blue I had ever seen. It was beautiful and for years it was my favorite color, and then I met Abby and noticed her eyes were the exact same shade.

If I had to choose, that crystal, whatever it was called, because I never asked, was my favorite. It looked like the night sky, like Abby's eyes. And I didn't even feel bad when I slipped it in my pocket to keep.

I pushed open the door to the vacant guest room. "So this is it. It's not much, nobody really stays here besides my mom. Even then it's only like once a year. But the bed is nice and ..."

"Kaiser," she says, effectively cutting off my stream of conciseness. Turned out acting like a normal human around her was difficult task.

This could possibly be either the best or the worst idea I ever had. Having people in my space was not something I enjoyed, I'd been on my own for so long that I'd need time to adjust. But I couldn't leave her there. Seeing her standing in the middle of her destroyed house pulled at a caveman-like instinct to protect her. My mouth asked her to stay with me before my brain had time to process the words.

And only after it did, did I remember why I lived on my own in the first place.

I'd deal with it when it came up, if it came up.

I was nervous, could she see it?

When I finally looked over she's grinning at me and my stomach flips. Actually flipped inside of me. This was a terrible idea, there was no way I would come out of this without all of my secrets spilling out and there were so many I wanted to stay hidden.

"Sorry, I'm rambling." My hand smoothed over the roughness of my beard as I avoided looking at her again.

"This is perfect, thank you again." She reached out, placing her hand on my upper arm. The warmth seeped through my thick flannel and radiated to every corner of my body. It was too much. I slinked away before I could act on my urge to lean into it. Her smile dropped a fraction, but it was for the best.

I was no good for her and I needed to remind myself that. I was going to fix her house and get her back over there as soon as possible. That was the plan and I was going to stick to it.

"Don't mention it." My hand dug further into my front pockets as we stood awkwardly in the middle of this barren room. "Do you want something to eat? I can cook something real fast." It was going on ten o'clock, and I had no idea where she came from or what she had been doing before she ran to me.

The silence that passed between us seemed to last forever. "You cook?" She questioned, as it was a fact she never would have guessed about me.

A quick nod was all I gave her. She knew nothing really, it didn't matter how much time we spent together, I didn't open up to anybody. I preferred solace—in my work, in my home, in the very few hobbies that I enjoyed. Relying on other people was ripped from me a long time ago.

"I think I'll try to sleep." The softness of her voice matched the anxious way her fingers twirled around themselves.

I was a normal person, why couldn't I act like it?

She sat on the bed, her hand smoothing over the faded blue quilt.

I needed to get something newer for her. Better. The urge to re-do this entire room, hell maybe even my entire house, to make her feel comfortable and at home was suddenly the only thing I could think about. A mental checklist formed in my head of anything she might need to make her stay better. Maybe I could check in with Kaity, she was younger than Abby but at least she would know what to buy or what she might need.

"If you need anything, let me know. My room is the next one over." My hand motioned down the hallway while she continued to stare at me with these wide and night sky colored eyes before nodding her head at me. Her gaze lacked any of the brightness I was accustomed to. Behind the color that was the star in all my fantasies was a sadness that I'd never seen. Gone was the spark and nothing took its place, there was only emptiness. I wanted to fix it but I didn't know how.

I turned to leave.

"Goodnight Kaiser." She called out after me as I shut the door and was left standing like a guest in my own hallway. Having Abby here was filling me with dread and stomachache inducing anticipation at the same time. Each feeling wrestles with the other fighting for dominance in my veins. And I couldn't quite figure out which was going to win. Or which one I wanted to win.

The lock flipped over on the front door and I continued around to do a second lap to secure the rest of the house before stopping in my kitchen to look out the window. If she knew I did this most nights... Well, I didn't really want that to come out, it was embarrassing enough when I was the only one that knew but at least this time I had an actual reason. My eyes scanned the length of her property, checking for any sign of movement or cars I didn't recognize. I hovered for a few moments before I deemed it clear and then headed to bed.

Everything was dark, only the soft light of her room filtering from underneath her door. Even though it was late, I knew sleep wouldn't come, but I went through my routine regardless and hoped it would trigger whatever was in my head that refused to turn off.

This would be easy, she would stay here a week or so, I'd fix her house up quick and she'd leave. We'd go back to being neighbors, where I suffer in my longing for a woman eleven years too young for me and she would continue to live her life thinking I couldn't care less about her. This would be easy, I'd been living with these feelings for years, having her in the next room opposed to across the street would be easy.

TEN

Abby

THE SUN BEGAN PEAKING up from the horizon and I had been rolling around in the extremely comfortable guest bed for a few hours. I loved Sundays, usually. I'd normally sleep in, roll out of bed by nine, and drink my coffee slowly either lounging on the patio furniture in my backyard or curled up in the corner of the house, depending on the weather.

Sundays were for bagels, for vanilla lattes from Renaissance Cafe, leisurely applied skin care and slowly reseting my home for the upcoming week.

But I didn't know what to do with this Sunday.

I texted my boss and let her know I couldn't make it in Monday or Tuesday. I would have taken longer but I had to be in by Wednesday. Carina had a big trial coming up and there was a never ending mountain of work on my desk in order to prepare. The only thing I knew for certain would happen today was I would spend most of it cleaning up and seeing how bad everything really was at my house.

Finding a silver lining to this whole mess was like searching for the light switch in the dark. You knew it was there, but no matter how many times your hands traced the wall, you never found it. I liked to be happy, it was a curse and blessing really. Life was beautiful and for the most part it was easy to find good in everything around me, or at least it was until I met Liam. Then my world darkened. Even after he tainted everything around me, I still looked for anything that would make the world seem brighter. Even if I had to fabricate it. Which was the problem.

I was smart, I should have seen the signs that everything about him was a facade. The red flags were waving themselves in my face from the start but when I looked at him they were only a pretty shade of rose. Even with the glasses completely gone I still couldn't believe he might have done this.

Despite the bed being one of the comfiest things I had ever slept in, I didn't sleep for longer than a few hours. I missed my sheets that I splurged on a few birthdays ago and the little nightlight plugged in between my bed and bathroom. I pulled back the covers and set my feet on the cool wooden floors. Even from my short stay, I could tell Kaiser put a lot of work into his home. The floors looked original but in pristine condition, the walls a pretty shade of beige with beautiful crown molding along the ceiling. I hadn't seen the rest of the house but from what I could see, it was all very *Kaiser*. A plain sort of beauty. Flinging open my suitcase, I shuffled through the stack of clothes until I found the worn pair of overalls I liked to work in. They're covered in paint and glue and the most comfortable thing I owned. My fingers comb through my hair quickly after I realized I didn't pack a brush and I was thankful it fell in easy waves, versus my sister's unruly tangle of curls, and then pulled it into two quick braids. Once I was satisfied, I pulled the door open only to crash into Kaiser the second I stepped out of my room.

His quick reflexes were the only saving grace that kept me from face planting onto the floor. His arm wrapped around me lightning fast as my feet twisted under me, causing me to stumble.

Embarrassment should have been crawling up the back of my neck. Instead it was a familiar red hot blush. And as fast as it came it was gone as his hand dropped from where it was clutched at my back. His eyes scanned me from head to toe.

"Where are you going?" He asked simply.

"I-um, I was going to start cleaning up." He made me nervous, I shouldn't be nervous.

My attempt to push past him was interrupted by him stepping back in front of me.

"Let me give you a quick tour, since you didn't get a chance to look around last night," he said.

"You don't have to do that, the room is great, I don't need to be in all your stuff." There was look of determination in his eyes.

"I don't think of it like that. I want you here, and if you need anything I want to make sure you know where to get it and that you're comfortable here even if I'm not." It wasn't a demand, it was a soft welcoming into his personal space, an invitation to know him better. And there was almost no way for me to say no.

His house couldn't be much bigger than mine, and I realized it's actually the same layout but reverse.

"So, you know your room," he points behind me, "I'm the next one over." He walked a few steps backwards. I peered around his door frame for a look. A pristinely made bed, hospital corners and everything, was stood in the middle and one nightstand with nothing on it, not even a lamp, were the only furniture in the room. Exactly what I expected from a man like him. "Another spare room, there's nothing in it but a desk. This closet has extra blankets and towels and of course the bathroom."

When I stumbled in during the night, I never switched on the light in an attempt to keep my eyes heavy with sleep. I expected to see a bathroom that matched the house, plain, but I was almost taken aback by the stunning craftsmanship that stood before us.

Up against the wall sat a porcelain, claw foot bathtub. It was by far the most stunning piece I had ever seen inside someone's house. It looked more like something you would find at a hotel or some swanky bed and breakfast, like the one that sat at the top of the hill overlooking the town. I stayed there once years ago and thought of that bath regularly. This was exactly like that, I couldn't believe it.

"Wow this tub is everything. I don't think I even fit into my bath at home," I mused half aloud, half to myself.

Kaiser shifted from one foot to another behind me. "Whatever you need to use is yours. There's coffee and bagels in the kitchen,

I need to run to my shop and then I'll come meet you," He said sharply before stepping away.

I followed, but before he walked out the door I stepped around the corner, coming into the kitchen. My eyes caught on a familiar brown paper bag with a large stamp of hands almost touching on the front, immediately I knew what I would find inside.

"Those are from Renaissance Cafe? I love that place."

"I know that's why I got them."

"What?" Confusion wracked through my brain. He didn't meet my eye.

"It's just breakfast."

Before he could slither away I swung my arm out and caught my hand onto his arm.

"Have you been watching me, Kaiser?" I asked with a half a laugh in my voice. As I said the words I realized how desperate I was for them to be true. Because if they were, it would mean I wasn't alone, and it would mean that I wasn't crazy for playing up every simple conversation we've had.

"It's just breakfast, " he repeated and looked almost annoyed as he said it. "I spend a lot of time in the garage and have seen you a few times leave and come back with the same bag and it didn't take a genius to figure out. I wasn't watching you, Abby."

What a complex Kaiser was. I expected to be met with a look of indifference before he left but when our eyes met his held so many emotions I couldn't focus. His look bored into me with flashes of concern, annoyance, sympathy. All the things you didn't want to see when man looks at you. And he didn't speak. We stood there in awkward silence that had me shift back and forth where I stood. Out of habit, my teeth tugged on my lower lip while I waited for anything to happen since I was effectively trapped by him.

I also didn't mind the close proximity, it allowed me to really look at him. It had been years since I was this close to him. Years since I was so close that all it would take was a slight tilt of his head to have his lips brush against my forehead once more. Years since I'd tracked the depth of his eyes with my own, watched them morph from a beautiful blue grey to the stormy green they were at the moment.

My bottom lip was pulled between my teeth again and new emotions blared from within. With a shake, I cleared my head of the memories that began popping up.

"You don't have to help me clean up you know." I was stalling, for some reason I didn't want him to leave yet.

"I told you I'd help you." He said the words with an impersonal tone, the type you reserve for someone you didn't like when you tell them, 'ya, I'll watch over your house while you're gone'. You knew it was the right thing to say but you didn't really want to do it.

"You really don't have to do that." I was panicking. I rushed out in front of him to get to the front door. "Really, it's not that big of deal. Probably some glass and broken furniture to clean up and that's it." He wasn't buying it and his normal look of indifference was back on his face. His facial hair really added to it as it covered the lower part of his face, you couldn't really tell what was going on. He could be smiling but I would never know. Not that he smiled really in the first place.

"I'll be over soon," he repeated and I backed out the front door slowly.

Kaiser was an impossible enigma. Days, even weeks, went by without talking, and not for any reason other than that life got in the way. Or in my case I ended up with a new boyfriend and turn into one of the girls who poured all their attention into that person and let everything fall to the wayside. Then eventually I'd need his help or want to pick his brain about a project and he acted like I'd personally offended him with my silence. But even in his silence he would drop whatever he was doing to help. It gave me constant whiplash.

Much like his current disdain for me cleaning up but insisted that he would come over and help. It's impossible to keep up with.

I walked over to the bag and peeled it open to find an array of flavors to choose from and settled on a what I hoped was a cinnamon and sugar bagel. I tore off a pieces and popped it in my mouth while my eyes roamed the kitchen before they snagged on the cup Kaiser had mentioned.

It didn't take me long to realized it wasn't full of black coffee as I expected, but was a pleasant shade of tan and carried an aroma of vanilla. With no one around, I hid a smile before taking a sip.

ELEVEN

Kaiser

THE SCANNER BEEPED AS Kaity popped her gum, her eyes flicked up every other item she scanned. "This is an unusual assortment of items. Do you need it gift wrapped?" Kaity asked as another beep rang out and she set the amber glass bottle back on the counter. She held her lips between her teeth to fight her smile. It was a mistake coming here. I should have driven the few extra minutes to a convenience store or literally anywhere else in this town, other than my own store.

"Just bag it, will you?" My boot tapped against the polished concrete floor.

"So not a gift. I didn't think you used the products from here, Boss." She turned a cellophane bag in her hand to find the barcode. To be honest I had no idea what was even in it, I headed straight to the vendor section and grabbed anything that read bath, or relaxing then carried it all to the booth where Kaity was sitting with a book in her hand.

"I don't."

"So not for you. Got it." She popped her gum again.

Everything about this interaction caused my shoulders to tense. I rolled my head from side to side and kicked myself for the question I was about to ask. "If I needed to pick up hair stuff for someone else to use, what should I get?" I requested, knowing it would only open a door to a world full of more questions.

"Is this someone a girlfriend?" she quizzed right back.

"If I tell you what's going, will you help me?"

"I'm all ears and dying for something to gossip about."

Kaity was as loyal as they came, and while there was nothing to actually gossip about I doubted she would take this and start spreading it around. Fairvale bordered on being small enough to know most people and large enough that people didn't actually care about what the local woodworker was doing in his spare time. But sometimes you never know.

I came straight from my shop to my house to shove all the products in the bathroom cabinet. My only hope was she wouldn't notice they were all still wrapped in plastic, put two and two together to figure out I went and got them specifically for her. All I wanted was for her to be as comfortable as possible in my home and around me. And when you're like me, a man who bumbled over any words that have to do with feelings it was hard to get that point across. The best I could do was stow away products I thought she would enjoy.

Her house was in a right state. A majority of the day was spent simply sweeping up glass shards and broken trinkets that were littered around her home. The water from her leaky faucet, which finally gave out, was mopped away and fans were plugged in to hopefully dry up the place before we came back the next day.

It was after her second breakdown while sweeping up the glass that we left the house for the hardware store to pick up supplies to begin the actual work. We had finished scouring the hardware store with a flatbed full of counters, a new sink and supplies for new backsplash. After finding her fawning over sample pieces, gushing about how it would make it feel like a mid-century French country kitchen, whatever that was, it was a simple choice to do a complete renovation of her kitchen and not replace only what was water damaged. I would have built her a new house entirely if I thought it would keep the tears from falling or her heart from breaking any further.

We teamed lifted the last cabinet into the bed of my truck, and I latched the tailgate.

"How long do you think all this will take?" she asked as she slipped into the passenger seat.

"The new door, about a full day, and the cabinets, backsplash and sink... Maybe two if there aren't any issues. You should be back home by next weekend."

"Really?" Her back hit the seat as her fingers nervously tapped against the worn leather of the seat. "I can talk to my sister, I'm sure I could stay over there until at least the door is in. Get out of your hair faster."

She wouldn't look at me and I wondered if I had done something to give her the impression that I didn't want her with me. Actually I was sure I probably did and that was my own fault.

She exhaled loudly. "I have to go back to work on Wednesday though and won't be able to help, and you have to get back to your shop. What if it takes longer? Do you think I'll be okay with only the door? I don't need a full working kitchen in order to be in my house, right?" She rambled before looking at me, waiting for the right answer.

I turned to face her. "Abby, you can stay with me as long as you need to. You are not a bother, or in my way, or whatever it is you're thinking. And don't worry about helping me, we'll get it all done in time, okay?"

She nodded. "Okay."

My truck rattled to life in the parking lot. "Are you sure this thing will make it home" She glanced back at the new cabinets and the large sliding glass door that was hanging off the truck bed.

"Don't talk about her like that, she'll make it just fine," I admonished as I rubbed my hand over the dash before giving a couple of taps. "She's a classic, built to last."

"This truck is a million years old, I think it was made the same year you were." She snorted, causing the dimples on both sides of her cheeks to appear at her own joke.

"Funny, Dimples." I deadpanned. I watched from the corner of my eyes as she smiled at the nickname, and briefly brought her hand up to touch the side of her face before dropping it back into her lap.

My faded green Ford 100, which was made in 1960, and not the same year I was born, pulled out of the parking lot. With the sun sinking toward the horizon at our backs we wove our way through town and back to our neighborhood. The air was cool but that didn't stop her from cranking the window down and letting the dusk air breeze through the truck. She sang along, badly, to some early 2000 pop song with her arm hanging out the side doing little rollercoaster movements in the wind.

She was content, happy even, and it was enough.

"Do you want to stop for dinner before we get home, or I can cook?"

"You keep saying you can cook, yet you still have yet to pull out a pan. I'm beginning to think you're trying to make yourself look better."

"I can cook, Abby."

"Sure you can. Let's stop and grab something before we get home, I'm too tired to wait." *Home*. I liked the way that sounded falling from her lips. I could get used to it.

TWELVE

Kaiser

SOMEONE ELSE IN MY home was such a foreign concept to me that I'd resorted to pacing the length of my room. I never lived with anyone outside my own parents; I had one girlfriend, decades ago, but I deployed for the first time before we ever moved in together and she wasn't around long enough to be there when I got home. Abby, being only one room over, threw off my routine. Instead of a quick shower, I stressed over if I should tell her goodnight or if that would be weird. Instead of trying to trick my mind into sleep, I was wondering if I should offer her another blanket or if the air needed to be turned on.

How did people in relationships move in each other's orbits without feeling invasive?

Not that what Abby and I had was a relationship. It was a... I didn't quite know what we were doing, but it was something.

No matter how hard I tried to push the feelings , they swam right below the surface between us.

Which was why I was pacing.

It felt like there was this tightly wound ball of string shoved in my chest. The more I focused on the fact she was here, in my home, the tighter and tighter the strings pulled. They were on the verge of snapping, I needed to do anything other than wear a track path around my bed.

Did I have a plan? Absolutely not, but I figured I would walk down the hall, casually, and if her door was open, I would tell her goodnight.

Easy, and not creepy. At least that was what I told myself.

With each step, I tried to convince myself it was normal behavior. Light flooded out of her open door and into the dark hallway. She was curled up by her pillows with her legs crossed underneath her and the blue comforter pushed to the end of the bed, writing in a notebook. The soft lamp on the nightstand illuminated the room, washing her in a golden color and turned her hair a fiery sort of red. The simplicity of the sight brought my focus back to the ball in my chest.

"Are your blankets alright?" I asked as my mental list rearranged in my head, new bedding suddenly skyrocketing to the top.

She looked up from her lap. For a split moment there was a wave of sadness that crest in her ocean eyes, but before I could ask what was wrong, she blinked, and like a switch was flipped, she beamed at me. It was so fast, I wondered if I'd imagined it.

"Everything's great, Kaiser, really." She snapped the book close, slipping it under her pillow and from my prying eyes.

The words were there, but her suitcase still sat in the corner full of her belongings, the crack in the closest told me nothing but an old forgotten box was behind the door. All of it a blaring reminder that this was temporary. She was here because I offered, she was here because her house wasn't safe. Not because she wanted to.

"You can unpack, you know?" I nodded toward the floor full of her stuff before I caught sight of the nightstand. "But I see you got your rocks out," I said with a tilt of my head.

"Crystals."

"Crystals, of course."

She shook her head at me. "Come here." I stepped forward without thought. "Hold out your hand." She requested as she reached over to the nightstand. I did what I was told and stretched my arm out toward her like an offering. It was easy, doing what she asked, and if it kept the amused look on her face, it would quickly become a daily ritual in my life.

Her fingers brushed the palm of my hand when she placed a small white stone with grey marbling in my hand as her gaze flitted from my face back down to my hand. But my eyes were locked on only her. The way her eyelashes seemed to be so long they brushed the apples of her cheeks as she blinked, the soft halo of untamed hair or the thin straps of her tank top that showed off the light freckles that dusted her shoulder tops that I never knew existed before. I couldn't tear my eyes away from all the fresh sights I had of her.

"This is howlite." I heard her say but all I could focus on was thrumming of my heartbeat in my ears. It took me a few seconds longer than it should have before I cleared my throat and took a small step back. Anything to pull myself from the thoughts that were floating to the surface. I held the rock between my thumb and forefinger, inspecting it. "This looks like a piece of counter top." Her nose crinkled as she shook her head.

"You place it under your pillow to help with insomnia." She lets me know as if she heard me walking around last night. That or it was a one hell of a coincidence. I didn't sleep much, it was almost impossible when all your dreams are nightmares.

The rock was plucked and replaced by a stone with all sorts of purple shades. "Fluorite. This acts like a sort of dreamcatcher. Filters out the bad, only lets in the good dreams. Among other things."

Skepticism and I went hand in hand, this was too far out for me to grasp, but I would pretend like I was interested if it kept me in here with her. "And you're sure they all do what you say they do?"

She took the stone back and slipped it under her pillow with the first. She shrugged her shoulders. "Maybe, maybe not but what's the harm" Her legs swung to the edge of the bed to walk over to the box in the corner and she began rifling around. Seconds later and a moment of me pretending like I wasn't watching the way her tight sleep pants stretched across her ass, she pulled out another of piece of dreamcatcher stone and handed it over.

Again, without thought, I took her offering. "Why bring these?" I asked as my fingers curled around the smooth stone.

She studied me for a moment, that small wave of sadness breaking through the sun again. "I think I needed something that felt familiar here. I like what they represent, the hope that these tiny pieces of the earth can fix whatever troubles you, as long as you believe in the change enough." Her long legs slipped back under the covers. "Try it out, see what happens," she proclaimed.

The room was quiet as I rolled the stone around in my palm, contemplating if there was anything to them after all. When I finally looked up, she was already watching me. Instinct begged me to look away quickly, like I'd always done, it yelled and screamed, but for once I ignored it. My pulse vibrated as we remained in a stalemate, neither one of us daring to be the first to look away. Her pink lips parted, but no words followed.

This must be it, the reason why people chose to be pulled into another's gravity. To bear witness to all the small moments where it feels like you're the only two people in the world. Where the tiny seconds could drag on into infinity and you would still wish you had more time in order to simply be near them.

She broke first, a quick blink and her gaze was torn from mine, and I took that as my cue to leave, still speechless. My hand closed around the doorknob and slowly pulled it closed behind me.

"Sweet dreams, Kaiser." Her soft voice was the last thing I heard.

I did not, in fact, have sweet dreams, but that was something I was used to. The late night air ached deep in my bones. It was a dull throb that wrapped around the long since healed cracks and breaks and in my joints from one too many times kicking down doors while overseas. My hand smoothed up and down my forearm as a chill rolled through me, failing to bring any warmth back. I was stuck on my back deck staring out into the deep blue of night and the greenbelt that my house backed up to. Sleep evaded me once again and I had been unable to talk myself into retreating back to my bed.

Smoke billowed lazily from the ash of my cigarette, soft tendrils that faded into nothing while the end burned like hot coals as I inhaled deeply. I loved how quiet this time of night was, after midnight where everything was still. No animals rustling in the trees, or birds chirping from the power lines. Barely any wind to disturb the leaves on the limbs of trees.

It was only me and the stars.

The exhale of smoke met the outdoor air as the silence was disturbed by a slow drag of the sliding door behind me. My body had yet to adjust to another person living in my home, and the noise had my fight instincts kicked into gear. I spun on my heel to face the intrusion, cigarette dangling from my lips, body clicked into fight mode, only to see the small stature of a woman who should have been asleep in her bed.

Abby slowly pulled the door shut behind her before turning back to me. It was as if she was brand new to me. Bare faced but with a slight sheen on the apples of her cheeks, like she went to bed wearing some sort of lotion. Her hair wasn't brushed and looked like she spent hours tossing and turning. Then there was the moonlight that drenched her in a soft glow that seemed to start from within her.

I never gave much thought to showing gratitude to the sky before, but I felt compelled to thank it for its contribution to the way she looked.

Midnight or noon, she was beautiful.

"What are you doing up?" The whisper of her voice sent shivers down my spine. She padded over on bare feet to stand next to me facing the forest.

"I could ask you the same."

There was a sad smile that ticked at her lips. Sadness that she carried over with the box full of belongings only yesterday and that sat with her on the bed when I left her room only a few hours earlier. "New house, I couldn't fall asleep, same as last night." She shrugged and pulled her arms around her body.

There was a lot of willpower on my end to not stare as she stood beside me wrapped in the thinnest robe made to man. I nodded and peeled my eyes away from her to turn and look back out into the night. There would've been no reason for her to look for me specifically, even if we're now under one roof. That didn't stop the thought from entering in my head that maybe in the cover of darkness I would be the person she would search for to calm her worries.

"I saw your bed empty and came to see what keeps you up at night." Her voice was soft, as if she didn't want to disturb the stillness around us. My heart didn't get the memo though as it pounded in my chest.

"Did the fluorite not work well?" I could hear the snicker in her voice.

"I don't sleep well most nights, your rock never stood a chance."

"How come?" What innocence that question possessed.

PTSD induced insomnia, nightmares, bad mattress. Take your pick, I thought.

I brought my cigarette back up to my lips and pulled in another round of toxic air. "Who knows." I lied on the exhale. Her eyes bore into the side of my head as she watched my movements.

My demons liked to find me in the middle of the night. Under the cover of darkness, where I straddled the cusp of dreams and reality and where I was most vulnerable. Every night was a battle and one I lost often. The place I stood in on the deck had permanent indents of my feet weathered into the wood.

Something compelled me to offer her a drag, if only to have her lips on the same place mine were. Her nose crinkled up at the offer. "Hasn't anyone told you those things are bad for you?" A snort of laughter exited my nose.

"Once or twice."

She didn't offer anything further but I kind of liked that she didn't press me to put it out or lecture me. Which was everyone's first instinct. I snuffed it out anyway and let the ashes mark the railing I was leaning on. If anyone could get me to quit it would've been her and she wouldn't even have to ask.

"Do you have any siblings?" she asked after a moment of silence.

"No."

"Did you grow up here in Fairvale?"

"No, I moved here when I sixteen. What is this, what are you doing?" I pulled back to look down at her.

"Just trying to get to know you better. I mean we're living together don't you think it's about time?" Amusement glimmered in her eyes as she stifled a small giggle.

My head rattled at the words, as if jail bars were slammed shut and self doubt seeped into my veins. The words were poised and ready on my tongue that I was no one worth knowing. That knowing me would to be covered in dark clouds and I would only rain all over her brightness, ruining her in the process.

But for a moment, a simple thought raced through my head as she went back to looking out at the darkness: if I was going to ever let anyone in, it would be her.

We stood shoulder to shoulder for a few minutes longer until she began to shiver next to me. The thinness of her robe doing nothing to hide the even thinner pajamas she had on underneath, I could see every last cold part of her. It was enough for me to question my own resolve to not look. Every part of me called out to wrap her in my arms, instead I pushed back from the railing and took a step away from her. "I'm going to head back inside," she announced and led the way.

Abby didn't even have to do anything for it to affect me. She probably had no clue that the way she walked stirred something up inside of me. I had this all wrong. One week was going to be hell and I had no one to blame but myself.

THIRTEEN

Abby

NOTHING FELT RIGHT AS we stepped into the house. I didn't know what I was hoping to feel, only that I wanted this to be over and walking through my empty living room was only a blatant reminder that it had happened. The glass may have been swept up and the shattered pieces of no longer littered the ground but I could still feel him here. His anger leeched into the walls, seeping into the foundation my house stood on.

The fans were still whirling but luckily they seemed to have done their job since we didn't have to wade through any puddles, though the water damage was evident. Water had seeped into the baseboards warping them and pulling them from the walls. The cabinet under the sink was crumbling away like cork from taking the brunt of the damage.

Holes spotted the living room walls where frames were ripped from their nails before being thrown on the floor. It wasn't until the morning breeze passed through the shattered glass door that the first tears of the day pricked the back of my eyes.

But I was going to fix this, I had no choice and there was no use in crying over broken glass.

A heavy sigh blew through my lips.

"Where should we start?" My voice broke the quietness of the house.

Kaiser appeared at my side, his hand skimming across the top of his hair. He did that a lot, it was like a nervous tick when he needed to think, as though the thoughts needed to be coaxed forward. There wasn't a problem he couldn't solve, so I waited for his instructions, because if I even tried to think about what to do I was sure I would start crying again.

"I'm going to take out the remainder of your sliding glass door and tarp it up for the night so nothing gets in. Then probably tear your baseboards off to replace them."

"And me?" I wanted clear instructions so I didn't have to think. His jaw clenched at my voice, his eyes sweeping around the room looking at everything but me.

"Have you ever patched a hole?"

Of course I hadn't, I wasn't a do it yourself type of women despite what I told myself when I bought this place. "No, but I could learn." I gently smiled up at him, hoping to ease the awkwardness between us.

He nodded and turned on his heel toward the kitchen before coming back with an armful of supplies. "It's simple, really, even you can do it." His voice carried a hint of amusement, before his face lost any trace of emotion.

Back and forth, back and forth. It was always the same with him. One moment he's all ice and scowl, and the next, I swore he's seconds away from laughing. Okay, maybe not laughing, that seemed a bit much for him, but occasionally he slipped into his version of relaxed around me. Those were my favorite moments, where it feels like I might be the only one who saw him without his guard. And it reignited the thought that maybe, just maybe, these buried feelings aren't so one-sided.

Until I knew one way or another, I would be happy with the little moments.

My jaw dropped as I scoffed. "I'll have you know," I snipped, plucking the mesh patches and tub of spackling from his hands, "I took a woodshop class in junior high. I know things." That wasn't a lie, but it was so long ago and I wasn't even sure that they let us use real tools in that class.

"I'll leave you to it then." He handed me the spatula that was left in his hand before walking away, with a slight shake of his head.

I turned back to the wall. Everything was fine, I could patch a wall. I pulled my phone from my back pocket and did a quick glance to see where Kaiser was. If I watched a quick tutorial on how to fix holes, no one would be the wiser.

The first two were a little wonky, I held my breath each time Kaiser walked by waiting for him to pick apart my work but he barely even looked my way.

With Liam, I waited in bated breath anytime he asked me to do something, because no matter how hard I tried nothing was ever good enough. But I kept coming back, kept trying no matter how defeated I felt once I was done. This wasn't like that though, Kaiser wasn't waiting around to berate me. I knew that and I was trying very hard to remember that.

As soon as the plaster turned white, I swiped my hand over the section. It was rough, but I didn't think you were supposed to paint over it like this. My hand snaked around to my back pocket to grab my phone for the next step in the tutorial when the sound of wood splintering pulled my attention. My head swiveled to glance behind me in time to watch Kaiser pull the sliding door from the wall.

A sudden intrusion of sensations torn through my body at the slight. My stomach dropped, a desert made a home in my throat and every muscle south of my waist clenched. And all of it caught me a little off guard.

I had a type—clean cut, polished. The type you find at a high end bar downtown with a suit jack tossed over a chair and a tie loosened around the neck of a man that looked like he was allergic to hard labor. Maybe it was a product of my environment. Working in a law office and all, there was no shortage of them. I knew what I liked but I was seconds away from throwing everything I knew out the window.

If you've never watched six foot something broad shoulder man, who only wore flannels of different colors, rip a door from a house, I suggest you do.

He lost the flannel he was wearing earlier because of the heat and was down to his jean and black tee. Thick biceps flexed under the weight of the door as he lifted and turned to prop the discarded door on the wall outside.

My throat worked to swallow.

I hadn't so much as looked at another man since Liam, but I was suddenly having trouble keeping my eyes to myself. But the rewarded me when he grabbed the hem of his shirt to wipe the sweat that gathered around his hairline. A quick glimpse of dark hair running down in to the tops of his jeans, I was done for. I was never looking at another man again, I decided. Not while Kaiser was around.

His eyes locked with mine as he dropped his shirt back down, and I made a quick but poor attempt to look busy once more.

Channels slipped past me as my vision began to blur. I sank back into the corner of Kaiser's couch, my feet tucked underneath me. We called it quits over at my house an hour earlier, and my body ached with the work we completed. The walls were a breeze, the baseboards were another story.

The previous homeowner had used more than nails to keep them in place. What should have been quick work to pry them off the walls turned into a few hours of removing sections only to have to repair the spots where the wall came off with the baseboards.

Kaiser walked into the living room, freshly showered, but his eyes betrayed him. He was tired. Faint purple circles adorned his face and there was an indent between his eyebrows like he had been scowling all day with no glimpse of happiness.

The couch dipped under his weight and I couldn't take my eyes off him. Again. He spared me nothing, no words left his mouth and his eyes never strayed from the tv.

"Are you hungry? I can put something together." I was halfway out of my seat before he answered. It was barely even a fully formed word, more of sound in his throat but I took it as a yes and headed to the kitchen.

If I could get away with ordering take out for every meal, I would. Cooking and I didn't mesh well. I get side tracked halfway through meals, often forget ingredients or burn the bottom of whatever I have in the pan. Liam hated it. *What kind of woman couldn't cook,* he would spit at me on the easy nights. On the harder nights the dinner would end up on the wall for me to clean up after he'd storm off.

There's exactly one dish I knew how to make and make well. I tossed open the refrigerator doors and pushed around more bottles of condiments than one person should have, until I found what I needed for a simple baked penne. Within the first few steps of the dish, I went into autopilot and my mind wandered for a moment. Back to when Lennon would make me this exact dish at least once a week. It was the meal she would make us on the night we were left alone and even though it was tied to some of my worst memories it was still my favorite.

Growing up was a mix of nightmares that never seemed to end and some of the best days I could remember. It had been years since I moved out of my mother's house but the memories lingered. Since Lennon was older she took on the role of parent when our mother would disappear in the night or be too drunk during the day to remember she had kids. But it wasn't always like that and Lennon had a hard time seeing past the dark to remember the good times, the softer times. I counted myself lucky; my mother often only forgot about us, but we always had a roof over our head, food on our table, and she never hit us. There were stints where she wouldn't drink at all and those were what I held on to. Where she would call me Blossom Girl while braiding my hair in the living room and I was the happiest version of myself.

My phone chimed from the counter. I leaned back from the pot of boiling noodles as random numbers flashed across the screen. I silenced the call and went back to cooking. With everything mixed together, I tipped the pot over into a pan and topped the entire thing with cheese. My phone rang again as I pushed the dish into the oven—I silenced it again.

This wasn't the first time a string of random numbers had my phone ringing off the hook. For a while I blocked them as quick as the calls came through, but that never stopped whoever it was on the other side. It's always a handful of calls in quick succession then nothing, and sure enough one more came through as I grabbed my phone and walked back to the couch. I sent it to voicemail before it even rang.

As I walked back into the living room, Kaiser looked as if he was seconds away from sleep. His gaze was heavy, each blink a bit longer than the last. I did my best to sit down without disturbing him but his eyes fluttered open as the couch dipped under me. Long limbs stretched up over his head before coming back down onto his face, the heel of his palm dug into his eye sockets. "Sorry," he mumbled between his fingers.

"It should be ready in about twenty minutes." His hand landed on the cushion between us. The urge to take care of him was overwhelming. To reach out and stroke my fingers along the back of his hand to see if he felt the way I had remembered. "Can I get you anything?" He shook his head the same time my phone began ringing.

Without looking at the caller, I declined the call knowing what was waiting for me on the other side. My movements must have been too fast or too suspicious because Kaiser was laser focused on me.

"Don't you want to get that?"

"No." It rang again. My eyes closed slowly, a sad attempt to will the call to stop.

"Someone is obviously trying to get a hold of you."

"I'm aware, it started a few months go. About once a week, I get all these spam calls at night. All different numbers, so it doesn't matter if I block it, another one will call, never leaving any voice-mails, and if I answer, dead air waves on the other side." I moved from the couch to seek the safety of the kitchen and away from his prying eyes.

Before I could get more than two steps away he spoke up. "Do you think it's someone you know?"

"I doubt it. I probably signed up for something that leaked my number. That's all."

By the look on his face, I couldn't tell if he believed me or not. I didn't even believe myself but being here has all but vanished any thoughts of Liam from my head. When I was in Kaiser's house I could forget about everything that happened and pretend, even if it was for little while, that I was wanted.

Dinner came out subpar, which was the best I could hope for, but he scarfed down the food without any complaints and I convinced him to let me clean up. When I made it back out to the living room, the TV was going with some show I had never heard of but Kaiser was focused on a pad of paper.

My steps were small to not startle him as if he was some rare wildlife animal. His hard brows quirked inward every so often as he scribbled back and forth before flicking the paper with the back of his pinky. At some point while I was in the kitchen, he shed the dark flannel and was down to the simple black henley that was underneath, each sleeve pushed to the elbows as he worked. It didn't matter that he wore the same type of outfit over and over, it never got old.

How did one stare without looking like a complete weirdo? However it was done, I was sure I was doing the exact opposite. I was locked in on his forearms, thick and flexing with every movement. It was distracting, to the point I was so focused on him that I almost missed what he was actually doing.

"You draw too?" I asked as I peered down. I was closer to him than I realized as our knees brushed against each other. "What other secrets do you have?"

He stalled and watched as I lowered myself onto the cushion closest to him. "No, not really," he stated before turning back to the notebook on his lap.

For a moment I thought about moving. Maybe this was something he did only for him, and not for prying eyes. But then he shifted. It was a small movement, barely even noticeable as he pulled the leg he had propped up on the opposite knee a bit higher, giving me a better look at the notebook. He never looked up but continued dragging his pencil across the page in short flicking movements. "I entered the shop into the competition during the fair and I need to come up with a design. I've sketched a few things but I haven't committed to anything yet."

"Can I see?"

His hand hesitated before looking at me with weary blue eyes.

"You don't have to, but maybe an outside opinion is what you need?" I said gently.

Without a word, he handed over the spiral notebook. The drawing that he was working on looked to be some sort of rocking chair, like the kind you might find in a nursery, it even had a rocking horse that would be etched in the head rest. I flipped the page to a chess set that I could only assume would be incredibly tedious to make with all the small pieces for the board. Each page was better than the last, and while I knew this was what he did for a living, the amount of talent someone would need to make any one of these was astounding.

"These are..." I flipped the pages as I searched for a word to capture how incredible these designs were. The last page caught my eye instantly. "This one would win for sure."

Fourteen

Abby

He'd been muttering under his breath for the past few minutes while we both stared at the French doors out on the deck. I wondered what went through his head when he's doing this, since I was never privy to the conversations. My sneaker tapped against the wood as I waited out his thought process.

"Don't you just, you know…" I made pushing movements with my hand. Seemed easy enough to me you just put the frame in the empty hole, and voila, doors. A few screws here and there for sure, but he'd been pondering it like it was rocket science.

The look he gave me was priceless. He physically recoiled at my words, brows lowered and eyes wild. "No, Abby, you don't just put it in," he said while mimicking my hand movements.

My shoulders raised and lowered. "Could've fooled me." He turned away, as I failed at my attempt to not laugh.

"Okay, I do need your help for this part, though. I'll need you to hold the frame in place while I place the first screw," he said in a serious tone.

Within minutes, the frame was in place and he got the first screw in without issue. I backed away once it was secure and walked back inside. "See, I told you, you push it in." His eyes fluttered closed on his next inhale. I decided it was in my best interest to walk away and go back to patching the holes in the wall. It wasn't only broken glass and tables. Picture frames were knocked off the wall and there were fist sized holes in various spots around the living room.

As I dragged the pink plaster along the wall, I tried to imagine what would cause a person to act this way. But I came up empty. I was tempted to reach out to Liam. I wanted to ask him point blank if it was him and why, but luckily the better, more reasonable part of me talked myself out of it.

The whirl of the drill drowned out my inner monologue, but I was chastising myself for the way my eyes kept sliding over to Kaiser and watching the way his shirt would ride up with each screw he put in.

It was like someone hit the slow motion button on the moment. Our eyes met and in that fraction of a second, his hand slipped, sending the drill piercing into his skin. Kaiser hissed through his clenched teeth, letting the drill fall to the floor with a thud.

The spackle filled spatula fell to the ground and onto the floor making more of mess I would need to clean up sooner than later. A few steps and I was kneeling in front of him, where he was crouched close to the ground rocking back and forth onto his heels. His eyes were squeezed closed so tightly that I was sure a headache wouldn't be too far behind. Small drops of blood were falling from his clenched fist. The pain was obvious in his silence.

"Kaiser?" I questioned.

He didn't move.

Talking would get me nowhere. I placed my hands gently over his, pulling open his clenched fist to see how bad the damage was and how much convincing was needed if it looked like he required stitches.

His breathing steadied once his hands rested in mine, melting into me like I was a refuge for his pain. The blood only looked bad and was already slowing, and thankfully, my stomach didn't even turn at the sight. A round puncture wound sat between his thumb and forefinger but nothing first aid couldn't take care of.

My thumb swept gingerly over the spot, the small drop of blood smearing at the touch. "Not too bad, I'll go get the first aid kit." I smiled gently, like it would ease some of his tension.

Instead his hand gripped me tighter, keeping me from raising. "Don't, I'm fine," he replied. His skin was warm and soft, much softer than I expected from someone who worked with his hands day in and day out. And when his fingertips grazed the inside of my wrist, I nearly exploded.

One touch and I was finding it hard to think, let alone keep my balance. I teetered on the balls of my feet but I didn't want to move. I didn't want to remove myself from his grasp as I might not find myself within it again.

Seconds passed and we remained in the same spot until his hand flexed causing him to inhale quickly at the pain. "Let me help you," I said quietly.

Reluctantly he moved his hand from mine. "First aid kits in the closet."

He had moved from the patio to the couch in the time I was gone. Without much thought I kneeled in front of him, placing the kit on the floor next to me and flipped open the box. I was using everything I had in me to not look up at him.

This was a reoccurring dream of mine or was it a fantasy. Was there even a difference?

Either way this scene had played out in my head, more than once, on particularly lonely nights.

I tore open the wipe, starting with a distraction, for me and him, seemed like a good idea. "What's your favorite food?"

"What?"

"Twenty-one questions, Kaiser, don't think just answer." I shook open the wipe and looked up at him. What a mistake. His heavy gaze was plastered on me. I swallowed. "What's your favorite food?" I asked again.

"Burgers."

I swiped the site, he hissed.

"Favorite season?" I blew lightly, trying to dull the sting. The fingers on his other hand curled into the sofa cushion.

"I like the cold."

I pressed a piece of gauze to the wound. "Favorite place to relax?"

"Wildflower Lake," he answered between his teeth.

"Hmm, don't think I've heard of that place."

"I'll take you some time."

I paused my amateur nurse skills to look up at him. There was a softness in his pale colored eyes as they danced between my mine, then my cheeks before flicking briefly toward my lips. My mouth went dry, my tongue darted out to wet my bottom lip.

He released a slow breath and dropped his shoulders before looking away. I grabbed a bandaid and peeled it open. I placed one side on, then took the backing off the other. I smoothed it down over the wound with my thumbs and hovered for longer than I should have.

"What's your favorite color?" I didn't want the game to end. I wanted to know everything about him.

"Midnight Blue." The answer came before I even finished the question, without thought, and he was back to staring directly into my eyes.

I ached for a soak in the claw foot tub Kaiser had in his guest bathroom. It had been calling my name since I first saw it. I hung another shirt up in the closet. I didn't mind living out of a suitcase, but since he made a point to let me know I could unpack, I thought it wouldn't hurt.

The space was small but easily fit the few blouses and trousers I brought. With the suitcase empty, I went to roll it into the closet to get it out of the way, but a box in the back caught my eye.

Snooping was frowned upon, I was taught that from a young age. Mainly that it wasn't okay when I was caught going through my sister's diary. I should have slid the box further back and shoved my suitcase in, but instead I dragged it across the floor before flicking open the cardboard flaps. My curiosity got the best of me.

It looked to be filled with momentos. My hands closed around a signed baseball in a plastic cube. I knew nothing about sports, it could have been signed by a world famous player and I would never have known. I rifled through the box of tickets until my fingers tapped on a glass frame on the bottom. When I dug it out I found myself looking a flag folded in a triangle frame.

My fingers brushed over the silver plaque.

SSG Kaiser Richard Price

In appreciation of your faithful military service.

Your selfless sacrifice and excellent performance of duty is reflective of the Army's Warrior Ethos.

I briefly considered if Kaiser and his father shared the same name. Wouldn't I have known if he was in the military? Wasn't that something you would be proud of? Maybe he wouldn't walk around boasting about it but surely it would have come up at least once over the years.

"What are you doing?" His voice came from behind me. My bones shook at the sound of his voice. The case that held the flag fumbled in my hands, but I grasped it tightly at the last second to keep it from falling to the ground. I wasn't trying to snoop, not really but the way he hovered over me was like I was caught with my hand in a cookie jar.

"I was unpacking and the box was there as I was putting my suitcase away, and I kinda looked inside." I looked up at him with the flag still in my hand. "I'm sorry."

He didn't say anything. He also didn't move.

"I didn't know you were in the military?"

"Not much to talk about," he answered before finally moving to take the case from my hand. It landed in the box with a crunch and with a quick nudge of his foot it slid back into the closet.

"It's admirable." When I stood to face him he didn't look mad, but a sad smile ghosted his lips.

"I didn't do it to be thanked, not by you or strangers in restaurants." It sounded like it was from a cue card, like he'd said the same thing hundreds of times and had the statement down to a science.

A thousand questions formed in my head and even though he wasn't rushing out of the room, there was a steady wave of *don't ask* coming off of him. But I wanted to know and not because I was nosey, I mean I was but I told him I wanted to get to know him and this only solidified that I didn't know anything. He would be the type of person to enlist purely out of love for his country and sense of duty.

Now that I knew, it's all I could see. The way he moved through my house after the break in, the way he carried himself, even the way he wore his hat. It was ingrained in him even if he didn't talk about it.

His hand flexed by his side. "I'll be out in the garage," he grumbled, turned on his heel and left.

I blew out a long breath. "Great talk," I announced into the empty room.

This feeling wasn't new, where it seemed like nothing I did would break through his shell. There's a part of me dying for him to either put me out of my misery and tell me once and for all that there was nothing here or that all the moments where I could physical feel the pull to him in my chest weren't all in my head. I was stuck in a weird purgatory with him.

The longer I thought about it the more likely it would be that I would spiral out and actually ask him. I needed to turn my head off and the one thing I could think of was sinking chin deep into the bathtub I had not stopped thinking about since I got here. The tub I had at home was whatever kind comes with a house and not the gorgeous porcelain clawfoot tub Kaiser installed. Mine was about a foot too short even for me, and never covered all my parts no matter how high I filled the water.

As the water rushed out, I held my hand under the spout and waited for it to run warm. My only issue was it might turn out to be the most boring bath since I brought nothing from my house other than hair wash. I hung my towel on one of the empty hooks before I turned to the mirror cabinet and pulled it open but there was only a bottle of pain reliever, toothpaste and a pack of q-tips. Under the sink turned up empty as well. Kaiser didn't look like the type to unwind under a mountain of bubbles, but I was hoping I was wrong for my sake.

The bath gods heard my prayer. "Jackpot," I whispered to myself as I opened up the last cabinet. I picked up two amber colored jars in the front, one lavender salts, the other eucalyptus. It was like shopping straight from a store, every scent to choose from and every product I could think of filled the cabinet. Bath salts, bubbles, even bath bombs that looked like they had flower petals pressed into them, and everything was unopened.

I took the first bottle I saw from the shelf and poured it into the stream of water, letting bubbles froth until they came close to cascading over the edge.

A quiet sigh escaped as I stepped carefully into the tub, sliding down until my chin hit the foam. This was exactly what I needed, a moment to not think about my house or that I had to go back into work or about Kaiser and what could be going through his head. It was me and my book and a massive of amount of bubbles. All was right—for the time being at least.

FIFTEEN

Kaiser

My bones were tired and ached something fierce after spending the day with my arms above my head installing that damn door. I rubbed the spot where the drill pierced my skin as it throbbed. I'd suffered through my fair share of cuts and bruises over the years, never had I been distracted enough to cause injury. Leave it to Abby to be the only thing that could pull my attention.

We were on track to finish by the end of the week and the dread of sending her back home was beginning to creep in. I'd spent the last five years helping her with any random project she wanted, new gutters, replacing windows and interior doors, anything she wanted I was there to help. There was always something she came asking for help with but now the closer we got to end of this project the more I was realizing that soon there would be nothing and I would loose my excuse to be near her. And who was I, if not the man she went to when she needed help?

I was minutes away from dozing off on the couch, when I started to search for my phone. Most of the day had passed without noticing as Randy and I finished the kitchen. I didn't know what a French country kitchen was but the items she picked out looked great with everything coming together.

My hands came up empty after patting around my pockets. I retraced my footsteps. Nothing in the kitchen. My bedroom was empty as well. By the time I got out to my truck to look I was annoyed. I reached in-between seats, under them, nothing.

I paced the hallway. I heard Abby turn on the water in the tub after I shoved the box back into closet and left without an explanation. A fact I had been trying not to focus on.

"I can hear you walking around Kaiser!" Her voice shouted through the door.

I swore silently. "Abby, sorry, but if you have your phone, can you call mine? I can't find it."

All I could hear was the sloshing of the water before she replied. "Okay, I'm calling it."

The ringing started but it sounded like—I took a step closer to the door.

Fuck.

"Um, Kaiser I think your phone's in here." Her delicate laugh floated under the door.

"Oh, uh, that's okay, I'll just get it when you're done." I turned to walk away. The shop was fine, Kaity was probably having the time of her life running the store without me or Randy around.

"You can get it if you want. The door's unlocked." I stopped mid step. If she could have see me she would watch in real time the way blood slowly drained from my face. I had been actively trying not to picture her in the bath, opening the door to see the real life thing didn't seem like the best way to keep that up.

This didn't mean anything, the thought blared at me. I was going to pop in, grab my phone and get out. My eyes wouldn't wander and everything would be fine.

Except cracking open the door enough to reach my hand in did nothing. I did a quick sweep of the counter and my phone wasn't there.

"It's on the shelf," she said.

Because of course it was.

I pushed the door open the rest of the way and kept my eye trained on the floor as I took a step in. The weight of her gaze was felt instantly.

"You don't have to shield your eyes. For a bachelor you have an awful lot of bath products so there plenty of bubbles."

I hummed in agreement, it was all I could work with a throat that was full of sand.

"And all the good parts are covered." There was a smirk in her voice as she swirled her hands around the top of the bubbles in my peripheral vision. She cupped a handful and blew them at me.

Everything was in slow motion when I finally looked at her. Her hair was frizzy from the steam, bringing out more curls than I ever remembered seeing. Strands clung to her forehead and damp cheeks, that had turned dark pink from the heat. A book sat wrapped around the edge of the tub, the corners damp and wrinkled.

A smile crept across her face before she sunk lower into the water and under a mountain of bubbles, only her glittering sapphire eyes stared back at me. I guess it wasn't a waste of money after all.

I never understood the appeal of baths, you're kind of just sitting in your own dirty water but this didn't seem half bad from the outside looking in.

She slid back up, out of the water, which was now dangerously close to not cover anything. "What?" Her eyes flashed a familiar look. Amusement mostly, but there was something deeper there.

I didn't realize I had said that out loud. I was preoccupied with where the water line met her chest and what was below the surface.

I needed to get out of here before I something wild came out of my mouth, like "can I join?"

Lavender hung in the air like thick, invisible clouds, fogging any sense I had that leaving would be the best thing. My foot lifted and I had no will to stop it as I took another step closer. She arched an eyebrow but made no move to cast me out. "What are you reading?" Not what I meant to say but my brain was refusing to tell my feet to move.

She picked the book back up, and thumbed through the pages, damping the paper further in the process.

"It's called the Power of Crystals." She wiggled her fingers a bit as she spoke, bubbles clinging to the tips.

"You don't know everything yet?" I teased as my body lowered on its own accord to take a seat. She looked up over her book, a smirk pulling at her lips. She looked like trouble and it felt like I had gone outside to lick the pavement as all moisture evaporated from my mouth. When was the last time I had been this nervous around a woman? Had I ever been nervous or was it just an Abby thing?

She shifted, and the water line dipped again. By some grace, I turned the groan that slipped up my throat into a semi convincing cough.

Definitely just an Abby thing; these feelings were brand new, and I had no idea what to do with them.

I should leave. I needed to stand up and leave and take a really, really cold shower. Or five.

But I didn't.

"I don't know everything but I know a lot," she said.

"I'm sure you do."

She handed her book over, with a look of determination. "Here, quiz me if you don't believe me." She shook the book and leaned over the edge to meet my outstretched hand, bubbles sliding down her wet chest. I really needed to get out of here.

But I didn't.

She was so fucking pretty. The type of pretty that made it hard to look at and impossible to look away all at once. Too pretty for a grumpy asshole eleven years older than her, that was for sure. I would say too pretty for anyone else also, but I wasn't the jealous type, or at least I was pretty sure I wasn't. It had been almost twenty years since my last girlfriend, I could hardly remember what I was like in a relationship. A mental image on Abby with another man flashed through my head. Scratch that, she *was* too pretty for anyone else, I wanted her for me and me alone. I could live with being labeled jealous if it meant she was mine.

All I knew was Abby was too good for me and it had nothing to do with the fact that underneath the mound of bubbles she was ... nope not going there. If I actively started thinking about it, I wouldn't be able to get up and walk out of here anytime soon.

I grabbed the book and flipped to a random page, thankful I had something else to train my eyes on, to focus on other than the way my jeans were beginning to tighten.

My hand smoothed over my beard as I sat back and propped my ankle up on the opposite knee. "Okay, it's a purple, sparkly looking rock."

"Easy, amethyst, another." She waved her hand as she leaned back onto the tile, letting her eyes drift close.

I laughed. "It's black and glossy looking."

She paused to think.

"It also looks a lot like that necklace you always have on."

"Black obsidian."

Correct again. "Why do you wear it?" I asked. She cocked her head at me. "The necklace, it says here that is helps cleanse the energetic field of disharmony, emotions and negative attachments. What are you trying to get rid of, Dimples?"

She avoided my eyes, choosing to sit forward, hugging her knees to her chest, the water precariously close to covering nothing at all. Finally she turned toward me, placing her cheek on her knee. "My last boyfriend wasn't a great person," she says quietly. "And sometimes it feels like he still has his claws in me. I wear the necklace because I'll do anything to keep him out of my head." My jaw clenched at her words, at the very thought that someone who had her could even think about not treating her like she was the most important thing in the world.

I flipped a couple pages forward and we did this for a few more minutes. I was surprised that she actually got every single one right. We moved on to what they did and I used that term very lightly because even with her as pretty as she looked in this bath there was nothing to convince me rocks did things.

I wasn't a sentimental man, little things in life rarely got to me and there's never been moments where I was struck with overwhelming feelings. But this felt different, it felt right. I felt it deep in my chest. A sharp tug where my soul met my physical body that got my attention. There was something about this specific domesticated action of reading, not just reading, but reading to Abby while she lounged in a bath after a long day of work that made me feel some type of way about how this was the start of something. I may not know what yet, but it was something.

It was the same feeling I got years ago during the one night I actually had her and I had to remind myself how hard it was to go back to being nothing after feeling the tug. I didn't want to have to do that again.

I should've left, but I didn't, because what if I never got this moment again?

SIXTEEN

Abby

Taking a few day off was a mistake, even if it was necessary. By noon, I was still scrolling through the mass amount of unread emails from my short time off, trying to filter out anything urgent to keep it all under control. Work didn't stop because I wasn't here, it only piled up for when I get back.

"Hey, I missed you. I didn't know you were on PTO." Carina's voice floated into my office pulling my focus from the screen and onto her. She leaned on the desk on the far side of the cubicle while still looking over a folder in her hand.

I shouldn't lie to her but the truth was too much to lay on someone all at once. "Oh. A pipe burst in my house. Flooded everything. It's a mess. I can't even stay there right now." Half a truth it is.

She snapped the file close. "Oh, shit, that's the worst," she said before her eyes narrowed my direction. "I talked to Lennon last night, she didn't say you were staying over. Did you get everything cleaned up then?" Small blond wisps of hair fell along her forehead.

I swiveled back to face the computer screen so she wouldn't see the deception. "No I think it will take awhile to get things back in shape." My fingers plucked away at the keys aimlessly to avoid looking back at her.

"Then where are you staying?"

The afternoon sun shined in from a nearby window casting her in an angelic light, but I knew better. Carina was an instigator, through and through. She could smell a secret a mile away and knew when to push and how far to push to get the information she wanted. The follow up questions were coming I could feel them in the air.

"If you're not at Lennon's, and you can't stay at your house, where are you staying?" she asked again while moving her finger from one imaginary spot to another as she tried to work out the mystery before I could tell her.

"Oh. I'm at Kaiser's house." There were not enough words in the dictionary for me to fake type while I tried like hell to keep from looking back at her.

Her hands smacked against my desk. "Hot Neighbor Kaiser?" She probed as she leaned in closer, like the words were a secret.

How did I explain this so it didn't sound like the start of a bad porno. Desperate girl next door needs a place to stay, the hot hunky neighbor has just place for her. Bleh.

"My *neighbor* Kaiser, yes." I stressed the word so she didn't start floating away with whatever scenario was going through her head.

Her mouth fell open a second ago and she refused to close it. "Shut the fuck up." She smacked my shoulder with the back of her hand. Not once or twice, but in three quick motions that had me scrambling from my seat.

"Umm... Ow," I said as I rubbed the spot before having to block another incoming hit. "Knock it off Carina. Look, it's not a big deal, okay? Kaiser offered to let me stay and help fix everything up. It made the most sense. He's across the street, I can run over and get anything I need from the house. He's already helped me fix up most of the place from the start anyways so he knows what he's doing and I trust him with the repairs. Nothing weird is happening." I sucked in a large breath after and I didn't know if I rambled in order to convince her or myself, but I hoped it was working.

All were great points, perfectly normal answers to what happened.

Nothing, and I meant nothing was going to happen between us. Kaiser didn't see me in that way, and I needed to stop throwing myself at men who were uninterested in me. All that happened when I did was force love where it didn't want to be. I always end up jamming it like glue into the broken cracks of my heart only to be shattered when the pieces fell apart a few months later.

She pushed off from the desk to leave. "Whatever you say *Amore*. But if I know you, and I think I do, and I've seen the way he looks at you, you two will be in love by the end of the month."

She disappeared from my small fabric walled office before I had a chance to respond.

Carina knew me better than anyone, except for Lennon for obvious reasons. But I didn't want to fall in love again or at the very least I shouldn't fall in love again. That's my whole problem, I was always the first to fall. First to say I love you and the first to ruin everything. I couldn't go through all of that again, I wanted my next relationship to be my last and in the five years I have known Kaiser I wasn't even sure he had so much as brought another woman home, let alone date. He'd be the last person to fall in love with me.

I turned back to my computer and went back to actually working. But the longer I scrolled through emails, or dropped off files Carina's last statement played on loop in my head.

Maybe I wasn't making it all up after all.

SEVENTEEN

Kaiser

ABBY LEFT FOR WORK in a rush, barely stopping to grab the coffee I had made for her. I guess in theory she could have gone back to her house, the door was replaced so there weren't any obvious issues to keep her out, people stay in their homes all the time while they renovate their kitchens. But I had some sick urge to keep her close

I couldn't keep her forever though, and in order to get her home soon, I needed help.

Kaity was unlocking the doors and turning the open sign over as I approached my shop. Her bright pink hair even brighter in the sun streaming through the window. Abby and I might be from the same generation, albeit different ends, but Kaity and I were absolutely not. I was pretty sure I was old enough to be her father and she was defiant enough to remind of it often.

"Hey, Boss, I thought you weren't going to be in today," she said as she stepped aside to let me pass through.

"I need Randy's help, do you think you could manage the store by yourself today?"

Her eyes brightened at my request. Kaity was more competent than half the people her age, it's part of the reason I hired her. Hell probably even more than me at times, I trusted her not to burn the place down while I was gone.

"Absolutely," was all she said and went back to unpacking boxes of items for the front window. She was organizing bags of dried flowers in a wooden tray when I had an idea.

"Have you thought about putting some rocks out for sale?" She turned back to me, eyes narrowing into cat like judgmental slits.

Her head cocked to the side. "Rocks?"

"Yeah you know the ones that people say do things. Like for energy and stuff." I had no idea what I was saying or why I was saying it. My hands went clammy, sticking to strands as I tried to run them through my hair.

She looked at me like I was stupid. I felt stupid.

I watched as she mouthed the words rocks to herself while the gears in her head turned. "Are you talking about crystals?" She finally said once the light bulb went off.

"Yeah, crystals, that's what I said."

"You got a girlfriend or something, Boss?" A sly smile crept across her face

"No."

I answered too quickly.

"Yeah, sure. First, all the bath stuff, and now crystals. The only time a man willingly knows about healing crystals is when there's a woman telling him about them."

"There's a blue one in particular," I said, ignoring her, digging out my phone to show her a picture of the one I found in Abby's office, years ago.

"It's pretty," she said, touching the screen. "Do you know what it's called?"

I hadn't thought of that. "No."

"No worries, send me that picture and I'll see what I can find."

I was shaking my head at her when Randy's frame appeared on the other side of the shop and started walking towards Kaity and I stood before knocking into a table and stumbling forward. He was tall and lanky, had me beat by about two inches, and was hard to miss but he moved like a giraffe just after it was born. A little wobbly and always running in to things.

"You good?" I asked, as a his cheeks turned bright red as he nodded.

Kaity tossed me a two finger salute. "Off to buy rocks," she said, barely keeping the laughter out of her voice. Leaving Randy looking confused and me wishing I never said anything in the first place.

Randy was a diligent worker, between the two of us we ripped out the cabinet, patched up the holes that were remaining and installed the rock black splash by noon. The room was bare, with only her appliances left behind and I felt pretty good about the day's progress.

We sat on her back porch eating lunch in silence before he spoke up.

"Do you take these kind of projects on often," he asked with a mouth full of the deli sandwich I had him run out and get.

"Renovations?"

He nodded with his mouth full.

"No, this is for a friend. I live across the street, her house was broken into," I took a bite of the sandwich, "trashed. I'm just helping out where I can."

He said nothing more, we finished eating in silence and the rest of the day, for that matter. By the time Abby was close to being off, all the cabinets were built and placed so the next day all we had to was grout the backsplash, attach the cabinets to the wall, install the new sink and counter top. Friday, I'd finish up all the little details or last minute issues that'd come up.

I wasn't quite sure what Abby's schedule was or when she normally would get home. The only thing I knew for sure was that she had a work event the next day that she had to go to and to not wait up for her.

Randy pulled away leaving me to walk back home and headed straight to the kitchen. Throughout a normal week, I didn't keep much in the fridge, only enough to make quick dinners for a few days and enough vegetables to please my mother if she ever stopped by to check. I pulled a few ingredients to make the one meal I knew like the back of my hand and the first thing I ever learned to make.

My mother was one of my favorite people, and I needed to make more of an effort to see her but sometimes it was too hard. When my father died, I was fourteen and it was probably the best thing that could have happened to either one of us. We packed up what little we had and moved a few hours to Fairvale and started our lives without living in fear. I didn't make friends for a while so I spent each night with my mom, hanging out with her in the kitchen while she cooked.

"Here's the thing, Kaiser, if you ever want to impress a girl...or guy, no bother either way, cook for them." *She chopped the garlic before throwing it in the pan.* "Everyone likes to be taken care of, no matter the age or how stubborn they think they are, and food is the easiest way." *She added more ingredients, chicken and at least five different spice jars were in use.*

She plated the creamy garlic chicken over of bed a mashed potatoes not long after she started cooking and placed it in front of me at the table. She smiled warmly at me. "Remember if you like them, cook for them. It's the only failsafe way to let them know you care."

I never cooked for anyone besides myself, but mother knows best.

Eighteen

Abby

It was far later than I anticipated when I walked through the door and I was bone-tired. My keys clicked against the bowl that sat on the entryway table when I set them down, and then I hung up my purse.

The smell of garlic and herbs floated through the air when I walked in the front door. I turned toward the kitchen doorway and I was met with pops and sizzling of oil in a pan and the buzz of a timer ringing out.

"Good, you're home." His casual use of the word home startled me. It rolled off his tongue like I came home to him every night

I stepped into the kitchen further. "You made dinner?" I questioned as I peered around his shoulder to get a glimpse of what was in the pan, but he shoo'd me away with his hand. "I was beginning to think you were lying about knowing how to cook."

"I made dinner and it's about done if you want to go sit at the table." He motioned with the spatula to the dining room. His words were tender and caring but his delivery could use some work. With hesitant steps, I walked over to the small dining room and slid onto the hard wood of the chair. My hand smoothed over the table. Kaiser's work was amazing, it was no wonder that his shop on Main Street did so well. I didn't own any large pieces like this table, but I told myself that one day I would save up enough to buy one, one day.

He appeared back at my side and set a plate down in front of me. I glanced up to thank him but Carina's words echoed in my head and the words died in my throat. A small strained smile was all I could muster but he didn't seem to notice. He left and came back with his own plate and sat to my right. It was all very domestic.

The first bite was nothing sort of heavenly. Flavors exploded over my tongue and I had to bite back from moaning around my poor unsuspecting fork. I was so busy at work I didn't realize my stomach only saw three cups of coffee throughout the day.

"This is amazing. Where did you learn to cook?" I asked, my mouth half full and the words garbled together. He chuckled softly at my lack of manners. I should've felt embarrassed but I couldn't seem to find that emotion as I dug in for another bite.

"My mom taught me," he said fondly. "She would slide me up to the counter before I could reach and teach me almost every meal she made." Smiling down at his plate, he pushed the food around, lost in thought. "They were some of my favorite times even if I didn't appreciate it for what it was back then."

"And what's that," I asked in between bites.

He paused for a moment. "I like feeling useful, even at a young age, and helping her always made me feel closer to her."

"It's your love language."

"My what?"

I rolled my eyes. "Your love language, how you like to give and receive love, we all have them. There are five different types and it seems like you like to show your love with acts of service. Makes total sense, helping your mom cook, I'm sure you did other things for her growing up too or made things to help her or for your friends. You like to help but you're not big on words and you like your alone time, and it's probably why you work with your hands. I mean you help me all the time." My mouth snapped shut as a red hot blush crawled up my neck at the implication of my words. "I didn't mean it like that, I just meant you're helpful." I stared at my food as I shoved in another bit. Anything to keep me from talking.

He sat up a bit straighter in his chair, brows pulling downward. Not quite his common scowl but more like he was working through a problem in his head. "Hmm," he finally answered.

I needed a segue far, far away from any conversation about feelings, so I asked more about what he could cook and listened as he told me about the vast amount of dishes he'd learned since he was young. Time passed and when I looked down onto my plate and everything was gone. That's when my stomach started to turn and not because I was full.

Pressing the napkin to my mouth, I looked down at my plate. "Sorry, I didn't mean to finish my entire plate but it was wonderful."

His eyes snapped to mine as he searched my face for an answer to the unspoken secret I let slide.

"Are you still hungry? There's plenty more." He reached for my plate.

"Oh, no thank you, I don't need more." Please stop talking, I thought to myself. Please don't make this any more awkward than it had to be.

"But do you want more, Abby?" Concern cradled the words and there seemed to be no way out.

My breath quickened as I grabbed my drink and swallowed loudly and urgently. I was still hungry and I knew if I didn't eat more, it's a sure thing that I'd end up starving in the middle of the night. But the words wouldn't form to tell him that yes I want more, but I spent eight months with a man who monitored my food intake, so it's not that simple.

Liam ruined my relationship with food, like everything else. This was never a problem before him. When I was hungry I would eat, and if I enjoyed it, I would clear my plate.

It was about two months into our relationship, when we had stopped to grab lunch in a place I no longer remembered. What I did remember was the way he looked at me as I was about half way through with my meal and told me not to finish. I was so dumbfounded by his statement I thought I misheard him, so I asked him to repeat himself and he did. "You don't need to finish everything you eat, Abigail. I don't need you gaining any weight and you don't want to lose my interest do you." It rolled off his tongue so effortlessly, you'd think he was doing me a favor.

There's a part of me that wished I fought back. I could have told him off and let him know that what I ate and what my body looked like was none of his concern, but I didn't. The weight of his words fell onto me like a ton of bricks, I was trapped and unable to move. Instead, I packed up the rest of the food and threw it in the trash. That was the first sign that things were on a downhill spiral.

I never finished a meal around Liam from that day forward.

Kaiser's chair screeched as he pushed himself away from the table and grabbed my plate. I stared down into my lap as my hands twisted around themselves and sucked in air through my nose and held a breath in order to keep my regret at bay.

My mind wandered to the dark corner of my brain. Was I naive? Did all men care about the amount of food women ate?

His footsteps echoed on the floor as he made his way back to the table. My eyes opened in time to see him set my plate back down in front of me with a second helping of dinner. He sat back down with his own plate but instead of eating, he turned to me.

"If you're hungry, I want you to eat. Seconds, thirds, it doesn't matter, it's your body, you just tell me what it needs. I'll cook any meal ten times over if it's what you want."

There's a divot in the table top, I knew this because I couldn't seem to look anywhere else, especially not at him. Not until my stomach gave a large growl that I glanced up at him to see his eyebrows cocked in a 'see, I knew it' sort of look.

I finished the second plate of food without an ounce of guilt for the first time in forever.

NINETEEN

Kaiser

"No!" THE WORD ROARED out of my chest as my body bolted up right from my bed. It had been months since my last nightmare. Foolishly I thought they had finally stopped and I could be rid of them for good. My hands carded through my hair and came out slick. Curls stuck to the back of my neck and there was a steady flush of heat warming my body.

The sheet bunched around my waist as I tried to get my bearings. My head fell limp in my hands as I propped my elbows up onto my knees. It's the same every time, nothing ever changed. I never got to save them, my limbs were always too heavy and I never moved fast enough. No matter how hard I tried, I stayed running in place and I was forced to watch them slip over the edge and disappear into nothingness. Every single time.

Forcing air in through my nose, I made a poor attempt to calm down. But on the exhale, I knew it would do nothing to stop the shake in my hands. I tried a few more times in case I could trick myself into remembering I was safe but my heart still slammed against my rib cage.

There was nothing more I could have done.

Nothing more.

On the nights where my nightmares crawled their way out of the depths of my mind, the night sky was the only thing that grounded me. That, and the ritual of breathing in and out toxic air.

I tossed back the covers and slipped on the closest pair of sweats my hands found. Slowly I crept out of my room, careful to step around the boards in front of her room that I knew made noise. Although I doubted she would have heard anything. Not so soft snores ripped through the crack in her doorway, so loud they're almost endearing.

My first step into the night acted like a salve to my thrumming pulse, the fast beats slowing with every step out onto the deck. The flicker of my lighter hissing to life with a flame was the peace I was craving. My lungs expanded with the toxic air, soothing the agitation that had built in my chest. I held on to it as long as possible.

If there was a way to shut off the part of my brain that held on to every ounce of shame all my problems would cease to exist. Instead, I was forced to relive some of the worst moments of my life. An endless cycle that looped in my mind that I could never out run.

A familiar creak of the door pulled me from my thoughts and for a moment my head went silent at the thought of her close. Soft padding of her feet echoed into the still of the night. "You again," I said without turning, dragging in another inhale of my cigarette.

The soft titter of her laughter reached my ears and caused my chest to swell. "We've got to stop meeting like this." Her fake exacerbation was almost seductive.

"What are you doing up, Dimples?"

She shrugged.

We stood in what I deemed our unofficial meeting spot. Moments slid by like the night's air and it's the most calm I'd been in years. Abby must be the cure to my overactive mind. What I wouldn't give to keep her close, so that any time I found myself spiraling I could latch onto her.

Her stare snagged on where my cigarette dangled from my fingers. "Sorry," I said quickly. Ash darkened the railing where I stabbed the lit end out.

"It's your house." She shrugged and looked back up to the sky.

"Yeah but I know it bothers everyone."

People are due their bad habits, but it didn't make them any less of a bad habit. And I hadn't been able to bring myself to kick mine yet.

A wistful sigh passed her lips as she swayed slightly on her feet. "You really shouldn't smoke but I'm probably one of very few people who has a twisted love affair with it."

I lifted an eyebrow "But you don't smoke, I thought?" I quizzed.

She shook her head. "Oh I don't, like I said it's terrible for you. You really shouldn't. But..." She trailed her eyes from my fingertips, up the length of my arm, and across my chest before meeting my eyes. Hers narrowed at me, flooding me with a sense of impatience. "You're gonna think it's weird," she stated.

"Probably." My curiosity peaked. I wanted to ask more, but it was easier to tease her and watch her eyes roll in annoyance.

"Unlike most people, I like the smell of it. The oddly comforting way it settles into my chest when I'm near it. Or the way it tastes on another person's mouth when they kiss you." Her voice went dreamy with her last words. Almost as if she didn't mean for them to come out. "I spent a lot of time in dive bars in my early twenties," she said quickly as if was some sort of reasoning on why she would be kissing men with tobacco soaked mouths.

It wasn't an invitation, I was aware of that, but my mind flashed with visions of pressing her back against the desk railing and my mouth against hers. Give her a way to fall into her own bad habit. We caught each other's gaze. For a split second, her stare mirrored my desire. It knocked me off my axis, causing that thrumming in my chest to return.

Her fingers twitched where she hung onto the railing before tearing her eyes from mine and giving us back to the silence.

Normally a few minutes and a cigarette were enough to get me back to normal before I headed back inside. But with her here I wanted to drag out the moment, keep her close as long as possible and let the quiet wash over us. It was moments like this where I could pretend she was mine, if only for a little while.

"Are you doing okay?" She whispered the words, scared of the answer that might follow. I wanted to act like I didn't know what she was talking about, pretend that I was a perfectly sound human without a closet full of skeletons. That it was normal to be out on my deck in the middle of the night, night after night after night. It'd been a long while since I talked to anyone about the nightmares, and I knew that was what she was referring to.

"I've been better." I would spare her the bad details, pity and I didn't mix well but I would be lying if I said her concern didn't warm a piece of my cold heart. "I get nightmares, the type that chase sleep and make my nights longer than I'd like."

She hummed out her understanding before replying. "Do you want to talk about it?"

"No." It was harsh, cutting off her empathy at the head. I was too far gone for the sentiment. Too jaded and stuck in my purgatory loop.

She shifted on her feet. "So, do you come out here in hopes that the sky will listen?" I could hear the smile playing on her lips.

"Something like that."

The sudden intrusion of her hand on mine trapped my next breath in my chest. She looked at me with pinched brows and her pretty light pink lips turned downwards, regarding me as if I was fine china. I didn't want to seem weak or fragile because who would want a man like that. "If you ever need someone to talk to or just to listen, I can be that for you." She spoke the words softly and allowed the empty space between us to hold them. My fists tightened around the deck railing, my throat constricted, making it so I couldn't speak even if I wanted to.

Instead of wanting to dig in to my usual persona of nothing ever bothering me, or that I had no feelings toward them, I wanted to sink into her words. I wanted to let her know I wasn't always like this, standoffish and cold, but that the last time I reached for someone to talk to I was let down and I never crawled my way out of the rejection. I wanted to tell her I believed her and that all I wanted was to maybe one day take her up on that offer.

But of course, I said none of that. I simply nodded my acknowledgement.

I think she's trying to kill me. Between the achingly sweet sentiment and the way she tugged on her bottom lip with her teeth had my system shocked. My brain couldn't even form a response before her hand slipped off mine and she turned back to disappear inside.

For a moment I wondered if she could see through the front I put between us. Could she see that my walls were slowly crumbling the closer we got? Could she see that all I wanted was her? She knew, she had to. And yet there was some sick, twisted part of me that hoped she would run away instead of toward me because, at least with her at a distance, all my darkness and gloom wouldn't taint her warmth and light. We didn't belong together, but it was getting harder and harder to remind my heart why.

TWENTY

Abby

AFTER HOURS WORK MIXERS were my favorite, our firm shelled out big money to host a parties at swanky hotels downtown where free drinks flow like water. Carina and I normally stuck together at these things, to gossip about whose dress was slightly inappropriate and who might be hiding a pregnancy announcement when we saw them refuse a drink they would otherwise take. It was always fun but I found myself wishing I was back on the deck with my neighbor who didn't speak more than a few words at a time to me.

So when I came back to see him standing out back exactly like we were the other night, I saw it as opportunity and I took it. If only for a reason to stand close to him.

"Did you see that?" I asked, pointing at the spot where the light passed through, "right there?"

He searched the sky but it was so quick, if he blinked he would have missed it. "See, what?"

I squeezed my eyes shut and whispered a quick wish under my breath. "What are you—" he started to ask.

"Shhh, I'm making a wish."

"A what?"

"I said shhh." I opened one eye to chastise him, then quickly shut it to finish. It was silly, and not as if I actually thought anything would come of it, but what's life without a little whimsy.

Kaiser watched me from the side of his eye when I finally opened mine. And I didn't fail to notice that he put out his cigarette "Do you think we could see a meteor shower from here if there was one?"

"From the back yard?"

"Yeah."

"Maybe," he said. "But why?"

"It's on my list." I should have been embarrassed, but the alcohol was still doing its job.

"What list?" he questioned.

"I, uh…" My hands tightened around the railing we stood at. "I have a bucket list, kind of." He waited for me to elaborate.

"My last break up was a disaster, I won't bore you with the details only that I knew I never wanted to be in that sort of relationship again, where I gave every part of me for nothing in return. After we broke up I started thinking about all the things I wanted to do or learn now that I was on my own and it formed a sort of bucket list."

There was scrap piece of paper shoved in a pocket of my purse, its not even old yet but the folds along the paper were already starting to wear from how many times I opened to read it over and over.

"I haven't crossed anything off yet but I will soon."

"What's on it?"

"It's silly," I said shaking my head. I have't shared what was on it with anyone yet, but Kaiser would be the last person to make fun of anything I had on it.

"I don't think so, not if it's important to you," he responded.

My fingers fiddled with the sleeve of my dress. I couldn't remember the last time I heard a sentence like that. I was so used to being the one checking in on everyone, making sure they knew they were valued and that I would always be there to support whatever they need to reach their goals, that I forgot what it was like to have someone do it for me.

"Well I want to replicate my mother's chocolate cake. She's the only one with the recipe and we don't talk anymore, so I've been winging it and haven't quite figured it out yet," I turned to him and found him already watching me intently. "I want to learn to play a decent hand of poker, and learn to waltz, a Viennese waltz specifically." I started pacing the deck, a giddy grin splashed across my face as I finally shared with someone my plans. "I want to see a meteor shower at some point, oh and win a competition, but I don't know in what, I'm not really good at anything. Things like that."

"That's quite a list."

"I know." A pregnant pause followed my words and I was slowly being filled with regret of my rambling.

"I like you like this."

"Like what? Drunk?" I laughed.

"No, excited." There was a slight shutter in his stoic facade as his lips twitched into a smile.

My lips parted in a simple 'o' and the warmth that started in my joints after my first drink hours ago returned and began spreading like wildfire through my limbs. I had doubts about coming to stay at Kaiser's, purely out fear of the fantasy I had built in my head over the years would spill out into real life, but it was quickly quashed. Kaiser was exactly as he had been over the years, quiet and without emotion. But there was something more under all his stoney disposition.

He faced away from me again. "What's your favorite color?" he asked.

"Purple but dark purple. Like a plum."

"Favorite food?"

"I'm partial to lemon desserts and I love cotton candy."

"I said favorite food not dessert, Abby."

"I heard you, and my answer remains the same."

"Favorite crystal?" he asked after some thought.

"Oh, that's a hard one. Probably citrine but there's really too many to choose from, it changes daily at this point."

It was nice, standing with him, with nothing to answer and nowhere to rush off to. The stillness of the dark allowed us to be in a moment we created together, where we were only roommates for the time being but two people seeking something more. I allowed my head to loll to the side and came to a rest on his shoulder. If anyone asked, I would immediately blame the alcohol but I mostly I just wanted to touch him, if only for a moment.

His muscles tensed for a fraction of a second, before the brief tension of my intrusion melted away.

"Are we friends, Kaiser?"

"Yeah, Dimples, we're friends," he said into the dark.

"Good and as your friend, I want to say that you really shouldn't smoke, Kaiser, I'd hate to loose you any sooner than I'd have to."

"Okay, only since you asked," he said with a trace of laughter in his voice.

My head pounded with the consequences of my actions when I finally peeled my eyes open at the sound of my alarm. Staying up with Kaiser way past any reasonable hour only added to the fatigue that was setting in before I could even start the day. The only saving grace was in only eight hours it would be the weekend.

I rifled through my closest, pulled the first decent outfit I could find and got dressed quickly. With any luck, Kaiser would be up and gone already and I wouldn't have to face him after my embarrassing display of rambling.

Within record time, I stepped out of my room balancing on one heel, slipping my other foot in the heel in my hand and was only about two minutes late getting out the door. My hair was down and barely even brushed as I raced into the kitchen and hoped there would be enough coffee left in the pot for me, I was willing to drink it black at this point.

He sat with his back to me reading over a newspaper. Another dark colored flannel was stretched over the expanse of his back. Small droplets of water gathered on the tips of the curls at the nape of his neck.

Why did he have to be so attractive? The stupid kind. Where he didn't even have to try and barely registered that a mere glance at him in the morning sun sent my stomach into backflips. My body and my mind were not corroborating.

"Morning," he said from over his shoulder.

"Morning." I grabbed the nearest cup I saw and walked over to where the coffee percolated on the counter. "Do you mind if I grab a cup before I go?"

"You don't have to ask," he grumbled.

"Someone is spicy this morning."

"Spicy?" he deadpanned.

"Yeah, spicy," I laughed and plucked a mug from the cabinet.

He pushed back from the table. He placed his cup in the sink and leaned in, crowding my space and the laughter died in my throat. "You think that's funny," he said in low tone, that had a playful edge to it.

"Yeah, kinda of." I wished I had a better quip, but with him so close by I was caught off guard and I couldn't seem to find a better remark.

He cocked his head to the side and there was a flash of humor in his blue eyes. "Did you know you snore?"

My eyes flared "I do not."

Actually, I did.

"Like a trucker. It was so loud I could hear you through the wall." He took a step back and propped one hip on the counter, folding his arms across his chest.

"You could not because I do not snore." I do snore. Lennon complained the entire time we shared a room as kids until she finally convinced our mom to turn the spare room that was supposed to be an office into her room. Even Liam complained when we would spend the night together.

He doubled down on his teasing "The walls aren't even thin. It's a good thing I don't sleep much to begin with." A rare smile appeared on his face but by the time I noticed it was gone. I pushed past him with my cup, grabbing my purse from the entryway and walked to the door. "You're incorrigible."

The last thing I heard was the echo of a laugh.

TWENTY-ONE
Kaiser

I EXPECTED A WAVE of relief to wash over me once I finished with her kitchen. It was the last thing on the list to fix in order for her to move back in. Actually, she could have moved back in as soon as I had the back door replaced, but I was keeping that fact to myself. Her kitchen was done but there was no sense of euphoria that came with it. Part of me contemplated telling her there was still more to do but as I wracked my brain for anything to tell her, her car appeared and pulled into her driveway.

My knuckles rapped against the window pane to get her attention before she walked over to our house—*my house*. I had to remind myself. We didn't actually live together and she wasn't mine. Her head whipped at the sound, sending her hair flying to the side and a smile graced her face. She shouldn't smile at me like that, it was almost too much. If she knew that I didn't want to go back to being neighbors who only waved in passing or people who spent a few hours in comfortable silence while I lent her a helping hand, she wouldn't smile at me like that.

But fuck if I didn't like the way it made me feel.

I didn't have the words to tell her any of this, of course. Or maybe it was courage that I lacked.

She breezed through the door and made a beeline directly toward me. Eyes were bright deep pools of blue, and I wanted nothing more than to dive head first and never come up for air.

"Hi," she breathed out. "What are you doing over here?" She took a step toward me.

"It's done."

"What's done?" she asked, oblivious to the finished kitchen we stood in. It was cute.

Cute? Where the fuck did that come from.

I didn't think things were cute. At least not until her.

"Look around, Dimples."

We were close, too close, but I needed more. I needed to let my restraints go, if only a little bit. She was going back and I would never have her this close again.

I circled her slowly in less than two steps, leaving only an inch of space between her back and my front. My hands skimmed the tops of her shoulders, trailing down her arms before I grasped her elbow lightly and slowly spun her in a half circle to showcase the work.

"Oh." The word fell from her mouth and filled me with desire I shouldn't have. "It's finished."

"A bit sooner than I anticipated, but yes. You could move back right now if you wanted." The words pained me to even think let alone say. Her body tensed under my grasp. She spun to face me, her delicate chin titling upwards.

I studied her for a moment, I knew there was a chance I'd never be this close again. Her lips were pale pink and matched the color high on her cheek bones. She must have done something to her hair because it fell in soft waves around her shoulders, with no sun filtering in the red was almost non-existent and I missed it. When I finally pulled the courage from the depths on my chest I looked into her eyes. They really did look like those crystals, I had half of a mind to fill my house with them. Maybe then the absence of her wouldn't be so large.

"Isn't that what you wanted?" I questioned.

She looked crestfallen but gathered her emotions and plastered a look of indifference on her face. "Yes, of course."

"Or," I started.

"Or?" she mimicked. Her eyebrows rose with the word.

"We can celebrate and move your stuff later." I didn't know where that came from, only that I knew I needed more time. I wasn't ready for her to leave me, not yet.

"I think that's a great idea." She bounced on her toes, bringing her lips far too close. Dangerously close.

I stepped back and waited for the fog to clear. "Lets go have a drink?"

"Perfect."

It was like some weird paradox, the more time I spent with her the reason why I had been keeping her at a distance got farther and farther away, slipping through my fingers like running water. This could've been the nail in coffin for me, but I needed more time, I wasn't ready to let her go.

TWENTY-TWO

Abby

WHO KNEW HOW WE got here, or how long we've been here but I knew I never wanted to be out of this moment. Our backs were pressed up against cabinets in his kitchen, handles dug into my shoulder but the pain was getting further and further away with every sip. The moon and sun switched places without us noticing, with a soft glow filtering in through the windows above us.

We passed the bottle back and forth more times than I kept count of. Each of my limbs were warm and on their way to being numb, with tiny little pin pricks in my fingers and toes. And there was a stupid grin plastered on my face after I convinced Kaiser to play twenty questions with me.

"You ever been married?"

He looked up sharply, he opened his mouth but then snapped it closed. A second later he replied. "Married? No." He took another drink.

"Celebrity crush?" I quickly followed up with.

He laughed. Which was now my favorite sound. "Nicole Kidman."

"What?!" I exclaimed. "Really?"

"Yeah, if you've ever seen Days of Thunder, you'd understand." He took another swig as I tossed my head back in laughter. It struck the cabinet but only pulled more laughter out of me and Kaiser. I couldn't remember the last time I let loose like this. It felt like a piece of normalcy, like our lives were always meant to be intertwined. I wanted to keep him talking. This was the most I'd gotten out of him in the five years I'd known him. And I didn't want it to end.

"Tell me something I don't know about you." I shifted in my spot on the floor, and if I brought myself closer to him so that our legs pressed against each other and I could easily reach out to him if I wanted to then so be it.

His hand scrubbed down the side of his face while he searched for the answer. He was so pretty in the darkness of his kitchen, and maybe men weren't supposed to be pretty, but that was the only word my muddled brain could think of.

"I was in a band in high school," he responded finally. He placed the bottle between my outstretched legs. Static rang in my ears at the closeness between us and for a moment I had forgotten what my question was.

Our bodies breathed in tandem until I remembered. I took another drink to keep my hands busy. "What did you play?"

"The drums, obviously."

"Obviously, how is that obvious?" I asked.

"Drummers were always the coolest." This new version of him might be one of my favorites. Where he was loose with his words and his laughter. My hand snapped to the side, hitting his thigh while I continued laughing, but before I could move away his fingers wrapped around my wrist to hold it in place.

The dark was a safe space. In the dark you could act on feelings and when the morning came you'd have something to blame it on. That's what I was telling myself as his fingers threaded gently through mine. My blood became an overwhelming sound in my head, it was so loud I was sure he could hear it. But he didn't look at me, instead his eyes drifted close, like my hand in his was an overwhelming experience.

It was all almost too much.

"That's very early nineties teen of you but I guess when there's no internet, you have to entertain yourselves somehow."

He snorted. "Jesus. You make me sound ancient."

"You are, but that's okay," I said with a laugh as I gave his hand a pat that was only mildly patronizing.

He took another drink with his free hand. Maybe we should stop but any chance to get to know him was not something I would pass up. "Okay, when's it my turn to ask questions?" He gave my hand three hard squeezes before pulling me across the tile to close the small gap that was between us.

My head came to rest on his shoulder. He exhaled slowly at the contact. "I have one more, tell me something you've never told anyone. Tell me a secret."

Tell me everything, I wanted to say. Tell me every bad memory you keep tucked away, the ones I saw floating through your eyes like ghosts and made you pull back from life, from me. I wanted him to tell me he felt this too, the string pulling us together.

From the moment I met him I felt it weave itself between us. At first it was a simple loose knot, he was only a neighbor, someone that helped me when I asked. Over time, the string changed, like a simple slip knot, tightening and loosing with a pull. With every moment, every small interaction or heated gaze the string changed and wove itself tighter. And now it felt like a Palomar knot, simple yet strong.

He plucked the bottle from its resting spot and brought it to his lips, pulling a large swig. I tried not to watch his throat work to swallow but I was past acting coy. Watching Kaiser had always been my favorite past time, who was I to give that up now. His tongue slid across his bottom lips catching the droplets that were left behind.

Maybe my question was too much, and the longer he took to ask the more I began to berate myself for ever asking.

"Before my dad died, Christmas was always the worst. My mom would do her best to make it special for me but every year, I'd watch as she handed out gifts to me and him, while she got nothing. He couldn't even find an ounce of kindness in him to get her a fucking trinket. Nothing in her stocking and never a single present. So when I was about twelve, up until he died, I would steal cash from his wallet throughout the year so that when Christmas came around she would have gifts to open too."

His thumb swiped gently across my hand, repetitively. Like these words were the first time he'd ever said them out loud and this was the self soothing technique he chose to keep himself grounded. It was small, but I knew in this very instance that I would give anything to be that for him again. And again. And again. For however long he needed.

"But I would sign his name on the presents. The first year he looked so damned confused when I handed her that first box with the tag that said it was from Dad. He didn't really want to deny it so he kept his mouth shut and took the credit. And it was worth it, seeing that look on her face as she unwrapped the present. It was some of the only times she looked genuinely happy when I was growing up." A sad smile graced his face.

Finally, he shook his head. "Your turn, tell me a secret."

I should have expected that. My secrets stayed buried in my chest, deep enough that nobody saw but large enough that I always felt them. I slipped my hand out from his. It would be impossible to say anything while holding on to him, and if I had to feel him let go after spilling my secret it might have been unbearable.

Maybe I should have made something up, there were plenty of issues I could have pulled inspiration from. But it would have been a disgrace to do so after the realness of his words. My fingers rolled around each other in my lap and then the words poured out.

"Sometimes I think I'm the reason my mother drinks. That it's my fault my sister had to work so hard to give me a better life."

He didn't pull away like I imagined, but he didn't reach for me either.

And there was the right amount of alcohol in me to keep talking.

"Lennon doesn't talk much about our childhood but I know she remembers our dad. They were their own little family until I came along and everything went downhill from there. I think that maybe if I had never been born my dad wouldn't have left and then my mom never would have started drinking. And Lennon..." I took a deep breath in, held it in my chest to keep from crying. "Lennon wouldn't have had to give up her life for me. They could have all been happy if I just never existed."

I tipped the bottle back and emptied the last remaining drops.

The words lived in my head for as long as I'd been able to think. Since I was barely old enough to form thoughts, I lived with the notion that my family was barely a family and it was all my fault. It didn't matter that I got older, or that I understood the dynamics of addiction, it was always my fault there was little love in our home.

Which was why I would try and force it into existence in my own relationships. But it never belonged in the first place, like I never belonged.

"Do you ever think about getting back in touch with her?" he asked.

What a loaded question but it was easy enough to answer.

"All the time. Though I think it's more that I miss the idea of her. I can't be the one to reach out to her only to be let down again." The air seemed to still around us at my omission. "I used to drive by her house sometimes, to catch a glimpse of her. I'd park my car across the street and wait for her to appear in the window but it's been a long time since I've done that, even now it's still hard."

Aching silence that began to fill my lungs. I wanted to run. Just get up, walk out the door and never come back.

My eyes were closed, so I didn't see it coming. All I felt was his hand back on mine, stilling my anxious fidgeting and it was like I plunged into ice filled water. A simple touch from him and the swirling thoughts dissipated, a break in the dark clouds that allowed a light to shine through.

"I know what you mean." One touch from him and I was drunk on more than our shared bottle. "We make quite the fucked up pair, don't you think?" he said.

My laughed echoed into the night.

"Yeah, I guess we do."

When I turned to him, he was already staring at me. It's not the first time it'd happened but it always made my stomach flip. I was rarely, if ever, this close to him but at this distance even in the dark I noticed that his eyes are flecked with silver. They're pretty in a haunted way, windows that said he'd seen too much and kept it locked away.

"For what it's worth I don't think any of that is true and I for one am very happy that you exist," he whispered.

"I thought nothing made you happy, Kaiser."

He reached out and brushed my hair back behind my shoulder, finger tips grazing the side of my neck in the process. That one small movement sent shivers to every corner of my body and soul.

I was boneless, willing putty for him.

"Turns out there's at least one thing."

I could kiss him. It would be so easy, like breathing. What I wouldn't do to reach across and feel the scruff of his beard under my hand. To haul him in close and feel his body weight on top of me. I wanted to remember what it felt like, it had been so long since the last time. And well, that time there was a lot going on for me to focus enough to savor the moment.

But before I could do anything he was on his feet pulling me up with him.

"Thanks, Kaiser." It could have been for a million things and something told me he knew that too. It was quick, he tilted my head up a fraction.

"Anytime, pretty girl," he said as his fingers trailed up my neck and along my jaw until his thumb gently pulled my bottom lip out from my teeth's grasp. The moment seemed to drag on into infinity as his thumb traced my bottom lip until he blinked, locking down the feelings that were right in front of us, dropping his hands from me completely.

Pretty girl.

The name echoed in my head and spiked a fever that crawled across my chest. I knew this feeling, it was one of my favorites, but currently it was sending me into a panic.

"Come on, I'll walk you home."

And then I came crashing back to Earth. I didn't actually belong here. Despite what the past week made me feel.

We crossed the street in silence, arms swinging gently in each other's orbit. Close enough to touch but he didn't reach for me again. My hand was poised on the door. It was easier if I could walk inside and not have to watch him walk away from me. I was a second away for doing that when he spoke up.

"I want to take you somewhere tomorrow."

"Okay." The word came out in a winded rush.

Too needy, I thought. The dark chuckle from him said that he could tell. "Don't you want to know where we're going?" he asked, his fingers laced in between mine slowly and I hadn't even registered that we were still touching.

"No, I trust you," I replied. His face softened instantly at my words, relaxing into an inscrutable expression, relief sweeping across his features.

He stepped away, his hand trailing from my grasp. "Be ready in the morning," He walked to the door, paused before turning back to look at me. "Goodnight, Abby." He left swiftly. I hurried inside and I watched from the window as he walked back to his house.

My body itched to be back in the sanctuary of his home. Barely a week I spent over there and yet it felt more like home than my own four walls ever did. This would be fine, Kaiser and I would go back to being neighbors only, and I could go back to pining in secret.

After turning out all the lights and checking each lock compulsively, I stood at the kitchen sink staring out the window, the one that looks directly into his and willed him to appear. I wasn't scared of being alone in my house, but I got so used to him being the last thing I saw at night.

Then, as if my screaming thoughts could be heard, there he was. My shoulders relaxed and the tension melted away. I lifted my hand

and waved and he did the same, for a second we stood there staring at each other.

My phone buzzed in my hand, I tore my gaze away from him to look down.

Goodnight pretty girl

That was it. Simple. Understated. So very Kaiser, and yet I yearned for more.

When I looked backed up, his window went dark but there was a small smile playing on my lips.

It seemed Kaiser was also used to me being the last thing he saw before bed.

That beginning feeling of falling pricked along my skin. When you're standing on the edge of a cliff with the tips of your toes teetering on the edge, talking yourself into either jumping or scrambling back from the edge.

Could I have this without ruining it? The inevitability of me being me told me no, but I would leave that for future Abby to deal with.

TWENTY-THREE

Abby

I WAS READY FOR him bright and early. I had no idea where we were going so when his eyes raked over me when I pulled the door open, I second guessed my entire outfit. He seemed like the type of man who preferred the outdoors. His garage was open anytime he was working, he had the entire outdoor shop area next to his store front. It was like he couldn't stomach the thought of being caged in. Someone like that would definitely prefer the outdoors.

My cut off shorts shouldn't have been so shocking then, but he was staring and I was feeling torn between to wildly different emotions.

Kaiser and I stood in a stalemate, eyes locked on each other. We'd been in this moment before, many times over the years. I never knew what it meant, or if it ever had a real meaning. But when he looked at me, with eyes full of a stormy fight, I was pulled toward him.

I wanted him, in a plain and simple way that almost scared me. I wanted him in shared dinners after long days at work. I wanted him in lazy mornings and breakfast in bed. I wanted him for comfort, for cuts and bruises or broken hearts, and not as some careless rebound. I wanted him, and unless it was some trick of the light, I could see that he might feel the same.

"Hi," I said, breaking the silence. "Is this okay for wherever we're going?"

He slipped his hat to thread his fingers through his tousled hair, then nodded. "I wanted to take a look at the back door before we go if that's alright."

I stepped sideways, letting him breeze past me. He checked, actually I had no idea what he was checking. Whatever it was, though, he seemed pleased with it because not even a minute later he was back at my side.

"Hi," I greeted softly, looking up at him.

Last night played on a loop and I wanted nothing more than to slip my hand into his again.

Before either of us could break or lean into the moment, a loud knock came from the front door, leaving barely enough time to break apart before the door flung open and bounced off the wall. Fear spiked through me; neither of us were expecting anyone. He must have been thinking the same thing. In one swift movement he placed himself between me and whoever was coming through the door, my hand tightly clasped in his.

Maybe I should be filled with a little bit more fear than what was coursing through me, but I was easily distracted.

"Abby?" The voice registered immediately followed by the sound of another singing out the word 'hello'. My shoulders relaxed and I moved quickly from around Kaiser to greet Lennon and Carina.

"What are you doing here?" They came around the corner from the kitchen to see me in the middle of a barren living room, I hadn't had the chance to replace any of the ruined furniture yet. My eyes darted from them back to Kaiser who was hovering around me. They both stopped as they took in the weird state of my house. They glanced at each other, then at Kaiser and back to me.

Shock, amusement and something that resembled confusion began forming over their features.

Lennon spoke first. "Carina told me you had some water damage and you had to take some time off of work." Her auburn curls moved with her head as she looked around. "This doesn't look like just water damage. You have a whole new kitchen." She stepped into the dining room and looked into the living room. "And back door, it seems."

Guilt began its steady crawl up my throat. She had a nose for when I was in trouble, and I was foolish to think I could hide something like this from her. I'd been running to her for help for as long as I'd been able to stand on my own. I knew that if I came to her, she would pull me out of the dark without a second thought. It was practically second nature at this point. She was a force to be reckoned with when it came to me and there were plenty of times where I thought it might have been worth it to let her know, but embarrassment was a powerful thing.

Where she was made of strength I was made of anything but.

"Abigail Catherine, what happened?" The use of my full name sent a chill through the house. Kaiser's head perked up while Carina's face pulled into a slight grimace. They began to blur in front of me and it took a moment to realize it was because of the tears. Then their arms wrapped around me and whatever dam I had constructed to keep everything at bay broke. Words were impossible to find, so I stood in the warmth they were willing to lend me.

At some point, I was gently coaxed to the makeshift dining room table and I began to tell them everything. About finding the door open after coming back from seeing them last week, the break in, the cops and staying with Kaiser since. Carina quietly muttered what seemed to be every curse word the Italian language had to offer. Lennon on the other hand, said nothing, barely moved. She sat like a statue with her hands folded delicately in her lap. When I finished, I mustered up enough courage to look at her, only to see her regarding me with a face I'd never seen. She rapidly blinked a few time before pushing back from the table and slowly stood up.

She was leaving, this was her tipping point. The point where she decided I was no longer worthy of her protection. My heart as I locked eyes with Kaiser who had wandered on to the deck but watched me with an intense look.

Panic was ensuing.

She couldn't leave, she couldn't do this. I was her sister. I needed her.

I was no longer worried about looking desperate. My chair toppled over as I tried to reach her before she disappeared. "Where... Where are you going?" I stammered out.

Her curls nearly smacked me in the face when she spun around. "It was him, wasn't it?" she snapped and I didn't know how to answer, I hadn't even told Kaiser about my suspicions but Lennon knew immediately.

I nodded. "I think so, but I haven't told the cops or Kaiser. I... I don't know."

"I'm going to kill him." It was so matter of fact and calm that you would think she was telling me her grocery list. Her brows were set in a hard line, while her eyes burned like flames on the ocean.

A laugh bubbled out of my chest and suddenly it was the only thing I could focus on. It echoed out until my side hurt and they started looking at me as if I needed to be committed. "Sit back down." I pulled on her hand to lead her back to the table.

"At least let me hit him with my car or something." She sounded wistful at the idea. Her hand never left mind and I clung to it like a life raft. "Why didn't you tell me?" she asked while her eyes lingered on the patched holes in the living room. They may have been painted over but it was easy to see.

My sister was my church, I sought my solace and comfort in her arms. I would go to her for guidance and when I was broken she would lead me home. When I was younger I thought the sun rose and set on her, she was everything I wanted to be. She took care of me so the absence of our parents was never felt. I owe her my life.

I could try for a thousand years but I would never be able to repay her for the childhood she had to give up for me.

"You can't always be the one to save me. Sometimes I need to do it myself," I said when I really wanted to tell her I was too ashamed to let her know.

She shook her head. "No." Seeing Lennon cry was almost second nature. After the death of her husband it seemed to be her constant state of emotion. But watching her shed tears over me ignited emotions that were hard to name. "No, Abigail, I don't care how old you are or where you are. If you call, I will come."

My sister was my religion, and the only place that felt like home. Even on days where I felt unworthy she saw room for redemption and granted me salvation.

Her eyes slid above my head to where Kaiser must've been. She gave her head a tilt. "So you've been staying with Kaiser?" she asked with a smile.

"Uh.. yeah. He's been..." I searched for the words. Kind didn't feel like it did what Kaiser has done for me justice. A godsend sounded a little too dramatic. A force that has rattled me to my core with his closed off demeanor that only seemed to soften around me, but I doubted she wanted to hear anything like that. I must have taken too long to answer because both Lennon and Carina shared a look before snickering. "He's just being nice."

"I bet he is," Carina said, and Lennon hummed in agreement.

"Well, can we help with anything, since we're here?" she asked. I looked back at Kaiser who in the time it took us to talk installed the doors completely. I turned back to them already dreading their reaction to my next statement.

"No, we were actually about to leave."

"Where are you going?" They asked simultaneously.

"We're going to Wildflower Lake." He was unusually light on his feet because I never even heard him coming up behind me; I looked up at with him with a smile.

Lennon and Carina watched us carefully before looking back at each other, a strange look passed between them.

My sister was the first to scoot her chair back. "Well, don't let us keep you." She motioned for Carina to get up then Lennon did something that was rare, for her at least. She wrapped me in a hug that threatened to squeeze the air out of my lungs.

And as quick as it came on, she was done, releasing me from her hold and stepping around me and moving toward the door. Only she didn't leave, she stopped where Kaiser was hovering awkwardly around the entryway.

Carina hugged me a little tighter than normal also and I almost didn't want to pull away. From over her shoulder I watched Lennon's mouth move as she cornered Kaiser. I couldn't hear and reading lips was not something I was good at, but I would have gave anything to know what was happening a few feet from me.

He looked almost scared, well as scared as six foot, two inches tall man could be when they're on the receiving end of some sort of triad given by red head who was a head shorter than him. He nodded solemnly at the end of her inquisition, then slowly a small smirk played at his lips. He muttered something that made Lennon beam and left me jealous.

Carina was halfway out the door when Lennon turned back. "What was all that about?" I asked.

"Oh, nothing, just wanted to make sure of something." She tugged me in for another unexpected embrace. She was never the one to initiate prolonged contact and it took me by surprise. "You deserve someone good in your life if that's what you want, you know."

My throat worked to swallow the insecurity. "I just got back into my house and I have the list, you know." *And I have a tendency to ruin everything I touch.* My half hearted response barely phased her. "That's what I should be focused on."

If I said the lie out loud, maybe it would make it true.

Her nose scrunched up. "That's when they liked to find you, when your life is in shambles and you're trying everything to fight it," she said.

"Who?" I asked.

"The love of your life," she whispered, and then walked out the door.

TWENTY-FOUR

Abby

AN HOUR IN THE car and Lennon's words had been ricocheting in my mind. Pinging around in a failed attempt to get me to ask him what they spoke about. Kaiser and Lennon had spoken barely a handful of words to each other over the years. So what on Earth happened in those quick two minutes that would lead her to say something to him?

She had the whole situation wrong. Kaiser and I were friends, only friends.

Sure, maybe there were moments where his eyes lingered a touch too long. Or moments where the air was thick with tension you could cut in half. But I liked whatever it was between us and I knew that I would only ruin it if I acted on any of the desires. Like I ruined everything else.

Kaiser pulled off the highway onto a two lane road that began weaving through thick trees. It was the beginning of fall, where the days were still warm but nights carried a chill. The trees were still green and not yet barren and dull.

I had never been up this way. Growing up, camping trips or vacations in general never really happened.

The drive, although quiet, was incredibly peaceful. Vivid greens and earthy brown tones blurred by as we continued to climb up the mountain towards the lake. I sat up a bit straighter in my seat, leaning towards the window to gaze out down into the valley between the mountains. "Why does it feel like we're going up the mountain?" I peered out the window. The drop down was farther than I could see, but the trees were endless. It was breath taking and made me feel a million miles from all my issues. "Shouldn't we be going down to get to a lake?"

"No, Wildflower Lake is on top of the mountain," he replied.

I sat back in the seat and refocused on the road in front of us. "Really?" Why didn't that sound right?

He nodded. "It's a man made lake, technically a reservoir." He launched into a spiel about how it was made for mining at some point in time. There was a new lightness to his voice as he rambled and I had a feeling this man's hobbies involved random lore about the area we lived in.

"Huh..." I didn't get out into nature much, that was plain to see.

A break in the trees allowed me my first glimpse of the lake. Sunlight bounced off the top of Wildflower Lake like glittering diamonds in the late afternoon sun. Dark blue waters lapped gently against a small and rocky shore and I was dying to get out of this truck for a closer look. My face was practically smooshed against the glass.

Kaiser didn't say much as the truck came to a halt in one of the camping spots at the far end of the area. I guess we're back to minimal conversations. I swung the door open and slid out from the seat. I should help set up or whatever people do when they come out to the lake but I had my eyes set on the short trail that led to the water.

Without a thought, I bounded down the trail through the tall green grass that swayed in the slight breeze. It was beautiful here. The wide lake sat in the basin of rolling green mountains. The sun warmed my skin as I tilted my head back to meet the morning rays. I wouldn't normally consider myself an outdoorsy type of person, probably due to lack of exposure, but being here gave me a feeling of comfort like I'd never experienced.

"My father used to bring me camping here during the summer." I jumped at his words, loosing my foot and stumbling forward. His hand grasped my upper arm keeping me from flying head first into the water. It was all over within a second and yet his hand remained on me, falling slowly down my arm, grazing my skin with his fingertips in the process.

"Why are we here, Kaiser?"

"Come on, let's get everything set up before it gets too hot."

Fishing poles, that's what we had to set up. Was I a person who fished? No. Absolutely not. But I was right about him being an outdoor person, so I should have guessed that meant some sort of outdoor activity.

"Do you come out here often?" The silence was getting to me and being out in the woods with only the faint bug chirping and birds calling out as they swopped into trees was starting to get to me.

Without looking up he replied, "Not as much as I'd like to, but enough." Vague, so very vague.

"What is it that you like about being out here?" He bent down where his pole was rigged to stand between a stick he found that looked like the letter Y.

"The silence," he replied.

Dually noted.

I didn't do well in silence. In silence, the negative came crawling to the surface of my skin.

Kaiser pulled his chair up next to me, facing out towards the lake.

"After my first deployment, I was a mess. I never slept, was angry at everything and everyone and just didn't know how to move on. A buddy of mine noticed all the signs of PTSD before the thought ever crossed my mind. He got me help and when we came back home he stayed in the area and every weekend for months he hauled my ass out of my house and into the woods. Something about the air and the stillness seemed to quiet the thoughts in my head. It was hard to hate myself when I was surrounded by beautiful landscapes and a friend."

"That, and we'd get rip-roaring drunk which helped." He chuckled as he scratched at his beard. "This was the only place I felt like I could talk about anything. Without judgement. I thought this place could be that for you too."

Before any words came out, tears gathered in my vision. I rapidly blinked them away and then smiled at him.

I couldn't remember the last time someone checked on me. Sure, Lennon and Carina asked if anything was wrong but there was never any follow up after I would brush off their concerns. Yet Kaiser set up a whole day trip to the mountains in case I wanted to talk about my feelings.

It was softer than anything I thought he might be capable of and it was like I was looking at an entirely different man. Or has he always been this thoughtful and I was only now noticing? Either way, I think he's right, this might be exactly what I needed.

"I feel like a failure," I started. "My whole life, I've tried to be the best. Never caused trouble, got good grades in school so my mother wouldn't have an excuse to hate me more than she already did. I got into a good college, then went straight to work to help pay back Lennon for everything she's done for me."

My throat was thick with the truth, making it hard to swallow and once I started I couldn't stop.

"I was the perfect girlfriend, and it was never enough. I was never enough. I am never enough for anybody it seems." His face morphed into a new expression that I'd never seen before. But I still couldn't stop.

"If he didn't like something I changed it to fit the image he wanted to portray. My clothes, my eating habits, the movies, shows, places I liked to visit. And I did it, even though something inside me was screaming to stop. I did anything he asked and it didn't make a difference. In the end it didn't matter. He never saw the lengths that I was willing to go to for him and what's worst is I lost myself in the process. It wasn't love but I wanted it to be, and now I feel pathetic. I'm a failure, again."

Tears spilled down my face as I tried to wipe them away with the palms of my hands. When I got the courage to look back at Kaiser he was pitched forward, elbows resting on his knee, staring out across the lake. Stillness surrounded us and I was beginning to get what he meant. I seemed to hate myself a little less than I did when we got here.

I liked how quiet he was. That he let me pour out my thoughts and didn't interrupt and ask for anything further. He was content in the details I was willing to spare and it made me feel seen. Like I was finally able to shed the different layers I acquired to keep Liam happy. I could be me and for him that was enough.

"Feels good, huh?"

"Yeah," I breathed out.

We spent the next hour prepping for lunch. We ate in near silence, with only the soft wind blowing around us.

He disappeared into his truck while I sat with my face tipped back to look at the sky until his voice pulled my attention back.

"The rules are easy." He swung his long leg over the bench of the picnic table and the other followed. He hit whatever was in his hand on to the table and then split it in two. I walked from the chairs we had set up to the table to join him when the familiar sound of cards being shuffled hit my ears. "First thing is to place your bets. We have no chips but I had quarters stashed away in the truck." The coins clinked together as he dumped them on the table.

I sat opposite of him on the table. "What is this?" I asked pulling a few of the coins over to my side.

"Poker." He shuffled the cards again and my hand stilled over the coins.

"Poker?"

He placed two quarters in the middle of the table from his pile then motioned for me to do the same. I dropped two more and he dealt two cards to each of us.

The cards slid easily over the rough wood of the table, but I didn't look at them. Not yet. Not until he finally met my eyes. "You said you wanted to learn poker," he remarked casually as he pulled up his hand to look over.

"You remembered?"

He held my gaze, sun bouncing off the dark brown waves in his hair. "When it comes to you, Dimples, I remember everything."

It took over an hour, but I eventually I got the hang of it. "Royal flush." I fanned the cards out in front of us.

"Not quite."

"Don't be a sore loser," I teased before taking the quarters from the middle of the table.

Then Kaiser did something I had been dying to see.

He laughed, actually laughed out loud. His eyes crinkled at the sides, his mouth pulled into a wide grin that showed off his perfectly straight teeth. The sound shot straight through me, filling me with an indescribable amount of wonder. It was like winning a lottery you never bought a ticket for, and I didn't want him to ever stop.

TWENTY-FIVE

Abby

It was intoxicating, the feeling of being at ease around him already. A week in his presence and addicted. It'd been a few days since the lake with only glimpses of him in the meantime. I couldn't stomach it any longer.

"Thank you," I called out as I pressed my back against the door of Vince's Pizza and walked out on Main Street. This was a brilliant cover, but I needed to get to Kaiser's shop fast before I talked myself out of going all together. It was a 'thank you' pizza for Randy mainly, for helping Kaiser out at my house. And a really bad excuse to see Kaiser in the middle of the week pizza.

It had been almost a week since I last stayed at his house and almost as many days since I last saw him. I wished I wasn't counting the days or that they didn't feel like they stretched on longer with every hour that passed, but I was getting desperate. With the house in better shape than it'd ever been, there was no reason to show up unannounced.

The door chimed as I walked in. The smell of pine and wood stain hit my nose in an oddly comforting way. It smelled like Kaiser.

"Hello?" My voice echoed into the emptiness of the store when a pop of pink rolled out from where I assumed the office was.

"Hi, welcome to Price and Company," she said brightly as she got up from the chair and started toward me

I shifted the box into my other hand. "Is Kaiser around?" I looked past her and it seemed to be empty beside her. Maybe I missed him, or maybe he liked to go out for lunch. She smiled brightly up at me, her eyes crinkled shut, showing off the septum piercing in her nose as it scrunched up from her laugh.

"You must be Abby!" she exclaimed like she had been expecting me, but I had no idea who she was. She seemed out of place and right at home in the store all at once. Her bubblegum colored hair and tattooed arm a striking contrast to the natural colors of the store. "I am, but I'm sorry, I don't know—"

She cut me off swiftly and then stuck her hand out. "Kaity, I work the front of the store for Kaiser, and some office work, and oh... " She pulled my hand slightly as she shook it while staring directly into my eyes. "I do the ordering for the window display." She let my hand go and breezed past me back to the front of the store. With no Kaiser in sight, I had no choice but to follow her.

Her hair swished over her shoulder as she glanced back at me. "Your eyes are beautiful, the blue reminds me of the crystals we have up front." She held back a small smile, like she was avoiding unraveling a secret.

We stopped in front of the display and she pulled the box from my hand, setting it on a stunning dining room table next to us. I winced slightly, thinking of the grease that might seep through the cardboard box and stain the table. Kaity must have seem my face, or at least had the same thought and quickly moved it to the table mat that was there for staging purposes.

"Come look." She nodded toward the window display. I've walked past the shop countless of times in the past, but had only been in once or twice when I was looking for furniture for the house after I bought it. I quickly learned you would need to give up small fortune and your first born child for one of the larger pieces in Kaiser's shop. But once you had them, it was worth it.

My fingers brushed over the wooden salt and pepper cracks, a faint smile pulling at my lips. He was really an artist. The attention to detail on every piece was astounding.

My eyes caught the wooden bowl which had a heaping mound of different crystals.

"What a funny thing to carry in the store," I said, picking up a piece of sodalite, turning it between my fingers in the ray of sun that was streaming through the window. It was a deep blue stone with an almost silver marbling throughout it, that was tumbled making it round and smooth. I had a similar one in my office, they said it was good for organizing the mind. I lost it at some point though and never replaced it. I like it because it was almost the same shade of my eyes.

"Kaiser asked for that one specifically," she said, glancing up at me again.

I looked at her, my eyebrows drawing inward. "Really, I wonder why?" I turned back to the stone, letting it roll off my palm and back into the bowl.

"Oh, I have an idea." She threw her head back in laughter right as Kaiser and Randy rounded the corner.

Kaiser's footsteps faltered for a second when he saw me. There it was again, an elusive smile that felt like it was just for me. "What are you doing here?"

"I thought I'd bring lunch. To thank you and Randy for all of the help with my house."

He looked from the box on the table back to me. "You didn't have to do that."

Randy walked in and Kaiser stepped back from where he was encroaching on my space.

"Randy, Abby brought lunch."

"Oh nice." The box was plucked from the table and handed it over to Randy. Kaity smacked his shoulder with the back of her hand. "How about a thank you Randy," she said. A blush appeared across the top of Randy's cheeks before he shyly thanked me and walked away with Kaity and the pizza.

"What's with those two?" I jerked my head to where they could still be heard bickering back and forth.

"You know, the less I know is probably for the better." His voice taking on no inflection like he really wanted nothing to do with whatever was going on between them.

"Kaity was showing me the display."

"Oh yeah, she's in charge of all of that." He waved toward the display without much care.

Kaiser teased me about my crystals for as long as I could remember. Laughing when he would find them tucked into the corners of my house, or rolling his eyes when I explained their purpose. I didn't exactly believe that they cleared my mind or calmed my anxiety but they were fun to have around, even if he teased me about them. But why would he have them in his store?

"I was just stopping by on my lunch break, I should get going." I started toward the door. With nothing left to keep me here, it felt awkward to hang around. I didn't even know if he wanted to see me.

"Do you have a few extra minutes? I have something I wanted to show you." He shoved his hands into his front pockets, and rocked back onto the heel of his boots.

"Yeah, a few more minutes," I answered immediately and tried not to sound too eager but I think I was past that. So, when he reached out his hand, I slipped mine in it without a second thought and let him pull me to the workshop attached to the store.

He positioned me in front of a large board with pages and pages pinned into it. Some with drawings, some with what looked like calculations. I stared at the wall for a few minutes before turning to him. "You're gunna have to tell me what I'm looking at, Kai." He stepped behind me, our height difference on display as the top of my head barely grazed his chin.

"It's the cabinet I was sketching. Or it will be, these are just preliminary drawings."

Once he said it, it was impossible to unsee. It looked like it would be tall enough to scrape the ceiling of a normal house, four glass doors with a row of square drawers underneath and it would all sit on top of a cabinet. It was beautiful and it was only on paper so far.

"You will definitely win if this is what you enter." I reached out and traced the design with the tips of my fingers. It amazed me that all this could come from one man. Looking at him as only a stranger on the street I would have never guessed so much beauty could be created from the tips of his fingers, but he had an entire store to prove me wrong. "I bet if you could do some sort of bead detail along the edges," I said out loud, but mainly to myself as an observation.

He shifted behind me, his chest grazed my back with the movement. I pretend not to notice, but I didn't dare move. It had only been a week since I was this close to him. I told myself that it might have meant nothing, but I was never a good liar, especially to myself.

"Do you like it?" His voice was low outside my ear, questioning me with a hint of need of validation behind it. Like my words will make or break him.

I wondered if this was why I hadn't seen him since I moved back home. Did he feel what I did at the lake, like the space between us was infinite and not enough all at the same time? Could he feel the change in my heartbeat as it kicked up a notch at the centimeters of space between us?

He stepped closer, if that was even possible, and with each deep breath his chest brushed against the fabric of my shirt.

All my coherent thoughts seemed to vanish, surely this wasn't normal. I've had my fair share of relationships, casual flings. Hell, I developed crushes more often than the average twelve year old, but nothing had ever been like this. At no point in the past had I lost all my words from simple touches or flushed with heat over even the possibility of being touched. This wasn't normal and yet it was the only thing I knew I wanted. Even if it meant never finding our way out of the will he, won't he, purgatory I was in, I'd happily spend my days in near contact with Kaiser.

He cleared his throat. "I should have it done just in time for the competition." Another breath and his presence vanished from my back, leaving me blinking away the haze.

Was that it?

Nothing more? No arms around my waist to pull me closer? No lips pressed against any part of me? Nothing from him to ease the fire dancing on my skin.

Without him encroaching on my space I felt an odd sense of loneliness. It was something but nowhere close to what I wanted. My shoulders twisted as I quickly moved my head side to side as I tried to regain conciseness. "You can do all this in five weeks?" It seemed impossible with the amount of detail he'd have to put in. I turned in time to watch his shoulder lift then fall.

Kaiser was back to being his old, old as of ten minutes ago, nonchalant self.

I couldn't wait to see how it turned out or for the fair in general. It was one of my favorite times of year in Fairvale; the rides, the terrible yet addicting carnival sweets, and when the heat that finally disappeared leaving the air brisk but without the storms. Through those usually rolled in soon after but the fair was always perfect.

"I'm sure it'll be perfect, and I have no doubt that you will win based off these."

"You have no idea how much that means, Dimples."

TWENTY-SIX

Kaiser

THE SUN'S RAYS BEGAN their morning dance, bouncing off the front window pane and illuminating the store front. Golden wood tables and chairs were displayed in the front, months of back breaking work went into each piece bringing it to life. I was always a bit sad whenever they found a new home but my wallet would be happy.

This was my favorite time to be in the store. I could work without having to interact with the public, where the silence was comforting but I was having a hard time grasping it. She was everywhere and I could no longer concentrate even if I was already a few hours into one of my current orders. It was a pretty enough cutting board, but unchallenging. Normally, I kept these types of projects in stock, but the woman who ordered it had to have a custom size.

The last clamp squeezed the wood blocks together forcing beads of glue to seep through the cracks. I dragged a damp cloth across the surface for a quick clean up and then moved it to the table across the room for drying. I tugged at the tie of my apron, letting the string unravel under my fingertips before pulling it above my head and casting it aside when a familiar voice rang out from the front of the store.

"Kaiser," the voice called out. The softness of the syllables floated through my ears and I followed it like a lost stray being called home. My head popped out of the side room and was met with the sight of my mother. She hovered by the front door, eyes darting around until they found me. That's when she smiled, it's the only time she smiled it seemed.

"Mom." I responded as I strode toward her, the heavy heel of my boots thudding against the floor. She tugged me down for a brief hug, the top of her gray streaked brunette hair barely brushing my shoulder. My mother was a small, willowy woman, who was so used to making herself smaller that she always seemed to disappear anytime she entered a room.

With her hands clutched on the strap of her purse she followed me further into the shop. "What are you doing out here?" I questioned while pulling out one of the display chairs for her to sit on. She waved off my attempt at chivalry and continued to stand. "I'm here to shop, actually. I have a birthday dinner tonight and thought I'd take the opportunity to show off your work."

There's a glow in my chest at her words. If there's one person I credited all my hard work to, it's her and I'd never get used to her incessant need to tell everyone how proud she was of me.

"Whose birthday?" I questioned and I approached the shelving on the far side of the room. We kept a few different baskets on display for this reason exactly, it wasn't often that people thought to come here for a birthday gift but when they did we were prepared. I placed the deep brown wicker basket on the register counter while scanning the shelfs for what items might be best. All while trying not to read too far into that she hesitated before saying a friend.

The bell chimed and both our heads turned to see Kaity strolling in. She greeted my mother warmly before taking over my half assed attempt of putting together a gift basket. "Mama Price, it's been forever since you've been in here, how are you?" My mother seemed to light up at sight of her before pulling her into a tight embrace. I had to hand it to Kaity, she really knew how to make people feel wanted.

I'm an only child, and for a long time, I was grateful for it. At least there was only one kid in the house being subject to my father's wrath. But there was always a wistful longing in her voice when she would talk to Kaity or really any younger woman. Like she wished life had dealt her a better hand and she had the opportunity to have a daughter. It caused an uncomfortable sort of feeling in my chest and for a second it made me think of Ivy and how happy she was to have her around.

"He's dreadful. You should know better than to have him put together anything that isn't made out of wood."

"Kaity, do you ever have anything nice to say about me?"

"Absolutely not," she said without missing a beat as she slipped a set of cheese knives with custom handles into the basket.

"Isn't there anything else you can be doing around here," I snipped.

Her hand paused reaching for a cutting board. "Just because you stopped smoking, doesn't mean you get to take your irritability out on me. Boss, or not." She stood a bit taller as her said the words.

And she was absolutely right, but I never told anyone that I had been trying to quit. So how did she know?

"That's so good to hear, Son," my mother chimed in. Kaity resumed putting together the gift, slipping the board off the shelf.

I stood there a bit dumbfounded. "How?"

"Oh, please, you're almost too easy to read. You took an afternoon break like it was your religion ever since I stated working here and would come back into the shop smelling like an ashtray. Obviously, I would notice that it stopped after you came in to buy all the bath stuff a few weeks ago."

I could feel my mother's eyes on me.

"Uh huh," I mused, shoving my hands into my jeans pockets. "You're right, and I'm sorry."

She took the apology with a smug look on her face and left to pick over the rest of the store for the basket.

If she was waiting on me to elaborate on what Kaity meant, she didn't say it. She did however look at me and made me feel like a teenager again.

"Who ever she is, she must be quite the woman for you to finally give that up," She stated.

"It won't work between us," I admitted, not wanting to get her hopes up.

"Says who?"

This was not the place, or time, or person I wanted to talk to about this.

"Mom," I said with a warning tone in my voice.

"I'm not saying be pushy about it, if she has a boundary respect it, but there was obviously someone who has done her wrong, who has made her feel like giving up is the only option. Show her that you can be all the things the others before lacked."

Kaity looked just about done as she walked down the middle of the store back to the register counter. "Okay," I said, effectively ending the conversation. The last thing I needed was both of them telling all the things they thought would matter, because in the end it was me, and I wasn't good enough for her.

TWENTY-SEVEN

Abby

FOOD HELD MEMORIES. PEANUT butter and apricot jelly sand-wiches tasted like lunchtime summers when I was nine. Spaghetti and basil meatballs sparked memories of my mom coming home early from work to spend time with Lennon and I. Chocolate cake tasted like birthdays.

It was funny though, if I asked Lennon what any of them meant to her she probably would say she had never even had basil meat-balls before. I'd never understand how we were raised in the same home and yet seemed to have wildly different accounts of what happened. Lennon seemed to latch onto only the bad memories, which I understood, I swear I did, but it clouded all the soft and tender moments we experienced. To the point she couldn't remember them at all. Normal existed within our home, it wasn't all chaos and that was what I clung to like a raft.

I smoothed the weathered paper my list was scribbled on, against my new gleaming counters. It was tattered and wrinkled almost beyond recognition. Faded black ink seemed to mock me as I stared at it, like I was waiting for it to talk back to me. To tell me this was the right thing, that there was no harm in wanting more out of life even if it seemed trivial. That bucket list items didn't have to have some big life altering meaning to mean something.

The only item that did mean something was the first one I wrote: **bake the perfect chocolate cake.**

But not any cake, my grandmother's triple chocolate cake.

Every birthday until I was out of the house I had the same cake without fail, so did Lennon. One of my earliest memories was watching my mother break the eggs into the batter of a chocolate cake, her combining powdered sugar and coco powder into the mixing bowl while she whipped frosting together and of me climbing up onto a chair next to her, insisting that I put the chocolate sprinkles on the top. The recipe had been handed down, from my great grandmother to my grandmother to my mother. But it never made its way to mine or Lennon's hands. Lennon's birthday was soon and I wanted to make it for her, but since I couldn't ask for it, I'd have to figure it out myself.

The ingredients I did know for a basic chocolate cake were lined up on the counter, while my shiny new oven pre-heated. I worked through the beginning of the recipe as I had the last half a dozen times I'd done this, but this time I was going a little out of the normal realm and was doing a mayonnaise chocolate cake. Which sounded gross but I was desperate to find the right recipe. I was getting close, and out of everything on the list this was what I wanted the most and the only one that was up to me and me alone to figure out.

Everything was in the oven within a few minutes. By the time I turned back to the sink and looked up, Kaiser's truck was pulling into his driveway. I hovered in the spot to watch as he slipped out of the truck and ran his hand down the truck side he glided toward the bed, a stoic expression barely visible from my viewing point. Strong arms began yanking out wood and heaving it up onto his broad shoulders, keeping one arm around the materials. He then walked toward his backyard and out of my view.

The back and forth trips were nearly hypnotic as he continued to unload his materials and I realized I had never felt more alone. It was a dense feeling of loneliness that swept though each of my senses and left an aching pain in its wake.

My feet burned to carry me across the street to him. It was impossible to remind my heart that we were simply neighbors, that one week couldn't possibly change that much between us, but it was a stubborn organ who wasn't grasping the concept.

There was a few facts I was sure of. One - Kaiser and I were neighbors, that was it. Two - I made this stupid bucket list to not end up in my same pattern of falling heart first into relationships. Three - I was sure I would be stuck in a loop trying to figure a way to change the first fact.

Kaiser never came back out after his third trip. By the time the cake was out of the oven and cooled down, the sun was long gone and my home felt as empty as ever.

I unfolded the crinkled paper that held my bucket list and placed it beside the plate. If this was the right recipe I wanted to cross it off immediately in triumph. But when the first bite of cake passed my lips, a tear rolled down my face. It wasn't right. And all it did was serve as a reminder that I never got what I wanted.

TWENTY-EIGHT

Kaiser

IT WAS A RARE day I was alone in my shop. Customers were few and far between throughout the day, and I was trying not to be bothered by it.

I slid the goggles from the top of my head into place and pulled my ear protection over my head. When I flipped the switch, the machine in front of me whirled to life, bringing a sense of calm to my racing heart. I notched the first piece of wood through the saw and I let my mind drift, just for a second.

It had been weeks since I was last close to Abby. My house lost the smell of her the morning after she left and I felt like an incomplete man since, which was pathetic. Abby was not my woman, I had no claim to her but I wanted to.

I wanted to see her whenever I pleased, have her in my home so I never had to miss her and I would give anything to kiss her just because I could. I wasn't a romantic person, I was constantly reminded of that in my last relationship and it remained a constant weight on my shoulders. I was made to believe in order to keep a woman, you had to go out of your way with grand gestures and poetic words about how you felt. But that wasn't me. It wasn't that I didn't feel those things, but I didn't know how to translate what I was feeling into the right words. Which was probably why I was the lucky solider who received a Dear John letter about a month into my first deployment.

Since then, I stayed closed off to anything that resembled a relationship. But Abby made me rethink everything I had been doing.

the last piece of wood was cut, I switched off the table saw and pulled the ear protection from my head in time to hear the front door chime. I tossed the gear on to the table and brushed bits of saw dust that clung to me as I walked out front.

My head was down as I rounded the corner so the first thing I heard was the customers voice.

"Does anyone even work in this dump?"

My head snapped up, mouth ready to yell back that they could get the fuck out if they didn't like it when I registered a man leaning against the front window display. He was my height with dark brown hair cropped short and a shit eating grin plastered on his stupid face.

"Woods, you son of a bitch," I roared with a laugh and took a few long strides as he pushed off from the display to meet me in the middle. I stretched out my hand which he immediately swatted away before pulling me into a vice like hug.

I didn't know if grown men had best friends, but if they did, Woods was mine. It was hard not to be when we spent weeks in the field together, with no electronics and only the voices in our heads.

His deep laugh echoed into the otherwise empty store. I pulled back keeping my hands on his shoulders, using one hand I gave him a rough pat on his cheek. It had been months since I saw him last, I never knew when he would blow into town since he was still enlisted.

"How have you been, man?"

"I'm good, I got back to the states last week and came out here to see you as soon as I could."

Woods and I are the same age, we came up through the ranks together. He supported me when I decided to leave the Army instead of staying until I could retire and never judged me for when the clouds in my head became so dark that they rained down on me until it felt like I was drowning in them. He had this weird sixth sense for when I needed someone to talk to and always showed up when I called for help.

"Actually, there is a reason for me showing up, " he said with a wide grin. "I'm getting married."

My eyes went wide.

"On Saturday," he followed up with.

I looked at him waiting for the punch line. It never came. "I have a lot of thoughts but no words for that statement."

"How about congratulations and yes I'll be your best man?"

At least he was smiling.

"Who's the girl?"

I wasn't lying when I said we saw each other once every six months and the last time he was here, there was no girl. Not that you couldn't meet someone and fall in love in that amount of time, but Woods was Woods. When he found out I had a girl back home during basic training, he laughed in my face and told me he'd never be tied down. Sure that was over twenty years ago but he kept his word this entire time.

"Her name is Rebecca and she is the light of my life. We met on my last R&R at a bar and just clicked. I don't know man, I can't explain it. I spent every day of my break with her and when I got my next orders, I didn't want to leave. For the first time I didn't care about getting back over there and putting my life on the line, I wanted to stay with her." He looked lost in a moment as he spoke. "I'm PCSing to Korea and I want her there, but we can't do that unless we're married and I don't want to spend another second without her as my wife. So we're getting married on Saturday, at the courthouse, and I want you there. All I do is talk about you and I'm pretty sure she thinks you're made up at this point."

I laughed and shook my head.

Woods was the only guy I told about the Dear John letter I got from Ivy and when I cried, he slung his arm around my shoulders and let me know it would be alright. That in the end everything would work out how it was supposed to. He was as tough as they made them but didn't let the world tell him how a solider should act or feel and helped spread that mindset to the rest of us. If he said he wanted me by his side then that's what he'd get. He's as good as they come and deserved this.

"Will you come?"

I didn't hesitate this time. "Absolutely."

We sat in my office for an hour as he told me about his recent stint overseas and I was, for once, happy customers weren't flooding my store.

"Enough about me." He smacked my knee. "What have you been up to?"

"You're looking at it, running the shop, keeping my head on straight. The usual."

He nodded along. "Anything new with that girl you were moping around about last time I was here?"

Like I said, a weird sixth sense about when I needed someone.

Last time Woods was here, Abby was dating some guy I never bothered to remember the name of. He was blonde, wore suits a lot, and every time I saw him across the street, he looked like a total douche bag. Woods and I went out to Wildflower Lake to fish when I needed to get away from the reminder that I would never be with her. Woods listened as I complained about how often she asked for my help, how obnoxious I found her dark red hair, cliche dark blue eyes and the way she smiled at me with the dimples I found childish.

Granted I was well past my drink limit at the time and was word vomiting all over him.

I didn't remember much from that day except Woods simply telling me, "Oh, so you like her, is what you're saying?" I denied any feelings to his face but that was the first time I realized what I was feeling wasn't indifference and it was the first time since Ivy that I felt like I wanted anything other than a quick hook up with a woman.

A smug look crossed his features. His wide set eyes looked back at me waiting for an answer.

"No, nothing," I said, which was the truth. He waited for more of an answer, swiveling back and forth in the spare office chair I kept stashed in the corner. "Okay, not nothing, but there really isn't anything going on," I started with. "Someone broke into her house a while ago and wrecked a lot of it, so I offered to help her fix it and redo the kitchen while I was at it."

"Naturally. Go on." I could hear a twinge of his country drawl in the words. Didn't matter how long he'd been out of Georgia, the accent never fully went away.

I rolled my eyes. "I offered to let her stay at my house while I worked on hers. She stayed a week then went back home and nothing happened."

His eyes lit up like a casino slot machine hitting the mega jackpot. "I'm assuming you mean you told her how you felt and she fell into bed with you because you're so irresistible and you spent the week playing house together," he said with a grin.

"No. She stayed in the guest room, ass. Nothing happened."

Nothing but late night deck meetings, locked gazes over hand wounds and bath side book reading.

"So, what are you going to do about it?"

I wanted to say nothing, that I was going to do nothing about it because it was the safe option.

"Price, you are the best guy I know, and you are worthy of love and being loved." My head drooped between my shoulders as my elbows rested on my knees and my hands were clasped so tight that my knuckles turned white. "What Ivy did to you was rough, but it wasn't your fault. What happened in the desert wasn't your fault. Your father wasn't your fault. You've been dealt a shitty hand, but you can find new cards to play with. "

"I should really stop telling you things." My eyes burned but I needed to hear the words.

He barked out a laugh. "I've been telling you that for years Price, and yet you continue to spill your guts to me anytime you're feeling a little blue."

I knew this but the words in her letter burned into my mind twenty years ago and never left.

"You like this neighbor girl, right?" he said with a tone of authority.

I nodded my head. There was no use in lying.

"Invite her to the wedding, tell her that you love her."

"I don't love her."

"Or tell her you like her, if you want to be all middle school about it. If not for you, then for me. Sheesh, I'm tired of seeing you sad and mopey." A break in the dark clouds appeared and forced me to laugh.

"I'll think about it."

"Don't take too long, because if she doesn't know to wait for you, she'll slip through your fingers."

We sat around my shop to bullshit and talk about nothing for another hour before he left. When he finally did I made a decision that I owed it to myself to at least try.

People kept showing up to tell me I should let Abby know how I felt. I didn't know what would happen if I did or what I would say to her but Woods was right, I would wait forever for a chance with her but she wouldn't even know I was an option unless I told her.

Twenty-Nine

Abby

I was in a rut. I woke up, went to work, came home, and went to bed. Some weekends I'd see Carina and Lennon, but they had their own full lives. So I was alone on a Sunday but I didn't want to be.

This could be a mistake, I thought, as I stood on his porch, knocking on the wooden door with one hand and balancing two coffees in the other. The drinks teetered slightly in my hand but I was able to catch them before they spilt all over Kaiser's front porch and I made even more of a fool of myself.

He opened the door and instead of my nerves quieting they kicked into high gear. They buzzed down my spine making it hard for me to form words.

"What's up, Abby?" he questioned again, looking at my hand full of goods.

"I was just wondering if you wanted breakfast?" That was dumb, I was dumb. "I mean, it's been a while and I wanted to see what you were up to." That was no better. "I brought breakfast…" I lifted the coffees and bag of bagels.

"Why did that sound like a question?"

I blew out a frustrated breath. "I don't know. Do you want it, or not? I've been doing nothing all week and I wanted to see you." He lifted one eyebrow at me. "There, you happy?" I said. I didn't wait for an answer before walking inside.

There was a faint chuckle from him as he closed the door. I handed him his coffee and reassured him it was black, nothing in it, the way he liked it. Then opened the bag of bagels from Renaissance for him to choose from.

"Thanks, Abby," he said while holding my gaze. My throat bobbed as I swallowed down the insecurity that was rising.

We stood in the kitchen, sipping our coffees and eating in silence until he shoved the last bite into his mouth. I figured this was when he'd ask me to leave, but I was surprised when he asked me to follow him as he walked toward the garage.

Stepping into a mini workshop, I followed Kaiser carefully around the piles of wood, large machinery, and more tool boxes than I assumed one person would need.

Boxes were stacked in a far corner, tools that I didn't know the name of were neatly placed across his workbench along with nails, wires, and tubs of glue and paint. It was perfectly Kaiser. Was there ever a time Kaiser let loose, or was he always so *Kaiser.*

He stood next to what look like the beginning of a cabinet door. His hands were shoved into his pockets, back stick straight, uncomfortable with whatever he was about to present me.

"I went with your suggestion," he sheepishly muttered.

I ran my hand down the smooth unfinished wood.

"Hmmm," I hummed in question.

"For the cabinet, I added the beaded design to the doors like you mentioned."

My head moved from the door he was forming to look back at him. There was a swell of warmth in my chest. I didn't realize he was listening when I mentioned it.

"Really?"

He only nodded.

"Do you want to help?" he asked quietly.

"Are you sure you want me to? You know I'm pretty useless with the projects with my house. I don't think I know the difference between a saw and drill most of the time." I wanted to yell out yes as soon as he asked me but I was hesitant.

"You can leave that all to me but you can pick out the color of stain. I'll need knobs for all the doors and pulls for the drawers. And you have a good eye for that sort of thing," he rambled on. "What do you say?"

"I would love to."

"Okay."

"Okay," I repeated back.

He turned to his workbench, not really grabbing but clearly stalling and I wondered if I missed a queue to leave. Maybe he wanted to start later.

I was seconds away from asking him when he abruptly turned around.

"My friend is getting married, a small thing at the courthouse. Will you come with me?" The words ran together but there was no mistaking the slight wariness to the question.

"Really? Why?"

What was I saying? Why didn't I scream out yes the second he asked me?

I watched him deflate at my words.

I liked to pretend with Kaiser. Before I stayed at his house I would catch glimpses of him and wonder what it would be like to be his, to be with him, to be wanted by him. Little daydreams that weaved themselves into my every waking moment and made everything easier. Then I moved in for a week and little parts of the daydreams seemed to leech into real life. Moments where I'd catch him looking at me, causing a jolt of excitement to flood my system. Small brushes of his skin against mine during innocent interactions that left me longing for more. I thought it was me, maybe I was reading too far into him simply being a good person and my delusions were just that. Delusions I made up in my head.

There was too long of a pause between his question and my response. I was afraid he'd take back the offer if I didn't speak up.

"Kaiser," I said gently, placing my hand on his back, the muscles tensed under my touch but he didn't move. "Kaiser." I tried again, more gently, lacing as much care and affection into the word. When he wouldn't turn to meet me, I circled to his front. His eyes were squeezed shut. "Look at me," I demanded, and a moment later, they drifted open with slow apprehension. They were grey this time, a stormy color filled with anguish of a man who put his feelings on the line for the first time in a long time, if ever. He was walking a thin line of wanting to spill open and confess everything he'd been hiding and shutting down for good.

I reached out and cupped his face, the scratch of his beard a welcoming comfort. He exhaled a shaky breath of relief.

"When's the wedding?" I asked.

"On Saturday," he said simply, never taking his eyes off of me. He shoved his hands back into his pockets as soon as the words left his mouth and he rocked back on his heels.

"I'd love to." Warmth flooded my cheeks as I tried to bite back a smile as I said the words.

THIRTY

Kaiser

"How long have they been together?" Abby questioned as we parked in the closest spot I could find near the courthouse. My stomach felt like a lead ball was weighing me down. Which was stupid, I wasn't the one getting married today, so why did it feel like something big was going to happen? Like their wedding was going to catapult us from being one thing to each other to something else, something more.

It was a mistake, my brain screamed at me. This was all a mistake and I needed to run as far as I could in order her to keep her safe, but I couldn't find the strength to do it. So I stayed close but the longer I was around her the more that feeling of not being enough for her seemed to slowly flicker until it was gone completely. And that would only result in a disaster for me, but I didn't care anymore.

I barked out a quick laugh at her question with my hand hovering over the door handle. "They met six months ago." In reality, that was the only thing I *did* know. If Woods said he was going to do something, who was I to talk him out of talk of it?

"And they're already getting married?" I balked. It wasn't a question of concern, more like surprise. "Well I guess, if you know, you know," she justified with a smile.

I hopped out once traffic died and rounded the front of the truck to the passenger side. Once I pulled the door open and she stepped out, I let myself finally look at her. Her black heels touched the ground, as I dragged my eyes slowly up her body. The dress was silk, maybe, I didn't really know. What I did know was it was the same color of her eyes, dark blue silk that grazed the her ankles when she let the fabric go.

"Is this okay?" she questioned with a slight worry as she pulled her hair over one shoulder and then slid her hands down the front of the dress. "Everyone gets married differently at the courthouse and I didn't know whether it was get in and get out sort of deal or if they're doing the full ceremony or what."

"I didn't ask," I said after I cleared the lump in my throat. The sight of her made my knees want to buckle and worship the ground she walked on even if it was public sidewalk.

"Well if they're getting married in jeans you'll stick out like a sore thumb with me." Her eyes raked over my chest and I had to push down the urge to preen. I hated dressing up, anything with buttons I had to use, made me feel like the world was closing on me, but this called for a little effort. It was simple enough entire, black slacks that had never been pressed and a white dress shirt that had never seen an iron. It's what I wore when I needed to go to the bank to discuss a loan, or the few funerals I'd been to over the years. It was nothing special.

I felt like I should have asked so I could have given her more insight on what we were walking into, but with the way she looked, I couldn't find it in me to be mad about it.

More silence surrounded us as we entered the large marble building. Light filtered through the windows from the dome top casting spotlights inside the building. Gold accents dawned every surface while the shiny tiled floor echoed under our footsteps and from the dozens of other people who were around. "I'm surprised so many people are here," I leaned over to Abby and said in a whisper.

"Oh, yeah, this place is really popular for weddings nowadays. My sister got married here not that long ago, it can be really beautiful. Especially if you don't care about doing the whole 'I pledge my life to you' sort of thing in front of people."

The last time marriage crossed my mind, there was no real thought behind it but I was too young for anyone to talk me out of it. I bought a ring and everything but I never even considered it as pledging my life to someone as Abby put it. I never thought of the wedding, I never thought of what she would have looked like if I ever made it down the aisle and I never even thought what would come after. Nothing. I was in love and I thought that's what we were meant to do.

"Is this how you'd want to get married?" I asked without thinking it through. We stopped at the staircase and waited by the bannister where Woods said he would be, but was nowhere to be found. She looked up at me, eyes wistful and wide before turning away to stare out at the people around us.

"No, I don't think so. There is something profound about standing up in front of your friends and family and professing your love, your devotion to another person, your unyielding desire to be there for one person for as long as you live. I think it's beautiful act of trust and I think I would want that." Her voice was full of passion and eyes gleaming like sapphires. "But most of all, I just want a partner who sees me, all of me and still chooses me. Someone who knows everything about me and still thinks I'm worthy of love. As long as I had that, nothing else would matter, you know."

Moments passed between us before I looked at her and knew exactly what she was talking about even though a minute ago I would have said I didn't. "That sounds nice," I mused out loud. We were standing much too close, my fingers twitched at my side and for a brief second, they ghosted along her hand and I felt whole again.

A shout of my name broke the moment. I turned to see Woods walking up to us with a woman at his side, clutching a bouquet in a simple white sundress. He broke away from his soon to be wife and pulled me in for a hug and clasped my back in two quick succession. "My brother, thank you for being here," he said. He pulled away as the slight woman approached his side. "This is my wife, or is about to be, Rebecca." The words were simple but you could hear how proud he was to be saying them.

We shook hands, while Abby stood at my back. I didn't even have a chance to turn before Woods was introducing himself to her. "I've heard a lot about you," he said.

She chuckled. "Really?"

"Oh, you have no idea," he confirmed.

She quirked one of her brows up and I wanted turn in on myself.

"Well, shall we," Woods said as he clapped and rubbed his hands together.

"Is there anyone else?" I questioned. There was no one else walking up to us or with them when they came in.

"Just us, it will be a quick in and out. We'll all sign some papers and you two can go back to your lives."

We climbed the stairs to a small room where he gave his name and the clerk told him it would be only a few moments. As we sat on the hard wooden bench Abby leaned in. "Are we their witnesses?"

"I think so."

"Are you sure they want me here? Shouldn't it be someone important to sign their marriage certificate?"

"Price is important to me, and you are important to him," Woods said after obviously listening to us, while his soon to be wife nodded at his side.

"Oh," was all Abby answered with as the door opened and the judge called us back. His black robe swayed with every step he took. It was an unremarkable room, with boring thin carpet, a large desk with files neatly stacked in one corner and a computer in the other, but the couple barely noticed. Their eyes remained locked on each other.

It started like any other generic ceremony, the judge asked if they were both there on their own free will, had them each repeat routine vows, but right before the ring exchange, they asked to say their own words. It was short, yet powerful, and in that moment I understood what Abby meant about the profound feeling of declaring your love for another in front of your friends.

We sat near the door while they spoke to each other and in such an unremarkable room, something remarkable happened. Every feeling I ever had of inadequacy, every fiber of my being that fought against allowing myself to be happy, seemed to vanish.

Maybe it was watching my best friend get everything he deserved.

Maybe it was the closeness of Abby, and her sweet scent of vanilla and the way it seeped into my skin, fogging my way of thinking.

It didn't matter.

"I'm not..." I started in a hush voice. Her hair draped like a curtain over her face as she turned to me. I reached out to move the strands blocking her eyes, tucking them behind her ear. Leaving my thumb to brush the top of her cheek bone. "I'm not good with words, or actions, but I know that I don't like being away from you. I've known for a while actually, but the other day when you said you came over because you wanted to see me I knew then that I needed to do something about it. I don't like that I am only a neighbor to you." My voice carried such brazen confidence that it anchored me to the moment. "I tried like hell not to, I swear I did, but you have been stuck in my head since the day you moved in and I can't get you out. I don't want to get you out."

Her fingers flexed on the fabric of her dress, dragging it up an inch higher on her skin.

I leaned in. My lips inches from her ear. "Tell me you feel this too. Please tell me I'm not alone." I begged, full of agony as I walked a razor thin rope of mercy.

Time halted.

Every moment ticked by at a sluggish crawl and it was like an eternity stuck in purgatory.

She never took her eyes off me, offering me a glimpse at those deep blue irises that lived in my head. They sparkled as they pinged around my face in search of an answer. Any second now she would speak and I would be a changed man, one way or another.

Her lips parted. My breath stalled.

"You're not alone," she answered.

I exhaled, and time began again. A new lease on life.

"Are you busy after this?" The words tumbled out quickly.

She laughed and the judge's eyes flicked toward us. "Wide open."

"Can I take you out on a date, Dimples?" I almost didn't know what I was going to ask, but what popped up in my head was a memory of my mother telling me actions have meaning and every second counted. Words are nice, but if you don't back them up then they might as well mean nothing.

Telling her that I didn't want her out of my head was one thing. I needed to show her that I meant it. That I wanted her close, and I wanted to start immediately.

"I thought you'd never ask."

Most of my life was spent drifting. I drifted away, drifted through, drifted alone and never felt like I belonged. Or at least I did because the moment her hand trailed down my arm and her fingers laced into mine an anchor dropped. I was finally finding my way home.

THIRTY-ONE

Abby

THE CEREMONY WAS OVER as quickly as it started and the new-lyweds were gone before we even blinked. We were left standing in the middle of City Hall while other couples breezed past us. All of them on their way to the next chapter of their love story, unknowing that we were at the start of ours.

Kaiser smiled at me with relentless storm colored eyes that roamed over me. They traced every plane of my face, each curve of my body, from the top of my head, to the tips of my toes. Time slowed to a crawl under his gaze, as if he was savoring the sight of me. Vastly different from all the other times where he would stare only at my face, it was like he had given himself permission to finally stray. I think I liked this version of us better than anything that came before.

"Where did you want to go?" I finally asked, breaking the spell and allowing time to finally move once more. It didn't matter where we went, not really. We could end up back at either of our houses, simply sitting on the couch and I would relax into a bliss like state.

He flipped the blinker and merged into Saturday afternoon traffic seamlessly. It wasn't until he brought the truck up to speed with the surrounding cars that he looked over at me, the light of the sun turned his eyes into molten pools of ocean waves. "You look beautiful, I don't think I mentioned that earlier." I blushed before quickly turning to look out the window. "There's a restaurant in Palm Grove that's new, I didn't have a reason to try it out before now. Seems like I was waiting for something important." I could hear the smile in his voice. Palm Grove was only a few towns over and a forty minute drive on a good day, but I rarely had a reason to venture out that way.

This didn't feel like a first date. Our conversation flowed, no awkward lulls, or time spent trying to figure out if the person across from you was here for just one thing or generally interested in you. It felt like a typical Saturday, as if we'd always reserved this day for time together.

I recognized the restaurant name as we pulled into the parking lot, Carina had mentioned wanting to try it, saying something like 'know thy enemy' since it was an Italian restaurant. The building was beautiful. Tall cypress trees lined the long walkway toward the entrance giving off a countryside charm even though we were on the outskirts of town.

The door creaked open and Kaiser's hand appeared to help me out. I slipped mine into the rough calloused skin of his, it was one of the many things on the ever-growing list of things I liked about him. It was different than what I was used to, a sign that he worked hard for what he wanted.

We were a few steps away from the truck when I spotted a familiar flash of blonde breezing out the restaurant doors that were being help open by a man. I was a second away from dropping Kaiser's hand and calling out to her when the man let go of the door and slipped his arm around her waist to tug her in close.

My jaw dropped and for an unknown reason, I pulled Kaiser behind the nearest tree. "Oh I fucking knew it," I spoke out loud and peaked around the tree. Kaiser didn't miss a beat, he tucked himself in close behind me.

His hands dipped down to my waist, my heartbeat kicked up a notch. "What is it?" His breath warm on my neck as it cascaded across my skin.

"Look." I nodded toward where the couple was walking toward the parking lot looking every part of two people in love.

"Isn't that your friend?"

"Sure is."

"Then why are we hiding from her and her boyfriend?" I looked back at him and smiled.

"That's Levi Decker," I responded. Kaiser only stared back at me, no idea of the significance that statement held.

Carina didn't date, she has loudly and adamantly proclaimed this for as long as I'd known her. She liked her freedom too much. At least she did until Levi Decker. They were about as opposite as two people could be and yet more in tune with each other than one could imagine. Carina pretended like it wasn't obvious to see how they interacted and she would shut down any attempt to pry more information out of her about him or them.

But I saw it even if she didn't.

"It's not her boyfriend, or at least she tries to pretend like they're not together," I said with a smile. "Carina is very private, I'm her best friend and there are things she prefers not to discuss with me or Lennon. Which is fine, we're all entitled to our privacy, I'm just surprised they're out in public."

"Maybe that's why they're all the way out here." He dragged the tips of his fingers along my shoulder, pulling the hair with it and out of the way. "Maybe they wanted privacy?"

We were not in private, we were haphazardly hidden behind a tree trunk, but that didn't matter any longer. The movements were slow and calculated, I knew what I wanted as I turned to face him. My back pressed against the rough bark of the tree with his hand still pressed against my waist. The other skated up my arm, across my collar bone and trailed slowly, so fucking slowly up the column of my neck. Tiny shivers wracked through my system.

"Kaiser?"

"Yeah, Pretty Girl?"

That damn name again.

"Kiss me."

That was all the invitation he needed. Before the final syllable left my mouth, his was on mine to claim what I offered. Soft lips met mine as he pulled my body flush with his. Fireworks, electricity, every cliche reaction someone could feel or think of zipped through my mind as his hands cupped each side of my jaw and deepened the kiss.

Reverent.

That was the word that creeped out of the darkness of my mind. He held me in his hands and kissed me slowly, savoring the moment. Not like I was a prize won, but as if I was a divine experience he never thought he would have the chance to obtain. I was being savored. Explored. He was etching me into his mind, with each stroke of his fingers against my skin, as his tongue dipped into my mouth and when his teeth nipped at my bottom lip. He was collecting small pieces of me to burn into his memory. I could stay in this moment forever, let the seconds soak into my skin so that days, months, even years from this I could remember a time where everything felt right.

His lips barely left mine before he said, "I've waited years to do that again." Soft strokes of his thumb against my cheeks lured me into a bliss induced haze.

"You've thought about me since then?"

That night remained a hazy memory. I was so exhausted, and mentally drained from taking care of Lennon and grieving Camden that my mind blocked it all out. I remembered him though, I remembered feeling like I could let go because he would be there to catch me.

"I remember everything." He pushed closer into me. "And I haven't stopped thinking about you since."

We've never talked about that night.

He only nodded before dipping his head back down, pressing his lips to mine once more.

Thirty-Two

Kaiser

FOUR YEARS AGO

I imagined this piece of wood splintering on the wall across from me in vivid detail for the past twenty minutes. The pieces weren't fitting and it was getting under my skin. A crisp breeze blew through the open garage, carrying fallen leaves from my front yard. I looked up briefly to see Abby's car pull into the driveway across the street. It had been days since my last glimpse of her and I was surprised at the gnawing feeling it created in my chest.

Fucking stupid, but what could you do.

Twenty minutes later and I was still forcing wood that refused to hold together into clamps when I finally gave up and dropped the project onto the workbench. I paced the garage length with my hands laced above my head for a few moments. Air escaped from my chest in a heave as I glanced back over to the house across the street.

There was a small movement in the vehicle, she was still sitting inside. Faced forward, hands on the wheel like she was still driving. It almost seemed as if she was frozen in the spot.

I turned back to pick up the scraps of my trashed project, but my mind stayed on her. Abby had been a thorn in my side, a rock in my shoe and somehow the best parts of my day since she moved in.

I'd never let her know that, but it didn't stop the feelings.

The more time that passed, the more the feeling crept in that something was wrong. She was still sitting in her car. I couldn't take it, I started across the street. My steps slowed as I approached the window on the driver side. She didn't move. Eyes trained forward, no indication that there was an outside world.

I had no clue what I was doing over here. There was an unspoken separation between us. She asks for help, I helped. We didn't hang out, we didn't talk on the phone or even text. I came over when there's a project she needed done and then I went back home, and it was like I lived on another planet entirely. She didn't think of me the way I did of her. It didn't matter that simply looking at her most days stirred emotions up in my chest that I thought I buried a long time ago. I was her neighbor, nothing more.

I reminded myself of that as my knuckles rapped on the window. The longer she took to move the faster my heart beat, until slowly her head turned toward me.

She was looking at me but she didn't see me.

A sudden wave of panic crashed over me and I yanked open the door.

"Abby? Are you okay?"

Wide blue eyes blinked up at me as if that was an answer. "Oh, Kaiser. What... What are you doing here?" Her voice was soft, a slight quiver in the letters.

"You've been sitting in your car like this for like half an hour."

She mouthed the words half an hour but no sound came out. I crouched down beside her, my hand darted forward to catch myself from leaning too far in and fell onto her leg. She latched onto it without thinking, and returned to staring out the windshield.

Time passed but she barely acknowledged it, until finally she spoke.

"My brother's dead. He's not really my brother, I don't have one of those. Although I think I would have liked to. I've only had Lennon, having someone else would have been nice." She rambled, barely filling her lungs with air in between the words. "I would have liked a younger sibling, someone to else play with, to love." She trailed off, her eyes went distant as if in trapped memory. "On second thought, probably not. My house wasn't so great to grow up in. But he was good to me, and it was nice having someone else in our family when they started dating."

I wasn't scared of much, even after multiple tours in the Middle East, but this was clawing at an unknown feeling inside of me, watching her ramble without making sense.

"Abby, look at me." She didn't move, still trapped somewhere in the past. "You're not making any sense." I reached for her other hand and tried pulling her attention to me. I needed her to snap out of it, or to at least tell me what was happening, I needed to fix this. Whatever it was.

She still didn't move, but replied. "I'm just tired I think. I've been with Lennon this whole time."

"Dimples, please look at me." It slipped out, I never called her that out loud before. It was a name I reserved for her in my mind, but I was desperate for more answers than she was giving me.

Finally, she turned toward me and the tears I could hear in her voice filled her waterline.

"What happened?" I pleaded.

"My sister's husband, my brother, he's dead." A single tear tracked down her check, splashing onto where our hands were joined in her lap. I had never touched her before. Dreamed of it of course, daily even, and somehow this simple act had surpassed anything I was ever able to concoct.

"He's dead, and my sister is…" She couldn't bring herself to finish the sentence. She shook her head back and forth. More tears followed, cascading down her face like white water rapids, unyielding and unforgiving. "How does someone come back from that, Kaiser?" she asked. "When the love of your life dies without warning, how does life, how does anything keep going on?" She threw her arms around my neck without waiting for an answer.

The sudden contact of her skin on mine burned. Her hands grasped the back of my neck causing us to nearly topple over onto the driveway. I gripped her back, not knowing what else to do as she sobbed in my arms. In one swift motion, I scooped my arms under her legs and lifted her up, with nowhere else to go I shuffled toward her house.

My hand fumbled with the door but I eventually managed. I hesitated in the hallway for a moment, unsure of where to go before I decided on the safety of her living room. The couch dipped under both our weights as I sat down with her still in my arms. She stayed, almost refusing to move when I attempted to shift her off. Her breathing had evened out but she remained with her head tucked in the crook of my neck.

We stayed that way until my legs started to tingle, but I didn't have it in me to move her. Instead I passed the time simply watching her, noticing all the little details I was always too far away to see clearly. Long lashes kissed the tops of her red blotched cheeks, and there were clusters of faint freckles that dusted her nose. My fingers toyed with the silken strands of her reddish hair as she lapsed into sleep for the next half an hour.

I traced over every feature, committing them to memory. Perhaps I could stay like this forever. Keep her tucked into the safety of my arms and fight off whatever attempted to harm her. I think I would enjoy a life as her shield.

She stirred, eyes fluttering open and blinked up at me like a newborn doe.

"Hi." It was breathy and had me grasping for reality because surely I was dreaming.

"Are you okay?"

"No." She said immediately, turning her face into my chest and pulled me in closer. "But I will be." The words reverberated against my chest. With nothing left to do I gently rested my chin on top of her head.

"If you ever need anything you know you could always come to me, right?" I said.

It came on suddenly, the need to spill my heart to her, tell her everything that filled my mind since she moved in. That she was all I thought of, all I dreamed of and everything I could never let myself have. My heartbeat sped up as the stillness around us charged with electricity that seemed to come from where we were joined. Before I could blink, she shifted, pushed up and her lips were on mine.

They were soft and warm as they moved against me. My mouth, my jaw, down my neck. Surprise didn't begin to cover what I felt but I pushed it out of my mind, because if this was all I would ever get, then I was going to accept whatever it was she was willing to give.

Hands roamed over my chest, searching, pulling as she straddled my lap.

My name came out as whisper through her lips and into my skin as my shirt was tugged from my jeans.

It came out again, but more frantic.

I knew what this was.

A distraction.

I wanted to give in.

It would be easy but it wouldn't sit right with my conscience. I couldn't, not like this. No matter how much I wanted it.

Vulnerability made even the most sound minded people act rashly. The last thing I wanted was to have her for one night only to have her wake up the next day full of regret. I wanted her for more than that, and I couldn't risk being only a distraction for her.

Her fingers pressed at the button of my pants, flicking it open in one swift move that was nothing short of impressive. My hand tangled with hers, stopping her searching before I was too far gone in the moment.

"Abigail." When she looked at me I could see she already knew my next words and she silently pleaded for me not to say them.

"Please don't." She begged quietly and I almost gave in.

Brushing the fallen hair back behind her ear, I cupped the side of her face. "We shouldn't." When she tried to shimmy her way out of my grasp it only made me hold on tighter. I wasn't ready to let her go yet.

"But I want to," she confessed.

"Believe me, I want to but we both know this isn't the time."

Instead of letting her run off, I laid her down and tucked myself in beside her. Every inch of her molded against me as we laid face to face, noses brushing against each other on a couch three times too small.

"I'm sorry about your brother, Abby."

A weak smile graced her lips. "Me too." Her eyes closed and she was asleep in my arms within minutes again.

I might never get another chance with her being this close again but that was okay. This could be enough, I could live a life with only scraps of her. With my furniture in her house and me across the street. It could be enough, I was barely living anyway so what difference would it make. But if given a chance I knew I would enjoy a life as her shield.

THIRTY-THREE

Abby

"So, ARE YOU GUYS a couple?" my sister asked, bringing her glass of wine to her lips. She smirked behind the cup before taking a sip.

"No, or maybe," I stated. "I think so?"

I really didn't know. One date and countless week nights spent together cooking or watching TV. Weekends spent keeping him company as he built the cabinet for the fair. It was easy to fall into a routine when we lived so close, but as my sister asked the question that had been in the back of my mind I realized I didn't exactly know what we were.

"You think so?" She laughed gently. "How familiar."

"This isn't like you and Theo, this is different. I don't want to rush things or make a bigger deal out of what we are and ruin it. Like I always do." I drank from the wine glass in front of me, letting the acidic burn into my chest.

Everyone knew my sister and Theo were meant to be together. It was as easy to see as the sky in daylight. Maybe it had something to do with her as person, because I also thought her first husband was made with her in mind as well. Were some people simply more fortunate than others, and why was I never in that category?

"No, you're right, you'll never be me," she said playfully, practically reading my mind.

Before we could discuss it any further Carina slipped onto the open couch cushion smiling at the phone in her hand. I should let it be, not mention what I saw. That would be the polite thing to do but where was the fun in that. And if the roles were reversed, Carina wouldn't hesitate to poke fun at me.

"Oh, you know. Kaiser took me to that new restaurant out in Palm Grove, the one you have been talking about."

She barely looked up from the screen. "Oh, really, did you like it?"

"It was fantastic, not as good as your mom's place, but still, fantastic." It was the truth, nothing compared to Carina's Trattoria.

Carina only hummed in agreement as Lennon looked on without a clue. "Have you been there yet?"

Her head perked up as she set her phone face down and levied her glare on me. "What do you know?"

"What is happening?" Lennon cut in from the sidelines, gaze bouncing between us.

"I might know something, or seen something." I shrugged.

An opportunity to mess with her rarely presented itself, it would be a shame to not take the chance. The way her eyes widened amused me and I only wanted to know why was this such a secret. Levi and I have worked together as long as Carina and I have, I didn't have a negative thing to say about him, it would be hard to find a person who did. Why did he need to be a secret?

"And...?"

She really wasn't going to say anything.

Lennon leaned in. "What is happening?" She theater whispered.

"Carina's been keeping secrets," I whispered back. She rolled her eyes and made an annoyed tsking sound with her mouth. "but that's okay. We don't need to be all in each other's love lives all the time."

Lennon fake a gasped. "Does Carina Pera finally," she threw her hands up, "*finally* have a man?"

"You are the worst and there is not nearly enough wine in this house to get into details."

I jumped up, it was Friday after all, and there was nothing more important than spending time with my friends, my sisters. "I'll run to the store, I'll be ten minutes." I called out, already halfway to the door.

Cool night air washed over me as I left the house smiling. The weather took a turn from our usual dry start to fall and heavy clouds covered the sky. It went on further than I could see, like they would never dissipate. It made me nervous but I would deal with that later.

I looked for a light on in Kaiser's house and for a moment wished I was there instead of heading to my car, but life was all about balance. That was what I wanted for this new relationship, not to lose myself and this was a good start.

My purse landed in the passenger seat as I slid into the driver's spot. Something was wrong, I felt it the moment I fully sat down, but my gut couldn't determine what it was or I couldn't tell what it was trying to tell me. The air was different somehow, the smell was off but not my much. I waited to see if it came to me but after a minute I was still grasping at straws so I stuck my keys into ignition and started the engine.

What was different?

The thought stayed with me as I pulled out and headed two blocks over to the corner store. It stayed with me as I plucked a couple bottles of Carina's favorite red wine from the shelf and handed my money over to the cashier. The thought stayed with me as I headed home in silence, not even bothering with the radio.

The thought blared in my head when I arrived home and opened the car door. I kept crystals everywhere, even my car but as I pulled my keys from the car and pushed open the door it hit me. They were all missing.

Someone had been here, and that smell, I knew that smell. Suddenly, my gut and my mind clashed and caught up with each other. It was a sickly sweet sort of smell, the type that made you never want to look at a dessert as it turned your stomach.

I knew that smell.

THIRTY-FOUR

Abby

IT HAD BEEN OVER a week and I still hadn't told anyone about my car. My instinct was to run to Kaiser like I had when I came home to my door open, it was overwhelming, but I fought it. Instead I proceeded back into my house, sat around with Lennon and Carina and drank wine until we all decided that two in the morning was a good enough bed time. I wanted to tell them, tell anyone.

But I didn't.

Thunder shook the garage door of Kaiser's house. Metal rattled against the wood of the frame of his garage door the same way my bones did at the sound. I hated this weather, if I could I'd live in constant Summer without any threat of rain. Every day would be full of sun and I would never have the sense of fear crawling up my spine.

He looked up from where he was working. "You okay?"

"Yeah, not a big fan of storms, is all."

I should tell him, I started bargaining with myself. He would understand, I could make him understand. Maybe we'd both go to the station and I would tell Matty that I knew who was behind the break in and that they were still invading everything I owned. But I didn't. Instead I kept it to myself, set on ignoring it until it went away. If I didn't react he would get bored and leave eventually. Or at least that was what I told myself.

The crystals weren't the first things to go missing. It was only the first that I allowed myself to recognize for what it was.

The first was my mail. I would get the email from the post office saying it was arriving but then nothing ever showed up. It was always the more personal mail, nothing junk related. An invitation I was expecting from an old college friend for her baby shower or an anniversary card from work all disappeared somewhere between the post office and my house. Then some packages were delivered while I was at work and would be opened on the porch when I arrived home.

It was more annoying than anything so I allowed myself to believe that it wasn't a big deal.

I didn't want to think about it now, though. Instead I turned my focus onto Kaiser and his fair project. It was next weekend and I couldn't wait to watch him show it off.

"How much do you have left? It looks pretty much done to me." My feet swung back and forth where I perched myself up on his workbench. He was standing back from the hutch, rolling a screw driver around in his finger like someone would with a drum stick.

"I'm picking up the glass for the doors tomorrow afternoon and will fished those up tomorrow, then all that's left is putting all the handles and knobs on."

Even in the dim light of his garage that casted it in an orange glow, the piece was beautiful. The attention to detail was astounding, beveled edges with soft slopes, the intricate beaded strip that divided the credenza from the display case and the hand carved wooden appliqués that finished the top and bottom. Every single, little detail was done with so much care it was hard to believe one man was able to do all of it himself.

If you asked him, he would say that I helped but it was a bold face lie. One I continued to remind him of. As it turned out, I really was no help when working on a project. Which I told him, countless times over the years yet he always talked me into being a part of anything he tended to and this project was no different. In reality my helping was merely handing him whatever he needed for the next step but I knew I had never been happier than I was while working with him.

Kaiser stood back from the work table in the middle of his garage. "Does this look crooked to you?" He wasn't really asking me. I realized this after the third time he asked the question. He had been so used to working on his own throughout the years that he had taken to talking to himself out loud during a project. "Can you hand me that square over on the table?" he asked.

I flung my body off the workbench and stepped over to the table. My eyes swiped over the various items for what he asked for. Sure, I barely knew the difference between a Phillips and a flathead screwdriver, I could admit to that, but there wasn't a single thing on this table that looked like a square. I pushed sheets of sandpaper around and still nothing, swept my gaze across the floor and under the table but I was coming up empty.

"There's no square here, Kaiser," I called out over my shoulder. The wood he was working with dropped with a clatter, and a second later he approached my side, bringing a slightly annoyed disposition. His long arm reached around me and plucked the tool directly in front of me.

"This is a square," he stated. My brows pulled inward before I looked up at him.

Did we enter the twilight zone?

He was holding up a metal shape object that clearly only had three sides. "Uh, I'm not sure how long you spent in kindergarten, but that's a triangle."

"I repeated Kindergarten," he stated. He'd been doing that more and more, sharing tiny bits of himself without me prying at him first. It was my favorite part of getting to know him.

"Maybe you should go back?" I joked.

He snorted out a laugh, leaning his body into mine slightly. I liked making him laugh.

Thunder rolled over the house again, and I nearly jumped out of my skin. My fear of storms was so ingrained in me I almost forgot not everyone had the same knee jerk reaction to run home and hide once the storm began. One of my first memories was of me crawling under my sisters blankets for safety as the house shook under the clouds. I was six maybe, we had been home alone for most the day and into the night when we clearly shouldn't have been.

Kaiser didn't seem to notice the shake in my hands. We were still in the early stages, I didn't need him knowing every embarrassing fact about me. Not yet at least.

I ran my hand across his shoulders where he was bent down checking the that the door hung straight. "It's getting late, I'm going to head back home." A brief look of disappointment passed through his eyes.

Did he want me to stay? It was already past nine o'clock, any longer and I was liable to fall asleep where I sat, but maybe that's what he wanted.

He stood, and the look vanished, replaced with a gentle reassuring smile. "Want me to walk you home?" He kissed me gently on my cheek and I thought maybe it would be worth staying.

"No, I'm fine, but I'll see you tomorrow, right?"

Another kiss on the other side and my eyes fluttered shut. I could stay, right? One night. Our first night together, it would have to happen eventually.

Thunder cracked, lights flickered and I remembered why I wanted to go home. I needed the safety of my blankets to get through the night.

We met in the middle and he finally laid claim to my lips. It hadn't let up, that fluttering feeling I got in my stomach the first time he kissed me. It happened every time, and always felt never ending.

"I'll see you tomorrow," he said. A simple promise.

By the time I reached home, rain was pelting the ground in droves. It was unrelenting, it didn't matter that I sprinted into my house, I was drenched as I crossed the threshold. My clothes stuck to my body as I peeled them off my limbs and switched into warmer clothing for the night.

I was doing a lap around my house, checking windows and locks, when the power went out, plunging me into nearly total darkness. My head whipped around in the dark, waiting for my eyes to adjust as my pulse quickened. One thing I hated more than storms was darkness. It was an eerie feeling when there was nothing to remind you where you were. Nothing hummed, not a single power light to be seen, just endless darkness and total silence.

There was a chime from my bedroom where I left my phone. My hands skated across the wall to avoid knocking into anything as I made my way to the back room. I turned to the door and the light from my phone illuminated the rest of my way toward it.

> Are you okay?

> Just lost power

> It's the whole neighborhood

Panic sloshed through me. A brief stint in the dark I could handle, I was an adult after all. But all night, that was a tipping point for the pile of issues I was already dealing with.

My chest grew tighter as I attempted to pull air in through my nose and exhale out through my mouth. I was on my third deep breath when my front door creaked open and every alarm bell in my mind went off. My throat burned, I was on the edge of tears when the first rays of flashlight illuminated the room.

"Abby?" Kaiser's voice called out. A whoosh of air came out, relived that I wasn't about to be forced into dealing with an intruder and a power outage.

"I'm in here," I called back. My hand came up to block the light as he walked into my room. "I didn't know if you had any flashlights, so I brought over some things for you until the power comes back."

My heart melted. It was a puddle of warmth and desire that began seeping out into my limbs. Having him check on me opened flood gates that had been held close. A cry bubbled up my throat. In a flash he was in front of me with his arms wrapped around me. The light from the flashlight reflected off of the ground from his hand. Giving everything an odd ghost story vibe.

"I don't like the dark. Or storms," I mumbled into his chest.

His hand smoothed up and down my back until my breathing evened. My head tipped back and even though my eyes hadn't adjusted to the dark, I knew he wouldn't be looking at me like he couldn't believe a woman of my age had childish fears. Kaiser only thought of how to help me, about what he could do to make my life more comfortable, and it was all done with such ease you would think it had always been this way between us.

I pressed up onto my toes, running my palms up the length of his chest. He followed suit easily, dropping the flashlight to drag me closer, if that was possible, dipping his head and catching my lips with his. A gentle sigh made its way past my throat at first contact, only for the sound to deepen as his tongue traced my bottom lip. My hands found their way around his neck and into the soft curls of his hair.

There was a flurry of movement. His lips against mine, my jaw, down my neck. Hands that slipped through his shirt and over his shoulders, pulling the first layer of clothing from his body as his fingers dug into my skin. His kiss deepened, barely pulling away from me for his next breath of air.

In the dark it was easy to hide, but it was also easy to let everything go and act only on feeling.

My eyes had finally caught up with the darkness. Kaiser stood before me, chest heaving and a darkness that matched the room in his eyes. Until this point, we hadn't slept together, not for lack of wanting, but for whatever reason, neither one of us had been brave enough to cross that line. On some level, I was scared of what came next. It was where I always messed everything up and I didn't want to risk it. Falling for Kaiser had been easier and more natural than I ever expected and more terrifying because if this didn't work, I would never recover.

My fingers caught the hem of my shirt and tugged it off in one fluid motion. "Stay with me," I commanded as I took a step back and hit the edge of my bed.

Life was all about taking risks, and Kaiser was worth it.

THIRTY-FIVE

Kaiser

THE POWER FLICKERED BACK on at some point in the early hours of the morning. All at once a quiet hum started throughout the house as everything came back to left. The fan above Abby's bed began turning as I cracked my eyes open. There was something about going from utter silence to the quiet of a house on a normal day that messes with your senses and now that I was up I'd never be able to fall back asleep. Instead I took the time to admire the woman who had tucked herself into my side. Her hair had fallen across her face and would flutter with every breath. My fingers stroked the side of her face before brushing it out of the way.

There were dreams, then there were *dreams*. Having her in my arms was beyond anything I could have ever imagined. And now that I had her, I could never give her up. But the longer I laid next to her, soaking in her warmth, every thought of why I would never be good enough passed through my mind.

From the mundane, I was too old, to the shallow, she was too beautiful. Then there were the more realistic ones, she'd never want to be with me if she knew the things I'd done. The men I had to kill, the people I had to leave behind to save others, to the woman who left me all those years ago because she knew there was something in me that didn't deserve happiness. All of it was unforgivable and if I never managed to forgive myself how could I possibly ask for anyone else to see me as someone they could love.

Love.

It was such a simple word attached to a myriad of complicated feelings but I had them all.

A simple version of love where I wanted to wake up with her every morning, and fall asleep with her every night.

A possessive version where I wanted to sequester her away from the word to keep her for myself and only myself.

But it was the complex version of love that twisted itself around my vital organs and made her a part of me. If she hurt, I hurt. If she was happy, I was happy. Without trying, she's ingrained herself in me and I didn't want to go back but I needed to tell her everything.

She needed to know, to have all the facts.

I needed to know she was in this, that she wouldn't run because I wouldn't be able to survive her leaving. I would never be able to move on. Jagged lines from where my heart would be ripped from my chest would remain an open wound, festering until the end of time because the only antidote would be gone. And I would let it rot as a reminder of what was once there and what it once beat for.

Her.

Her eyelids fluttered open at the sound of the house turning back on around us, or maybe she could sense me staring, who knew. "Is it over?" she asked.

The rain stopped at some point during the night as I drifted off to sleep next to her. "Yeah, looks like the power is back on too." She rolled onto her back and looked up at me. Even in the darkness her deep blue eyes pulled me in like a magnet.

"Thank you for staying."

"All you ever have to do is ask."

A break in the clouds allowed the moon to shine through her widow, bathing her in soft light. Her eyes studied me for a moment, then asked. "Stay the rest of the night?"

And who was I to say no?

My hand began its search for her before I even opened my eyes in the morning. It swept across the bedding hoping to find her soft, warm body next to mine only to find the bed empty. My hands bunched the fabric and for a brief moment panic clutched at my chest that I had imagined the night before I rolled out and went in search for her.

Abigail Faulkner in the morning light was quite possibly the most beautiful sight a person could witness. She needed to be placed in the Lourve or the MET. Some museum where everyone could appreciate the splendor that was simply her.

My feet were light as I stepped behind her, snaking my arms around her waist to pull her flush with me. A quiet giggle fell from her lips as I pressed a kiss to her bare shoulder.

"Good morning," she whispered

She twisted in my arms to face me. Her fingers carded through the long pieces of hair on the back of my head and all I wanted to do was haul her back to bed. And then she smiled at me and I was gone. Further down a well full of Abby Faulkner and what it was like to be hers. My admission of secrets could wait. She yelped as I swept her up in my arms and carried her back to her room. If I was going to ruin this eventually, I was going to steal as much time with her as possible before I did.

She squealed as her back hit the bed and I slowly crawled up her body. Her eyes drooped into a sultry gaze that beckoned me further up her body and then her mouth was on mine.

I wondered if I would ever get used to this. The feeling of her soft, warm skin under my hands as they roamed over her body. The sound of her breath sticking in her throat when my lips would press against the sensitive spot below her ear. I hoped I didn't. I wanted each moment with her to feel like this, a fever inducing feeling that I wanted to stay drunk on for as long as possible.

She hummed in response. "What are your plans for today?" My lips dragged down her throat, before I kissed my way across her collar bone.

"I'm taking the cabinet over to the fair today." I pushed up and bracketed her in between my arms. Her tousled hair spilled across the pillow was like a dream. I was sure I had it before. "You're still coming with me tomorrow night, right?"

"Absolutely, I would never miss an opportunity to eat my weight in cotton candy," she said with a trace of laughter in her voice. "And to see you win, of course."

"I don't know about that but having you there will be enough."

I lowered my head down and captured her lips with mine. She arched into me as she looped her arms around my neck.

Win or lose the competition, this was enough.

THIRTY-SIX

Kaiser

"Jesus."

The word was supposed to stay in my head as Abby tore off another piece of soft blue cotton candy from her second, or was it her third, cone of the night. She didn't lie about fair food being her favorite, but she left out the fact that she only ate the cotton candy. I fell into some sort of transfixed stare as her lips closed around the digit before slowly dragging her finger out. Four would be way too many, but I was already looking for the nearest food cart if it meant being able to watch that motion all night.

A small piece of crystallized sugar clung to her bottom lip before her pink tongue darted out to capture the rouge sweet. This had to be real life, my fantasies never included this because I knew it would leave me feeling empty, knowing I did nothing to deserve her. I wanted to freeze time, bar it from letting another second pass because who knew what came next. At any moment she would see the darkness and she would run.

She continued to stare at me, with her sky colored eyes and before I could let my head run away with my what ifs I remembered that at this moment she was mine. I cupped both of her cheeks and swooped in, slowly pressing my lips to hers. A tiny surprised noise rose in her throat as I swiped my tongue along her bottom lip, collecting sugar and turning the kiss itself sweet.

She smiled. "What was that for?" she murmured against my lips.

There were hundreds of people around, breezing past us while I stood captivated by her. I couldn't quite put my finger on what it was, but there was something about being near her that made everything else fade away in a way that I had never experienced before.

The heavens could have been crashing down around us and I wouldn't have noticed. I had eyes only for her.

"Nothing," I said simply, "I just wanted to."

"Mmm," was all she said before kissing me once more.

Then I knew. It hit me so hard I was surprised I wasn't gasping for breath. This was what love felt like.

This was what it was like to be in love.

Simple moments where you realized all you wanted in life was to spend it with someone who made you feel comfortable in your own skin. And it was terrifying. I fell hard and fast, and barely even recognized the signs. What if she didn't feel the same? What if I ended up ruining everything? What if all I ended up with from our time together were scrapes and bruises?

This was too fast and too soon, wasn't it?

The questions floated around in my head as we wandered through the rest of the fair. Neon lights from the rides bounced off the ground while screaming laughter pierced through the air. She chucked the empty bag of cotton candy into the trash as we stepped through the tent flaps to the competition area. Yellow tinted lights illuminated the large area as people milled around the perimeter, stopping every so often to look over an entry.

Anyone could enter the competition and I always got a kick out of what was on display. We passed a small wooden derby car that had a boy in his Cub Scout uniform standing proudly by it. Abby stopped to admire a large, multicolored patchwork quilt that hung in the corner. The sign explained that a mother made the quilt from clothes from her daughter's first year of life. My favorite was a blacksmith's entry, a set of kitchen knives he forged himself from a damask casting with hundreds of layers, forming the swirled patterns in the steel.

The judges came out to let the crowd know they would announce the winners in 5 minutes. Abby latched on to my hand and pulled me toward my piece. With each step, the larger the sinking feeling in my gut got.

I didn't tell her about the changes I made, too afraid of what she might think or that she wouldn't see it the way I did. I waited while she looked over the piece we built together with an awe-inspiring look and I knew I made the right choice. I wouldn't have had a chance at winning without her input and help.

Any minute the judges would be back, and she still hadn't noticed. Her hand trailed along the row of drawers and the antique knobs she installed until she reached the last cabinet and glanced down at the entry sign. Her eyelids rabidly blinked before she leaned in closer for a better look. She stood sharply and turned to me. Of all the reactions that could have happened, crying wasn't on my list.

Abby's waterline filled with tears, making her already large doe eyes even bigger and they looked more like the lapis stone as they shimmered.

"My name's on your project?" It was a whispered question that I was sure she meant as a statement.

"Of course it is. I wouldn't have a project if it weren't for you." I reached out to stroke her cheek gently. "Now you'll get to cross one more thing off your list," she looked up with knitted brows. "You know, when we win the competition," I stated.

Suddenly, her arms were around me, her face buried in my neck. Sniffling filled my ears before she whispered she was just happy to spend the time with me.

"I know, Dimples," she didn't need to say anything. I could feel everything she wanted to say with her embrace.

She peeled herself off of me as the judges came back out. It was a panel of five people that included the Mayor of Fairvale, a husband and wife who helped put the fair together, and the rest were locals who volunteered. They stood up on a makeshift platform in the middle of the tent. Everyone's hands jumped to their ears as the microphone screeched as Mayor Torres turned it on.

"Welcome everyone to the 62nd Makers Competition." He smiled out at the clapping crowd.

Abby remained tucked under my arm and no matter who took first prize, having her next to me already meant I won.

"As always, I want to thank everyone for coming out and supporting our town's traditions. Every one of these entries is a testament to the hard work and dedication the people of Fairvale took to make life a little more beautiful." The crowd clapped politely. "Now, for the moment you've all been waiting for," he says as someone handed him an envelope. Abby squeezed in closer to me.

I didn't think I would be nervous, but I wanted to win. I wanted to give her this. I wanted to help her check every single thing off her list so she could make room to learn more and do new things.

"In third place, we have Mrs. Andrews and her book tapestry." Everyone's head turned to the bookshop owner who stood along the back wall. Thousands of threads were woven to create a beautiful picture that looked like pages and books spilling from a bookcase. The older woman looked ecstatic as she clapped her hands together in front of her chest. Her cheeks were already taking on a rosy hue from smiling.

"And in second place," Abby's hand slipped in to mine, "we have Dereck Leverett's beautiful set of kitchen knives." Mayor Torres announced.

Some people auctioned off their items after and I made a mental reminder to put a bid in for those if he did. They would look great in Abby's new kitchen.

The applause died down again. "And finally, in first place..." Mayor Torres unfolded the envelope with the winner's name. He smiled down at the page. "We have a second time winner, but his first with a partner." My heart dropped, and Abby squeezed my arm so tight I thought it might fall off. "Kaiser Price and Abby Faulkner!" he called out and the crowd all turned to us as Abby let out an ear deafening squeal and jumped up and down at my side. Eyes shining and fixed on me as I remained still and overwhelmed. Don't get me wrong, I wanted to win, but I didn't actually think we would. Relief washed through me.

The Mayor approached us to shake our hands, pulling me from my thoughts. She smiled from ear to ear, as she thanked him, simply glowing under the cheap lights. It was breathtaking, she was breathtaking. This was everything. Winning, having her with me as it happened.

A smile was plastered to her face as she turned back to me. "You won!" She squealed again, throwing her arms around me once more. I couldn't help myself. I swooped her up and spun her. She threw her head back, laughing, as the crowd hollered and cheered around us. I pressed my head into the crook of her neck, the urge not be as close to her as possible flooded me.

"We won," I replied, "and now you can mark it off your list when we get home."

She smiled. "No, now, we need a funnel cake." She stepped back from me still beaming. "I'll be right back." She disappeared in the crowd as I stood and stared back at our winning piece. It really was beautiful, and I was so proud of all the work I put into it. This was what I needed to kick my business back up a notch and would definitely be enough to attract the business I needed to keep both Kaity and Randy. I could feel it.

People milled around the tent, and I shook hands with more than I could count. Some congratulating me, a couple inquiring if it was for sale, those I spent a little more time with. If I didn't have to lug this thing all the way back to the shop an even bigger win.

"This is quite the piece of furniture." A man's voice called out from behind me as I handed over a business card to a woman who was asking about a pair of rocking chairs for her front porch.

When I turned to thank him, he was staring back at me with an amused looked. The hairs on the back of my neck stood at attention, putting me on edge almost immediately. "Thanks, man." I fished another card and extended it to him between two fingers. "If you are ever in need of custom work or want to look at what I keep in stock, just stop by the shop."

His ice-blue eyes flicked towards my hand as his tongue traced his upper teeth. It was quick but I caught it and for whatever reason it pissed me off. I was certain this guy was the most annoying person on the planet. This whole interaction had my hand twitching to form a fist to plant right in his face. "Sure, why not," he said while stuffing the card into the pocket of his pressed khakis. And who wears khakis to a town fair? He sticking out like a sore thumb in the midst of all the flannel, boots and kids covered in sticky candy running around.

"I'm Kaiser, by the way." I didn't offer my hand.

"How long have you been in Fairvale?" he asked without introducing himself.

He wasn't asking about my shop, but I wasn't going to answer him with any other information. "I opened up on Main Street almost seven years ago," I stated.

"You could make damn near anything you wanted, huh?"

"I can certainly do a lot." I mused. Where was Abby? This guy, whoever he was, was setting off all sorts of alarm bells in my head and making me antsy. It was like he was fishing for something, but I had no clue what he wanted. I didn't know this guy from the next, and if I saw him again, I was sure I wouldn't remember. So why was he hanging around acting like some pretentious, out-of-place asshole for no reason?

"I'm sure your girl loves that."

"Excuse me?" I straighten my shoulders and stood taller as I looked over at him. Who the hell was this guy?

His hands flew up. "Woah, no need to get all wound up, Paul Bunyan." I took a step toward him as a smile creeped across his face. His eyes flicked to something behind me and widened with recognition and something akin to greed. "I'll get out of your way. Keep up the good work, though. And keep that girl of yours close. You wouldn't want to lose her."

He vanished into the crowd before I could reply, leaving me with a sick, foreboding feeling from our brief encounter.

"Look at this, a funnel cake with strawberries, ice cream and whipped cream on top." Abby's bright voice dulled the feeling instantly, pushing it to the back of my mind as she came from behind me with a styrofoam plate balancing on one of her hands and a bite of her funnel cake loaded way too high on a fork in the other. She shoved the entire thing into her mouth and chewed with a smile.

There was a swell of pride that bloomed in my chest as I watched her eat with such satisfaction. Gone was the blank look in her eyes from when we sat at my kitchen table and she told me about a man who used food to control her. I couldn't imagine harboring the desire to control another person, wanting to put someone down to make myself feel bigger or stronger or whatever they were trying to get out of it. But what hit me hardest was that someone felt the need to extinguish the look on her face when she was happy and that it was somebody she trusted—a look so pure and innocent that I wanted to preserve it forever.

She took another bite. "God, I love the fair," she said around her mouth full of food.

I put the asshole stranger out of my mind and turned my focus back where it belonged, on her. Maybe that would be my bucket list. Finding all the ways to keep that look on her face.

THIRTY-SEVEN

Abby

Buildings blurred together in my peripherals as I sped down Main Street to meet Lennon for dinner. It had been too long since we sat across a booth and talked about nothing and everything all at once. I missed her. But I was late and the one thing my sister hated was tardiness.

Wind was blowing down from the far end of the street, pushing against me and making each step harder than the last. One end of Main Street to the other was about a mile and while I could have driven, but it seemed like a waste, but I was regretting every second of it. My shoes hit the pavement in a fast succession as I battled my way through people milling around and the families with dogs. I had completely forgotten it was Thursday and the nighttime farmers market was in full swing. Vendors clogged the last leg of the street before the restaurant, forcing me to weave in and out of the hoards of people on the sidewalk. Too many people if you asked me.

A box spilled off a table, sending vegetables tumbling across the pathway right in front of me. I jumped to the side to avoid stepping all over them but that only sent me bumping straight into a person in my attempt to move quickly.

"Oh, I'm..." The apology died on my tongue turning to ashes that were difficult to swallow. I stood frozen to the ground, wind whipping around my body, staring into my own eyes.

My mother was pretty, she always had been. Delicate features that reminded me of a renaissance painting with her wide dark blue eyes that were copied and pasted directly into Lennon and I. The longer she drank the more it warped the features that I once admired, until everything I loved vanished.

"Mom." It was a half question, half statement and barely more than a whisper. I wasn't sure she heard me over the crowd that continued on around us. Unaware that I was standing face to face with someone that I haven't spoken to in over a decade.

A decade.

I almost didn't think it was possible. The day I left was still so raw in my memory that it could have been yesterday. Looking back from where I was now, it was the best decision. I knew I made the right choice following Lennon, I would follow her anywhere in the world, but I often fantasized what would have happened if I had stayed. Would it have helped or made any difference at all?

"Abigail. Hi." Her voice was soft and full of surprise. I could see her fingers twitch but she didn't reach for me. "Look at you, you're so grown up."

My hands gripped at my jeans as I tried to process what was happening. "Yeah." There wasn't enough words in the English dictionary that could convey my racing thoughts.

"I know." Her eyes softened at the words, like regret filled her to the brim at the acknowledgment. Like she knew that one word was all I could manage, and knew that I stood in front of her, barely more than a stranger.

She was different somehow, and it's not that I haven't spoken to her in ten years or at least not only that. It was something about the way she carried herself. Her hands weren't shaking, she didn't hunch in on herself like it hurt too much to be seen fully. The air seemed lighter around her, and the delicate features I used to love were prominent and more beautiful than I could conjure up in a memory.

"I'm sorry, I have to go," I stammered out as I took a step toward the direction of the restaurant.

"Of course, of course. It was good to see to you, Blossom," she said with a voice that faded into the wind and eyes that broke over her last word. I meant to walk away but the mere mention of my girlhood name had me stuck.

The memory struck like a flash of lightening.

I was ten maybe, a storm had been beating against the house since the early morning. It was unrelenting, rain pounded on the windows and every time the thunder roared I would jump out of my skin. I remembered scurrying up to where my mother sat on the couch, tucking myself in-between her legs. I remembered the way she pulled her fingers through my hair to calm me down as she would whisper to me the rain was good. That rain would bring blossoms of new flowers, that rain brought out the beauty of the world around us.

She was sober.

The realization slammed into me, nearly taking my breath away.

She disappeared into the crowd and I walked like a ghost the rest of the way to the restaurant as I tried to wrap my mind around the fact that my mother was sober. Or at least I believed she was.

The doors into heaven on earth, or the local Mexican restaurant if you're a normal resident in Fairvale, breezed open with a gentle push. A quick scan of the dining room and I found Lennon in a corner booth with Theo waving me down. Each step was filled with lead as I walked toward them.

Should I tell her?

I shouldn't tell her.

Their relationship was the one that took the brunt of the beating. Like a rubber band that was stretched too far, until finally it snapped. The day Lennon left home was burned into my memory. I had graduated and it was as if that was what she was finally waiting for. Our mother did nothing to mark the occasion, which was fine I didn't expect much anyway, but Lennon flew into a rage over it and at the end she turned to me and told me that I didn't have to stay in this house any longer. That she had rented a place in town and my place was with her. We packed up and left the next day.

My body hit the booth with more force than I anticipated, both sets of eyes slid over to me. Lennon's suspicious, Theo's concerned.

"What happened to you?" she asked.

I needed to snap out of it. "Nothing." My voice full of false happiness. I plucked the menu to hide whatever emotions that clung to my features. I could do this, I needed to get through dinner, and then I could spiral in silence.

It was awful, keeping a secret from Lennon and it had always been the one thing I'd never been able to master. Only an hour later and I was about to burst open and word vomit everything that had happen all over them. Lennon and Theo were debating openly in front of me about where their next trip was going to be while I shoveled food to my mouth.

It wasn't working though, I swallowed the food and out came the words. "Have you seen Mom lately?" I asked abruptly in the middle of their bickering. As soon as the words escaped I wanted to scoop them back up and swallow them. Lennon's face paled instantly as she stared back at me.

Theo winced beside her. "Lennon, love, you're hurting me." His voice strained as he pried her hand open. I was sure there would be half moon nail marks in the palm of his hand. He smiled gently at her and never let go of the hand that attempted to maim him.

"Two years ago, when she rudely implied that Theo would leave me again given the chance. And thankfully never since," she said tersely.

I shouldn't tell her.

Don't tell her.

The word spewing continued. "I saw her on my way here." The words were out before I had time to stop them. My sister froze and looked as if she wanted to hear what happened next, wanted to run out the front door and pretend like she never heard me at the same time. "I think she's sober Lennon."

I watched as Lennon rocked side to side in her seat. She fiddled with a napkin before moving her fork from one side of her plate to the other. My sister got fidgety when she was uncomfortable.

"Do you think we should..."

"No," she abruptly cut me off. "I don't want anything to do with her."

"Lennon, maybe it's time to reach out."

She waved me off. "I said no." She stood from her seat, knocking the table and walked away without a second glance at either of us. The back of my eyes began to burn as Theo sat back into his seat.

"I'm sorry, Abby. I'll talk to her."

I nodded my head while looking into my lap. The waitress brushed by and dropped off the check. Theo reached for the holder, slipping his card into the slot and placed it at the edge of the table. "Did I ever tell you why I left?" Theo asked as we waited for it to be picked up.

This peaked my interest. I always knew there was some bigger reason than his parents moving, but it wasn't my place to ask.

I shook my head lightly. His lips rolled into each other before he continued. "I had a drinking problem."

My head pulled back in genuine shock. All the prying I did after he left and nothing even remotely would have led me to that conclusion. The love they shared was bigger than anything, and even at fourteen I knew nothing would pull him from Lennon. So when he left I knew it had to be something life changing, but I never figured out what. Not even after he showed back up in Lennon's life.

And now that I knew it still made no sense, he was eighteen when he left, how could he possibly have had a drinking problem?

"It's not something I am proud of but it is something that I work at every day to make sure it doesn't take over my life. At eighteen I somehow had enough strength to tell my parents and with their help I was able to get the tools and resources to not hit rock bottom and succumb to my addiction." He leaned in across the table. "If you want to reach out to your mom, don't let Lennon hold you back." He placed his hand on top of mine. "Like you said maybe it's time."

"Why now though? Why is she sober now? Why wasn't her rock bottom losing us?" I questioned him like he would have all the answers.

"Addiction rarely makes sense to those of us in it, let alone those on the outside. If she found what she needed to get sober now it's still a great accomplishment, no matter the age or time."

I found myself looking at this man across from me, someone I had known since I was barely a teenager. He had quickly become my confidant since getting back together with Lennon and I was truly grateful for the man he turned out to be.

We left the restaurant to see Lennon standing by the car door tapping away at her phone, barely even bothering to look up as Theo and I approached. She was everything to me and any other time I would have never thought about reaching out to our mom without her.

"I'm sorry." It was all I could manage.

Her head snapped up. "You don't need to be sorry, Abigail. I …" A haunted look passed over her eyes as her thought trailed off into the night. Theo slipped quietly into the car and left us to work through our shared demon in the chilly night. She took a breath, slipped her phone into her pocket and looked as if she wanted to be doing anything but have this conversation. "I guess I just don't understand," she finally said.

The words burned as I digested them.

"You don't understand why I would want to, I get it," I whispered, "but would you hate me if I did?"

"You have it all wrong." She pushed off from the car and wrapped me in her arms. I was taken back in time for a moment. Lennon didn't like affection, she wasn't a hugger and only reached out when her words failed her, like she could push everything she was feeling into the person. "I could never hate you."

"Promise?"

"Promise." She breathed the word out but the air was shaky on the way in. "But I don't think I can be a part of it." A long pause lingered in the air before she spoke again. "Not yet, at least."

We held each other a little longer, before she climbed in the car and left. I stood rooted in the parking lot with a new found sense of hope. It wasn't the outcome I was hoping for, there was a part of me that held on to some notion all she needed was to hear she was sober and that would be enough, but healing looked different for everyone. And for me, it was facing it head on.

Thirty-Eight

Abby

I slipped into my cubicle for the foreseeable future, scrolling through an endless amount of emails when there was a soft knock on the outside of my padded wall. It wasn't often I got a visit from one of the managing partners, so when Mr. Lane's kind smile greeted me, I had to school my shocked face from the sudden onset of nerves. A visit from the boss is nerve-wrecking, even if you knew you hadn't done anything wrong.

My chair slipped out from underneath me as I stood up quickly. "Good Morning, Mr. Lane." My voice was too high.

"Ms. Faulkner, good to see you. I have a candidate coming in for an interview for the last open associate position and I can't quite figure out the copy machine." He pointed to the large machine over his shoulder that stood outside my door. I pushed back from my desk and smiled at him.

"That old thing gives everyone problems." I held out my hand for the paper to which he happily handed over. "I'll have these copied in a quick minute," I said.

Carina would be happy to know this was being filled, less work that piled up on her desk, the less that would leak onto mine. Normally they asked her opinion on who they're interviewing, since she seemed to have knowledge on everyone in the industry and she would always let me know too, but maybe they didn't mention this one to her either. I mean, Decker was now back and they didn't tell her that either, surprising us all.

As I reached the machine I looked down at the cream paper of the resume. Blood ran cold through my veins, my smile faded and my stomach turned to lead. I turned to the older man, horror struck. "You're interviewing Liam Patterson?" My voice shook around the syllables of his name.

"Yes, bright young man from what I hear so far, do you know him?" The industry was small, and if you moved companies enough you ended up meeting and working with the same people. But Liam wasn't a family law attorney, so why was he being interviewed.

"Does Carina know he's interviewing?" I asked as I ignored his original question. He casted a wary look at me before answering.

"Of course," he said without an inkling of the weight behind the words.

Ringing began in my ears as I turned back towards the copier. I fixed the small jam in record time and handed him the copies in seconds, before turning and walking away. The clicking of my heels proceeding me as I rushed into Carina's office. Eyes wild and flushing heat coursing through my chest.

"You knew." My tone harsh and accusatory. Her eyes flashed before they hardened. Seven years of friendship and I have never, not once, ever talked to her like this. We bicker, mainly, argue on rare occasions when the topics got away from us but there was no way she knew he would be in this building and not tell me. I wanted her to tell me no right away, but the longer she sat in her chair the quicker my heart broke.

There was already a tightness in my throat as I slapped a copy of the resume on her desk. She looked at the paper, then up at me. "You were never supposed to know." I didn't wait to hear the rest of her betrayal as I turned and left the building.

I stumbled out the front doors of the office and into the windy afternoon. Cold air pricked like a thousand tiny needles as I doubled over and gasped for air. This couldn't be happening. Liam popping up in my life right as I finally placed him firmly in the back of my mind was like a cruel twist of fate. The universe saw me getting everything I wanted and took it as a sign to beat me back down.

My feet started down the street before my mind made up where we were going. Why did I have to wear heels? My toes pinched with each step and my skirt felt ten times tighter than when I slipped into it while getting dressed. Within minutes I barged into Kaiser's shop, a new record time from one end of Main Street to the other, with tears streaming down my face. His head snapped to the door. I could tell the moment he registered I wasn't some belligerent person off the street and that it was me. His whole demeanor changed as he swiftly excused himself from the customer he was talking to and with a few long strides he planted himself directly in front of me.

"What happened?" he demanded as his hands roamed over me.

"He won't let me go," I choked out. "He doesn't even practice the same type of law, he's only doing it to get to me. I've stopped taking his calls, I've blocked any way of him getting to me and yet he won't let me go."

He eased me back out the front, around the side of his shop and through the gate to a portioned he had enclosed.

"Randy, go help the customer inside." Kaiser barked the order. I barely even noticed there was another person around. I should have felt terrible, I did feel terrible, interrupting his work day without warning and crying nonetheless but he didn't seem to mind. Warm, large hands grasped my sides and lifted, setting me down on the workbench, bringing me eye level with him. But I couldn't bear to look at him. My lips trembled as I worked to keep from spinning out of control again.

Our relationship was too fresh for this. He was going to keep looking at me and wonder what he ever saw in the first place or I'd tell him about Liam and he would decide to wash his hands of me and my problems. Or at least that was what my anxiety riddled brain was telling me.

Kaiser gently brushed the hair from where it stuck to my face from the wind and tears, resting his hands under my jaw. My eyes drifted closed from his touch alone and as his thumbs rubbed slowly along my jaw line. I went from gasping and stuttering to slow and steady, and the voice that was telling me only minutes ago that our relationship couldn't handle something like this, quieted. When I finally opened my eyes he pressed his lips against mine. It was quick and reassuring and that small voice was gone altogether.

"I don't know what you're talking about but I want to help you. How do I help you?" he spoke as he leaned his forehead against mine.

His arms snaked around my lower back, pulling me closer into him. There was safety in his arms, a feeling like I had never known, but craved for as long as I could remember. I was allowed to feel and in turn it made me feel seen. He didn't expect me to not feel, or to immediately get over whatever was bothering me.

The lump in the back in my throat burned when he asked me if I wanted to talk about what happened at work. And I should tell him. I wanted to tell him, but there was a flicker of fear. I could tell Kaiser everything, all the small little details of what Liam did, what I allowed him to do but what if once I was done, he never look at me the same way again.

For the six months that I was with Liam, I lived with a constant stomach ache, this sick feeling that rooted around in my gut reminding me that something was off. It was as if my body was warning me long before my mind was able to comprehend what was actually happening.

That feeling was back at the thought of telling Kaiser.

I kept my eyes trained on the ground and my thumb between my teeth, gnawing at the flesh attempting to quash the shaky feeling that I was going to let him down.

"You're going to think... I don't know what you're going to think..." I shook my head and resumed picking at my fingers.

Kaiser made me feel strong, like I was in charge of my own life for the first time in so long. I wanted to be the woman he saw every time he looked at me but I didn't know where that person went in this moment.

His hand landed on my shoulder suddenly and I jumped at the intrusion. He gently pulled my hand from my mouth, I hadn't even realized I was still picking at the skin around the nail. "You don't have to tell me anything you don't want to you, you know that, right?" His gentle voice pulled tears to the corner of my eyes.

"Please don't hate me once I tell you," I said while looking at the ground. With the knuckle of his forefinger he softly lifted my chin to finally look at him. His face softened, his lips curved into a small smile as he dragged the back of his hand along my jaw, down the length of my neck before pulling me in closer.

"I could never hate you."

He only said that because he didn't know.

"I know who broke into my house. I've known since it happened." The words came out like a whisper.

He tensed grasp on my neck tensed, just for a second but he didn't let go.

"Have I ever told you why Liam and I broke up?" I asked, my voice muffled by the fabric of his shirt. I knew I hadn't but I didn't know where else to start. I pulled away from the comfort of his body. "Our entire relationship was built on the idea that I was the lucky one, that he was a prize and I was the one that should be grateful to simply be with him. That should have been enough for me to know to get out but I didn't see it until it was too late." I drew in the courage to continue. "It started slowly, he would make comments about how he liked my hair or my clothes a certain way and it was always different than how I normally would wear them. Or there was always an excuse to not spend time with my sister or Carina but conveniently enough time to see his friends or do whatever it was that he wanted. But I liked him and I wanted him too like me to so it didn't seem like an issue."

My chest tightened from memories. It all made me seem like a silly girl, like a person who didn't know how to stick up for themself. But when you're in that type of situation, it was all dense trees that obscured the sky and left me yearning for the forest. When you are hell bent on feeling something on the inside, it was easy to ignore what was happening around you and to you.

"Then it turned into things I wasn't allowed to do. Like finish a meal because he didn't want me to gain weight, or I couldn't go see Carina because he said she had it out for him and didn't want her influencing me. I was slowly being suffocated by him, until he was the only thing I saw and suddenly I was trapped. The first time I tried to leave ended in a screaming match but by the end he promised to change and I fell for it. It was a constant loop of fighting and making up that I was made to feel like a stranger in my own body. Until one day I snapped and left."

Kaiser had barely moved but the longer I went on, and the more that came out, the tightness began to lessen. I had been carrying around my shame like an invisible cloak. No one could see it but with every move I made I could feel it, tripping over it and tangling myself in the fabric until I was so intertwined I couldn't find a way out.

"I refused to listen to his lies, but the last thing he told me was that no one would ever want me but it was fine because I would never be rid of him. And he's right."

Strength was elusive, slipping through my fingers like running water. Instead I was composed of fragile twigs, snapping under the weight of even the faintest brush of someone else's words. Maybe I was too brittle for this world or too soft for anyone to handle. All I wanted was to be somebody's someone, but all it did was leave me a fool, scrambling at the first sign of specks of worthless gold.

"If you didn't want to see me anymore, I'd understand," I whispered the words. I needed to give him an out before it was too late.

He pushed off the bench he had been leaning against to give me space while I spoke. "I don't understand? Why would we stop seeing each other?" He sounded hurt at the thought.

"How can you say that after what I told you," I demanded to know. "Aren't you mad?"

"I'm furious, but not at you."

"Carina knew." He pulled back in time to watch hurt flood my features again. "She knew he applied and was coming to the office and didn't tell me. Didn't tell the partners that he was not to be interviewed, let alone set foot into the office."

He exhaled and rubbed his hand across his jaw and through a week's growth of a beard.

"What do you want to do about it?"

My shoulder lifted a fraction before dropping.

His hands trailed up my arms, over my shoulders, coming to a stop on either side of my face. "I have a couple of options. One, we could go to the police, try for a restraining order." He pulled me in and placed a kiss on one cheek. "Two I could go down there during his interview and put him in his place, preferably with my fists," He placed a kiss on the opposite cheek. "Or..." he continued to trail his lips across my jaw and down my neck, nuzzling into soft skin where it met my shoulder.

"Or?" I questioned. My erratic breathing reappeared but for an entirely different reason.

He smiled against my skin. "Or you could let me make you feel better." His hands were already gone from my face and trailing up my thighs and suddenly I was thankful for the skirt I was in. I did a quick sweep of the area, it wasn't out in the open exactly but not secluded either.

Feather light fingertips continued the exploration higher, and higher and higher. Until I was squirming from anticipation.

"But what if..." My neck craned to see if I could see the street from any angle. I couldn't so maybe that meant no one could see in.

"Do you think I would ever put you in a situation where someone could see what's mine, pretty girl?"

"What's yours?" I liked the way that sounded.

He hummed in agreement as his lips pressed against the base of my throat.

"I'm not a trophy, Kaiser."

"You're right, you're not a trophy. Trophies are placed on **shelves** to collect dust and are forgotten. You're a priceless painting, a rare jewel, treasure." Sinking to his knees on the hard concrete in front of me, he gripped the brim of his ball cap and twisted until it sat backwards on his head. "And what do you do with treasure?" He continued. "You covet it." A soft kiss to my knee. "treat it like it's the most important item in the world." One more to the opposite side. "You take care of it."

His hand slowly skated up my leg. "Will you let me take care of you, pretty girl?"

I couldn't form words, everything I knew zapped from my head.

"All you have to do is tell me to stop and I will but I want nothing more than to make you feel better." My skirt was pushed up and my knees slowly spread wide. My lip went numb from how hard my teeth dug into it before I gave him a small nod and his expression turned greedy, a hunger glinted in his eyes that I'd never seen.

I never went back to work.

THIRTY-NINE

Abby

WAS THIS WHAT IT felt like to be wanted? I had little to compare it to but this must have been what I was searching for all these years. Everything cascaded into place once I told Kaiser the truth. It had been only a month and yet it was as if we had always been this way. But that's what scared me the most because this was what I did. I got too attached in the beginning. Everything burned too hot before forming a supernova that would eventually explode. Until then I'd bask in the affection he was all too willing to give.

I never went back to work. It would have been too hard to face the betrayal, and a bit embarrassing to do with a fogged brain. I sent out a quick message to my boss that I was suddenly sick and went home. Kaiser finished a few tasks while I sat in his office before he loaded me in his truck and took me back to his house.

There wasn't a specific moment that I could pinpoint but at some point I found myself staying over at Kaiser's more and more.

It felt more like home than my own. He ushered me into the house gently, with a promise of my favorite dinner. That first meal he ever cooked that I quickly became attached to.

By the time dinner was ready, I hadn't said much. Carina's words were still ringing in my head when we sat down to eat when suddenly there was pounding at the door. Kaiser lept to his feet faster than I could register what was going on but relaxed at the next sound.

"Abby, I know you're in there! Open the door." Carina's voice was loud enough that it carried down the street.

He glanced at me for approval before opening the door. "Where's your girl? She wasn't at home so I assumed she went to you after leaving work." Carina didn't bother waiting for a reply as she brushed past him. She turned the corner and came straight for me. Carina was kind of scary on good days, but she looked unhinged. My head shouted danger but before I could react her arms were around me.

"Do you think that little of me?" The words were soft against my hair as she squeezed me tighter. When she let go, she kept her hands on my shoulders and gave me a small shake. "You left, but you *will* listen to what I have to say. I will not let you go around thinking I did something to hurt you when that was the furthest thing from the truth."

"You told me that you knew he applied, that he was going to be in the office and offered me no warning." I wanted to be mad but she wouldn't be here to try and lie her way out of a situation. It wasn't who she was.

"You were never supposed to know because I was never going to let him near you." She dragged me to the living room and pulled me to sit on the couch with her. Kaiser made himself scarce as I saw him walk out into the garage. "The partners usually run the resumes by me when they call people in for an interview. I told them that I did know Liam but they don't ask for any feedback until after they've completed the interview process. He was scheduled for Friday and I already knew you'd be out and then I was going to tell them that under no circumstances should he be hired." Her hands had a vice like grip on mine. "You have to believe that I would never keep something like that from you to hurt you."

There was a release of tension at her confession and maybe I should be angry with myself for doubting her but I was only relieved. At least momentarily.

"What if they don't care what you have to say? What if they hire him anyway and I'm forced to see him every day?"

"They won't. If they even entertain the idea then I'll let them know it's either him or me because I won't stand for working with him either."

Carina lived and breathed for her job, it was her whole life. She spent years cultivating her reputation in the industry and at our company so for her to offer to leave and to do it so effortlessly was touching.

"That's ridiculous." I shook my head.

"Why do you do that?"

I stopped to look at Carina. "Do what?' I snapped and luckily she was unfazed.

"You are always the one to step in any time Lennon and I need a kind word or someone to lean on. At a moments notice you're always the first to throw everything you have at all of our problems and you do it with a smile on your face. But the second someone shows you an ounce of the same kindness you give, you act like you are so underserving," she scooted closer toward me. Her light green eyes pierced straight through my cover.

"I-I don't know what you're talking about."

She tossed up her hands and she made an angry tsking sound, before she mumbled something in Italian. "You can keep telling yourself that, but I see you, Abigail. And if it comes down to it, I will choose you over working at ALA, over any job, over any man that comes crawling out of the gutter to try and get to you. You are worth choosing."

It was easy to fall into a routine and take for granted our friendships. And it's not until moments like these that we are reminded why we devote time to one another. She made being a friend look easy. Even when she was dealing with emotionally stubborn people, like myself.

Tears pricked behind my eyes at her words. "I'm sorry that I doubted you. I was caught off guard," I said.

"I know you are, and it's okay. I will always forgive you." She pulled me in for a rare hug. "Sei la mia anima gemelli."

As I gripped her tighter, it finally dawned on me. Maybe I was never hard to love, maybe the issues were never mine to try to fix. Here were two people who saw me hurt and scared and didn't hesitate to help me. They didn't let me spiral thinking I was the issue or that my problems were all fabricated. They came to me with solutions and answers and told me it was going to be okay.

I knew I loved Carina, but maybe she wasn't the only one deserving of those words. But until I could say them to him, there was something I needed to do.

FORTY

Abby

REGRET CARRIED A BITTER taste, it was acidic and vile. It lingered on the back of my tongue, so with every swallow I would be forced to remember memories I preferred to forget.

My car came to a stop in front of a house I left over fifteen years ago. In those years I never set foot back inside but the amount of time I spent driving past was a number I couldn't count to. A quick glimpse, that was what I told myself, a small fragment was all I needed to quench that dry and brittle feeling of desperation that was eating away at my insides. Most of the time I saw nothing but dark windows and an empty driveway. But on rare occasions I would see her, those became my favorite moments. The ones where she would be standing in the front window in the living room probably staring at the TV. Or when I'd catch her as she was unlocking the front door. Every time I would slow the car to a torturous crawl and in those moments I had to fight not to pull over and jump out, yelling for her to wait for me.

Yelling that I wanted to come home.

That I was sorry for ever leaving.

That I wanted my mother.

More than ever.

I cut the engine on the street across from her house. She was home and the taste of regret bubbled in my throat. What if she didn't want to see me? What if she didn't want me? All these years apart and she could be anybody, she was already certainly somebody I didn't know.

My hands shook as I opened the car door and my knees knocked together as I walked up the familiar driveway. My eyes caught on the patch of cement that didn't quite fit, and the two sets of small hand prints in them. It's funny the memories that wafted in when you least expected them. There was nothing special about that day but I remembered the way she smiled at us as Lennon and I giggled as the wet cement squished between our fingers. How she washed our hands with the front yard hose and her laugh as she sprayed us while we ran around in the yard after.

When I reached the front door, I was sure I would vomit all over the welcome mat. Instead, I brought my hand up and knocked on the weathered door.

"Coming." Her voice rang out from the back of the house.

Maybe I wasn't going to vomit but I was going to faint for sure.

The door pulled open and then she was there.

Her smile dropped the second she registered it was me on her porch.

"Abigail."

"Hi, Mom."

She looked over my shoulder, even she remembered you couldn't have one sister without the other. "It's just me." She moved to the side and gestured for me to come in.

The first steps inside my old home were tentative. Effectively I was a stranger in a place that I grew up in. There was no sense of home as I walked in, no feeling of belonging.

Her hands picked at her clothes as she fidgeted. "What...umm... What brings you here?" It wasn't a voice I was familiar with. It lacked the disdain I grew accustomed to growing up. In its place was a woman who was nervous and unsure.

I turned to face her, unsure of where to start. They said it was best if you ripped the band aid right off, right? "Are you sober?" Direct and to the point, giving her no option to skirt around the question.

"Yes." It came out quick and with an air of certainty.

"Why now?"

That question took longer for her to answer. Her head cocked to the side as a ghost of a smile tugged at her lips. "You and Lennon were always straight to the point, even as kids." She walked past me and left me to follow her to the kitchen. "I was making lunch, come sit down and I'll make you a plate."

I took my normal seat on the far side of the table. There are very few fond memories of dinners around this table. Mostly there were only simple meals I'd take to my room to eat in peace. My mother as a homemaker was an unusual sight. She flitted around the kitchen, pulling open a cabinet, dragging plates off the shelves like she was born to cater to those around her.

Within minutes there was a plate with a simple sandwich in front of me. My manners died in my throat, as nothing came out but she didn't seem to notice and sat across from me. I lifted the piece of bread out of habit. When you're as picky as I am, it was hard for me to let people make me food; I had a tendency to come across as ungrateful. To my surprise, it was perfect, it was even cut in half the triangle way.

Exactly how I would have made it for myself.

I looked up to see her studying me. It wasn't until I took my first bite that she touched her own food.

We ate in comfortable silence, for a few minutes. My eyes drifted to the front window and I lost myself in past memories while I took my final bites. It wasn't until the soft clearing of her throat caught me did I come back to the present.

I figured this would have been hard, but this was something else entirely. Inside, parts of me were screaming, some crying, others were angry and burning with rage. Then there was a small part of me, in the base of my heart, that felt content sitting in my mother's kitchen on a Sunday afternoon. I willed the tears to stay in my throat, I could deal with the burning ache. What I couldn't deal with was crying in front of her. I stopped doing that a long time ago.

"What do you want to know?" she asked.

Everything.

My heart pounded against my ribs. I tucked my hair behind my ear and thought about where to start.

"How long ago did you stop drinking?"

"Two years ago, after I saw Lennon and Theo, actually."

"Why now?" The words burned my throat as they came out again. Maybe this was a terrible idea. She didn't owe me an explanation, as much as I wanted one.

It wasn't mine to demand.

Her fingers traced the wood grain pattern of the table as I waited in bated breath. For her to tell me the reasons or ask me to leave. Either or, I would assume.

"Addiction is overwhelming. You think 'that could never be me'. A drink to celebrate, that's fine. A glass of wine or two after a rough day at work, normal. Then your father left," she sneered. Venom slipping into the last syllable.

My father was a hazy memory. A blur of a man who was never angry or happy but was barely there until he wasn't at all. "What happened?"

She turned her head to the side, looking out the window for a moment before answering. "I wish I had an answer for you but I don't. At least not one that will make you like him," she said with a small laugh. "He simply decided that a family wasn't for him and left. I had my suspicions that there was somebody else but it was clear that nothing I could say would make him stay so I didn't fight him."

There's a whooshing in my head. In my gut I knew she was telling the truth and that made it all the worse. Thinking you were simply not wanted versus hearing you weren't wasn't something you got used to.

She continued, unaware of the existential crisis flowing through me. "The harder life got, the more I found myself reaching for a bottle, any bottle. I felt like I needed something to help me over the feelings of sadness, regret, anger, bitterness. And then, suddenly I looked up and it had been years and I was lost, I couldn't function without it. I lived my life to keep a roof over our heads, food in our fridge and as many bottles of bourbon as I could afford to drink." She took a deep breath and a sip a her lemonade before continuing. "The past few years I have felt more empty than ever before. I wish I could explain it better, but I was nothing, felt nothing, nothing. Numb to everything around me. And then I saw Lennon. I said terrible things to her and as I walked away one thing she said to me stuck in my head. She said, 'You don't get to know what I do with my life anymore,' and she was right. I was a terrible person and an even worse mother. You two deserved so much better than I gave you. I got home that night and by instinct I pulled a bottle from the cabinet but I couldn't drink it. The next day I found a local alcoholics anonymous and went to my first meeting. There was a lot of falling back into habits and learning how to live with the choices I made but I have met some great people who have helped me be better."

Tears had welled up in her eyes and it called to the pounding ache in my chest. My hands shook in my lap as I looked across the table at my mother, she might as well have been a stranger and hearing the words made sense but didn't help ease any of the discomfort from the years of not having her a part of my life. She orchestrated this mess, there was no doubt of that in my mind and not having Lennon and I was her penance, but maybe it had been enough.

"My plan was always to reach out to you two, to see if there was any way I could repair the damage I caused but I haven't been able to find the courage." She said.

"Should I have not come then?" As a child I was always aware of other people's emotions and there was a sense of hesitation to the story that made it feel as if she never wanted to have this conversation.

"It's definitely a surprise, but there was a chance I would make excuses for a lifetime and never reach out so I will be eternally grateful that you showed up today." A hallow laugh followed her words. "I'm grateful you came."

We ate the rest of our lunch sharing small details about our lives. Nothing too deep that would put the fact we haven't seen each other since I was eighteen on a pedestal.

When I imagined this moment, I thought it would be this big event where she would usher me back into my childhood home with endless apologies and tell me none of this was ever my fault. We would talk and laugh and it would feel like no time had passed since I left home, there would be an easiness that would flow between us.

But there wasn't.

I thought the sharp edges of my heart would be filed down at the sight of her and I would finally feel at peace. I was grateful for this moment, not only seeing her after all these years but finally being able to connect with her now that she was sober, but I wanted out. This didn't feel like home, like I thought it would. Instead this house felt like a museum where each painting was a reminder of why sometimes looking to the past was never the way forward.

She walked me to the front door. We stood awkwardly on either side of the threshold. "I'd love to get dinner sometime or even lunch again. I want to put in the work to amend for my mistakes," She confessed and for the first time in my life I believed her.

I was about to turn away when the thought hit me. "Actually there is something I need," I stopped midway to the door. She looked back at me, eyebrows raised like she couldn't image what would come out of my mouth next. "What do you put in the chocolate cake?" I asked. I needed to know, it would be on my list until the end of time, no matter how many times I made it I could never get the missing ingredient right.

She held up a quick finger and disappeared toward the kitchen, returning moments later with a familiar piece of paper. The aged paper was a soft to the touch as she handed it over. I unfolded it and laughed. It wasn't hand written like I always assumed, it was a page ripped from a magazine, unfamiliar handwriting was scrawled in the margin.

"Thank you. Lennon's birthday is coming up, she is going to love having this again."

I left with a small smile and the burning feeling that we were on the right track to being something again. I'll never get back the years we lost but that shouldn't stop us from using the years we still had to cultivate something new between us and that's exactly what I was going to do.

FORTY-ONE

Abby

THE DOOR RATTLED IN its frame with each blow of my fist. "Kaiser," I called out before rapidly knocking a few more times. When it swung open I stumbled across the threshold and into his home.

"Are you the police? What the hell?" he growled.

"If you could forgive him, would you?" I asked as I barged into his house without a second thought.

Confusion swept across his face.

"Your dad, if he were still here and he asked for your forgiveness. If... If he sat you down and told you he had been wrong, that he was hurting and while it wasn't an excuse, it was the start of beginning to know the why behind the reason. Could you forgive him?"

"I don't know. What is going on?" he shouted after me as I walked deeper into his home in search of the safety I felt when I was near him.

"What happened?"

"I ran into my mom a few weeks ago and I can't explain it but I knew something was different. She called me Blossom, which sounds silly but it was something she only did on the days she was sober," My words came out in a winded rush. "I couldn't stop thinking about it so I went to her house. She's sober, Kaiser. And not for a few days, she's been sober for two years." By the end of my spiel, I was practically screeching. Not only in disbelief but confusion and anger almost.

He gently moved my hand from where I attempted to stifle my outburst. It wasn't until he swept his thumbs under my eyes that I realized I was crying.

"But I don't get it," I said to him with my face cupped between his hands.

"Get what?"

"I don't know." The lie was so transparent, I could see through to the other side. He only continued to hold me and wait for me to continue. "Listening to her explain how she fell down that path was supposed to fix me but it didn't." My hands hung limp at my side but there was no desire in me to slip away or feeling like he wasn't doing exactly what he wanted to. He was here because he wanted to be.

"It didn't fix me, all it did was remind me that I am no one's first choice." It was a whisper of a statement. "I have been second my whole life, in everything I've done. When will someone put me first, when will I stop being the person cast aside because something better came along? When will it be my turn?"

This was too much for him. He didn't want to hear any of this and yet I couldn't stop.

"I want someone to want me for me. Someone who chooses me and doesn't expect me to change. Who sees me and decides that I am still worth all the trouble it seems to be to love me." I lashed out without warning. "Everywhere I look I'm an option no one wants. When will it be my turn, Kaiser. When will someone put me first?"

I was conditioned to think the worst of myself, a lifetime of feeling like a burden to my mother, a six month crash course from Liam in you're not good enough and it stuck with me. I convinced myself that once Kaiser knew that nobody else has ever wanted me then he must not as well. His arms encircled my waist and I wanted to slink out of grip immediately, I didn't deserve it. He pulled me closer, bringing our chests flush.

"I can put you first," he whispered with his lips pressed into the top of my head. "I want to choose you. Every day, every night. If you let me, I will always put you first," he said firmly, without hesitation, like he had practiced the words over and over until he finally had the courage to say them out loud.

The words clung to the air, suffocating me. I was trembling, it came from inside my chest and cascaded out into my fingertips. Everything I had ever wanted was being laid in front of me, so why couldn't I find anything to say back to him.

FORTY-TWO

Kaiser

ABBY HAD BEEN OFF since she saw her mom, or maybe it was my reckless confession. Either way she's less bright and bubbly, and all around less her. The pull to cheer her up was like a constant ache in my chest.

I wasn't really good at this sort of stuff though, but I had to try and when I needed to remember why life was worth living I went to the lake. It was my spot but maybe it could be ours. There also happened to be a meteor shower that would take place if I timed it all right.

The truck rolled to a stop as we pulled into a parking space at the lake. Nothing about her perked up and I was slowly approaching a losing line. I reached behind the seat and grabbed the bag I packed for tonight.

"The sun won't go down for a few hours and I know it's not on your bucket list but I thought you might want to learn how to fish?" The words came out a bit awkward, and it was impossible to not to feel like I was trying too hard. She looked over from the seat next to me and surveyed me.

"What do you mean the sun will be down in a few hours? Won't we leave once we can't see?"

Surprising her might be one of my new favorite things. "That's the point." I threw her a wink, tossed my cap on and leaped out of the truck with the basket in hand. She shouted out after me as I made my way to the trail. "Come on," I waved my hand holding the fishing poles at her. "I'm taking you to a new spot." I slowed my steps a bit and allowed her to catch up with me.

She swiped the small table bag I had slung over my should and the pole that she used from my hand. Her lips curled into the first smile I had seen in days. We walked in silence up the trail toward the lake we would normally take but before we reached the water, I took a right and began following a small path. Honestly, it was more of a soft indent in the brush than a path, but it ran the perimeter of the lake.

After about ten minutes she finally spoke up. "Why aren't we fishing by the truck like last time?"

The grass started getting taller, brushing our knees and the trees thickened as we walked. Branches were still full of leaves that hadn't been taken by the beginning of fall yet. Everything was still clinging to the last bit of green from summer.

"Did I tell you my dad was the one to start bringing me up here, and taught me to fish?" I asked, already knowing the answer. She shook her head, the strands of her hair glittering like the water's surface in the sun. "I've told you he wasn't the greatest either. There were times where we would be up here and something would set him off, so to get away I would wander. I would walk and walk, for hours sometimes to get away. And one day I stumbled into a clearing, I forget how old I was but old enough to keep finding my way back anytime we would come up here."

"So, it's like your secret spot."

I wanted to argue that grown men didn't have secret spots but she was right. I never brought anyone this far. Even when Woods and I would come up here, we stayed close to the picnic area. This place was for me. Or at least it was.

"Yeah, I guess so." We were getting close. The break in the trees was up ahead and I was hoping the clearing was still full of flowers, but this late in the season was always a hit or miss.

"And do you bring all your girlfriends here?"

I moved a low branch up and out of the way to expose the way through. A tiny, barely audible gasp escaped her and for good reason. The early fall rain did the trick, flowers blanketed the area, a half moon shape clearing with the edge of the lake on the far side once you walked in. Oranges, reds and yellows of all types of flowers sprouted up along with tiny white flowers that dotted the grass.

She took a few steps in but reached back for my hand.

"No, Dimples, just you."

FORTY-THREE

Abby

I SAT A FEW feet from the lake, right where the grass met the rocky shore, close enough to get to our poles, if needed, but far enough from the waves that lapped slowly across the rocks. There was a only soft breeze that rustled through the trees as I picked at the flowers that surrounded me. Small daisy with white petals that would flake away with even the smallest touch, bright orange poppies that, despite what my sister told me growing up, are not illegal to pick. My fingers worked around the bunch until a small bouquet formed.

If I could make a home here, I think I would, but as far as I knew, no one lived on this lake. There's was only one building, I caught a glimpse of it a few times on the walk up but it wasn't a house. "Do you know what that building is?" I pointed to the structure barely visible across the lake. Kaiser looked up from his spot near the fishing poles and traced where my finger was leading to.

"That is a venue building. People have parties or weddings there sometimes."

Interesting place for a venue, out in the middle of nowhere. I dropped the flowers to the side and hugged my knees to my chest. "So why are we staying until after the sun goes down?" I said, popping a grape into my mouth. "I know fish don't go to sleep but what would be the point of fishing after dark." Kaiser had checked on our poles before walking around and began pulling items out of the bigger bag he brought up. I turned to watch him spread a blanket out on the soft grass a few paces behind where we set up near the shore.

"A little bold, don't you think?"

He only chuckled. "It's not for that. Although," he crouched down to smooth the fabric out and looked over at me, "I wouldn't say no," he said with a playful tone, and I rolled my eyes.

He sat at the edge of the blanket and looked out past me to the lake. The sun had been setting for the last half hour and the silence had a calming effect I craved. Everything was peaceful, and each time Kaiser brought me the more I realized I should've been spending more time outside. I joined him, lacing our fingers together as we sat and watched the sun sink beyond the mountains. The moon was already visible but only a small sliver of its size, and I wondered how many stars could be seen once it was completely dark.

My head tilted back toward the sky when I saw the first streak of light. "Oh," I exclaimed, pulling my hand from his and stood up abruptly. "Did you see that?" I pointed upward. "There."

"Come back down here, it should start soon," he said and tugged me back down before I looked at him, puzzled.

"What's starting?" I looked back to the sky.

He pulled me back on to the blanket, tucking me into his side. "If the internet is correct, there's a meteor shower starting soon, its peak is around ten but we don't have to stay that long. We should be able to see enough, even if we stay only another hour or so."

My head snapped to look at him. "A meteor shower?"

"It was on your list," he said casually and pulled me in tighter as two more streaks of light flashed in the sky. "Thank you," I whispered. He pressed a kiss to my head.

"If you keep helping me, I'm going to need to write a new list," I said and his quiet laugh echoed into the night.

The sky was beautiful once that the sun was fully beyond the horizon. Stars that shined like crystals in the ink colored sky as the shooting stars, or meteors, lit up every so often leaving bright dust in its trail. We laid on the blanket, surrounded by wildflowers and it was as if I had dreamt it all before.

"So you've really never brought anyone here before?"

"Never."

"Why not? It's beautiful." He shifted beside me. I could feel the uncomfortableness rolling off of him. I almost changed the subject entirely to get us out of it, but then he spoke.

"I struggle sometimes," he paused and took a deep breath. "A lot, even, with things I've done, decisions I've made, especially with my time overseas. When it's too much, I like to come here, to this spot." His voice was thick.

Men didn't cry. Isn't that what society tells us? Men are supposed to be stoic, unfazed. Our soldiers risk life and limb for us to live in a blissful state of existence, so we didn't have to be brave. But that wasn't who I saw when I looked at him. I saw a person who was scared. A person who agonized over the feeling that he let brothers and sisters down, a person who carried the weight of his decisions, whatever they may have been, on his back like a rucksack that could never be removed. Nobody has told him that everything he was feeling was valid. He'd been thanked for his service but who has told him he didn't have to carry this burden alone. Who's told him that the weight slung on his shoulders could be shared?

I propped myself up on one elbow and reach out for him with the other hand. The scruff of his beard pricked at my skin.

If no one has told him up until now, then maybe it could be me.

"It's okay to feel, Kaiser."

"It's easier when you're around."

"I can be around for you."

"Always?" he asked in a whispered breath, almost as if he was scared of the word. The silence of the woods around us only amplifying the desperation in his voice.

The feeling has been present for a while now, hell maybe even since that first day at his house. Flutters from the butterflies have been soft over the last couple of months. I conditioned myself to ignore their signals but the longer we spent together and the closer we got the harder they were to ignore. I told myself that I was making it up, that he was a nice guy and it was easy to get sucked into the feeling and a create visions of fairytales in my mind about what we were to each other. But as I looked down at him, I realized it was never a facade, or forced, or only in my head. He wanted me in his life, probably as much as I wanted him in mine.

It was terrifyingly beautiful.

I nodded my head. "Always."

FORTY-FOUR

Abby

Carina was meeting with the partners and it had me anxiously swiveling in my chair but after her feedback, they decided to go with another candidate. It had been almost a week until we heard anything, ultimately she didn't have to threaten to leave. She told them who he was, not everything he did to me but that he wasn't the type of person that belonged with their company. And they believed her.

Maybe this was it, he'd finally move on and leave me be. It should be easy, but he clung to everything I was. Tainting everything without so much as a touch.

As I shut down the various programs, I wondered if maybe that was the reason I couldn't tell Kaiser that I loved him. Easy enough to blame on Liam, one more thing he had ruined. One more thing he had taken from me without a fight. But that had to stop. I needed to stop giving him so much power over me. He was irrelevant in my life, so why should he have all the power.

I was halfway down the street to my normal parking spot when I remembered I was late and decided to park closer in the garage below the building. My hand fished around the bottom of my purse in search of my keys when a hand grasped my upper arm and pulled.

Panic bloomed, but before I could scream a hand came down on my mouth, muffling any noise and my back hit a wall. The sharp brick dug into the fabric of my shirt, piercing through the threads and into my skin. I couldn't process what was happening, this didn't make any sense.

Fairvale was a safe town. Maybe not in a keep your front doors unlocked type of way, because that was foolish no matter where you were, but nobody expected to be dragged off the street.

It was the faint scent of citrus and flowers that I latched onto as it turned my stomach. I'd know that smell anywhere. I spent hours picking it out only to have him sneer at the bottle because it wasn't the brand he normally bought. When my eyes adjusted he was barely an inch away from my face. Blonde tendrils had escaped his normal slicked back style and hung in limp strands in front of his eyes. There was no kindness or warmth, they lacked any emotion at all, really.

His hand pressed harder over my mouth and I struggled to pull in air. My hands clawed at his arms for reprieve, but it was useless. "You've ruined my life," he growled before he pushed off and I gasped for air.

Time felt sluggish as my hands pressed against the rough bricks and pain began to throb in my shoulder and on my chin. Short, shaky breaths escaped my lips as I worked up the courage to meet his gaze again.

Slowly my head turned to face him, his eyes were wild as he paced. "Look what you made me do!" he shouted, spit flying from his mouth. His hand gripped his blonde hair at the roots as he began to process what he'd just done.

Vulgar words were flung around as he paced in front of me while I remained glued to the wall. Too scared to move, too afraid to draw any further attention to myself. In his fury he ripped apart the fabric that contained the monster who laid beneath. He was now frantically attempting to figure out how to stitch the pieces back together. But it was no use, I could see all of him now. He was unrecognizable and it was because I saw him for what he truly was.

Get off the wall, I told myself. It was my moment to take back a part of my life. I just needed to get off of this wall.

And I did, even though my knees were trembling and I wanted to curl into a ball and cry.

"Liam, I've done nothing to you. This, all of this is because you have something broken inside of you that makes you want to take it out on people who you think are weaker than you."

He stumbled back at my words, and a whiff of stale whiskey on his breath made it all make sense and a lot more dangerous.

Instead of yelling, he just looked at me. His head cocked to the side like I was someone new. Suddenly I wondered what he saw when he looked at me. Did he see what reflected back at me in the mirror? Did he see the cracks life had etched into me as a way to rip me apart and keep me in pieces? Were the pieces of me somehow easier to manipulate?

But I wasn't in pieces any longer and maybe that's what he was seeing.

"I know it was you who broke into my house and destroyed it. You who's been messing with my mail and stealing things out of my car. And its stops now or the next time I will go to the police."

I was finally in a place where I felt whole and put together. There was something new inside of me, like I could do anything with my life, because it was finally my own again. And he wanted to take that from me.

All he ever did was take.

Liam's eyes darkened as he stepped forward and I wanted nothing more than to sink into the wall. "I get it." His voice was sickly sweet. "You think you can just replace me and move on." He leaned in, engulfing me in the cloud of rage he was holding on to. His lips hovered around my ear as I remained frozen. The words washed over me, spiking that little part in my brain that controlled my flight or fight. Everything inside of me was screaming to run but he was slowly pushing me further into the wall and I was trapped.

"I promised you that you will never be rid of me, and I always keep my promises."

He backed away and slid out the side door of the garage. In seconds he was gone and the silence he left behind was deafening. It was a promise he would die trying to keep.

FORTY-FIVE

Kaiser

CORNELIA WAS A FEW towns over and the only place in a hundred mile radius that carried the part for the busted timing belt for my truck. And if I didn't have to be all the way out here, I wouldn't have been, because my mind was stuck on Abby. Anytime I was even a moment away from her, I thought of her. What was she doing? Did she have a good day at work? Did she miss me?

It was a little pathetic and maybe a bit concerning, but I'd rather be this version of me than one who said I wasn't enough.

My hip propped up against the counter while the clerk looked in the back for the part I had called in about when my phone rang. It was the simple things I loved most, like her name scrolling across my phone.

"Hey, Dimples."

There was clanking in the background through the receiver. "Hey, love, do you have anything I can use to hang up my frames?"

"Yeah, check around my workbench you should be able to find something."

"Thanks, I'll see you when you get home." The phone clicked and the line went dead in time for the clerk to reappear. He rang my item up without a word and left me with thoughts that wandered. Abby hadn't brought up the fact that I all but told her that I loved her and she said nothing. I shouldn't read into it but it was starting to pull at memories from a place I didn't want them to escape from.

I turned the part over in my hand as I walked out the door. The shop was located in center I had never been to before and had no real interest in so when my name was shouted out I was more than surprised. At first no one registered as I scanned the area until my eyes fell on a familiar bright, blonde curls that made my stomach coil around itself.

"I thought that was you," the woman said with a bright smile. I felt like I fell down a time warp tunnel and came stumbling out twenty years in the past.

"Ivy." The two syllables were all I could mange.

Ivy had barely crossed my mind in over a decade and it had been longer since I'd laid eyes on her. Not since before my first deployment and the years seemed to warp my memory of her, turning it dark and hazy, until only the feelings of abandonment and resentment remained. None of the light and love I once held for her remained with me.

She looked normal, almost as if time never touched her, sure she looked older, more wrinkles around her eyes that makeup was failing to hide but all in all she looked the same. How was that possible when I felt like I was leagues away from who I was the last time we saw each other? We were starry eyed and blindly in love, planning to get married the second I came back home. Then six months in, she stopped taking my calls and the ones I was able to get her on were short and cold.

Then came the letter.

One page was all she wrote, it was filled with more cliches than I knew existed but none of that softened the blow or stopped the warmth of the dessert from evaporating. I confided in her my inner thoughts because I loved her, and I thought she loved me but in the end she decided that I wasn't worth the time.

I spent the remaining months of my deployment feeling like I would have been better off dead in the desert and I became reckless. Any mission that came up I put myself in a position to be sent out on it. The feeling of wanting to die consumed every waking moment and clouded my vision and there was a moment where I almost let it.

"Kaiser Price, as I live and breathe." The slight drawl in her voice pulled me out of my thoughts in time to see her give me a once over. Her gaze lingered on my left hand for a second too long. Twenty years had erased everything I had seen in her but I guess time did to all of us.

Her hair fell in waves around her round face as she looked up at me with her blue eyes that were too pale. I was accustomed a shade a bit darker and staring at this woman in front of me only made me antsy to get back home to see Abby.

"Good to see you, Ivy." It wasn't but I had nothing left in me for her. I stepped around her to make a quick getaway. There was an itchy feeling in my chest from being close to her after all these years and I had nothing to say to her anyway.

"Wait!" her voice called out after me.

I cursed my mother's installation of good manners; I could keep walking and pretend I didn't hear her if I wanted to but my body wouldn't keep moving. "What's up?" My hand curled around the rubber causing it to dig into my hand.

Her mouth opened then closed, like she didn't know what she stopped me for. "Do you think we could go out for a drink sometime?"

"I don't think so, Ivy."

"Are you sure? I'd love to catch up, it's been so long since we last saw each other."

"It's been so long because you sent me a fucking Dear John letter." I snapped.

She recoiled at my words but they were coming out too fast and once I started I couldn't stop. "Who does that?" The belt cracked as my hand tightened around it. I stepped closer. "How long did you wait after I told you, Ivy, before you decided to cast me aside? A week, a month? Or did you check out before I even told you what happen and used that to your advantage? At what point did you decide I was worthless and the best way to get rid of me was to write me a fucking letter?" My voice carried across the parking lot, people two lanes over were stopping to stare.

She began frantically brushing away stray tears that were streaking down her cheeks. "I'm sorry... I never meant to hurt you."

"It doesn't matter that you didn't mean to, you did and you did it in the most despicable way imaginable. I haven't been able to let anyone close to me because of that letter. Twenty years, Ivy, and your words have echoed in my head every single day. And now, I have finally found a woman who is everything I have dreamed about and I am terrified she is going to wake up one day and see whatever it was that you did and leave. Every day I live in fear that it will be my last with her and there will be nothing I can do to stop it." The thought had only been in my head, speaking it aloud only made it more real.

I was petrified Abby would leave.

Ivy was openly crying and I had never felt better, maybe that made me a bad person but I didn't care. Everything had been bottled up inside of me and now that it was out it was like a weight was lifted. The words were harsh but it wasn't my intention to make her cry. My grip loosened on the timing belt in my hand and I carded my other hand through my hair.

"Listen, I shouldn't have yelled, and I'm sorry, but what I said was true. So, no, I don't want to catch up with you."

Ivy pulled in a shaky breath and hung her head. "I understand." Without another word, she turned and walked away without ever meeting my eyes again. She was the last person I ever wanted to see, and the uneasiness I had been feeling about Abby was back and a thousand times worse. I yanked the door open of my car and slammed it shut behind me.

What if I was too much for her or my feelings were too big, or too sudden? I was telling the truth when I said Ivy's words had lived rent free in my head for twenty years. It's kept me at arm's length from everyone, because with distance they wouldn't be able to see the damage that would make them run.

Maybe Abby was better off without me. I did little throughout the years to change, so that selfish, overbearing man Ivy felt compelled to leave was still here.

Abby didn't deserve that. I didn't deserve her.

Forty-Six

Abby

You would think for a man who spends every waking moment in his workshop, he would try to keep it at least a little clean. I found everything except for nails to hang up the frames. My knees cracked as I bent down to check the shelf below but there was nothing but a cardboard box.

The box slid out easy, like it barely held anything. As I lifted the flaps there was a whooshing sound that took over in my ears and for a second I thought about giving up my search altogether. At first glance it only looked like a bunch of junk, items you'd find in a kid's bedroom. A faded baseball cap, a ribbon that seemed to have a half faded word that I was sure said participation, a few composition notebooks a folded up piece of paper and a small dust covered velvet box.

I needed to slide the box back into its place, but my hand reached in and picked up the box. I needed to put it back and tell Kaiser

I couldn't find what I needed and just have him hang up my frames for me, but I opened the tiny box to see a small single stone diamond ring. I should have put it back and never think of it again but I instead I pulled out and unfolded the piece of paper that was next to it.

Words were jumping off the pages with things I shouldn't know.

Out of all the seven deadly sins greed was the one I could never get far from, and snooping was my vice. Ink faded from the typed up letter a long time ago and the crease was worn to the point of no return, as if it had been opened and closed more times than the paper could withstand. My eyes skimmed the first paragraph and I knew immediately I shouldn't be reading it.

"What are you doing?" I nearly jumped out of my skin at the sound of Kaiser's booming voice. Never have I heard him yell. For a man of his size, one look at him and you would think he spent his time barking orders to anyone in his path, which couldn't be further from the truth. The only time I'd ever heard him even raise his voice it was usually directed at a piece of wood and never a person.

I scrambled to shove the letter back in the box but he was looming over me. He snatched it from my hand with such force it tore where the crease had worn out the paper.

"I'm sorry, I was looking for the nails and I came across the box. I didn't mean to read it." I shot up to face him.

A fire blazed in his eyes. "Have you never heard of personal space. Do you just go around snooping in everyone's things without a care," he snapped.

"I-I…" I was stumbling over my words, unable to grasp what was happening. He stuffed the paper in his pocket and the journals that had spilled out back into the box with little care. "I was looking for the nails like I asked. It was a mistake."

He barked out a laugh. "Yeah, sure, a mistake, just like the last time was a mistake when you rifled through a box without asking. You just take whatever you want, read whatever you want." He bent down and swiped the ring box from the ground and held it in his clenched fist as he began pacing, a dark cloud of anger formed around him.

It seemed as if I was no longer here in front of him. I was a ghost and he lost himself in his growing anger. He ran his fingers through his hair roughly, no longer looking at me as he paced. Back and forth, back and forth, muttering under his breath. The box remained clenched in his fist. "Kaiser," I called out softly only to be ignored. I took a step forward in his path only for him to change directions. He paced like I was never even here, as he retreated further and further into his head.

It was evident I was being shut out and I didn't know what to do. I'd spiraled out a few times in our short time actually and Kaiser never shied away from me and I wasn't about to do that to him. But being iced out wasn't the same and he wasn't going to make it easy.

As he brushed past me for the fourth time I reached out and latched onto his arm. "Kaiser," I said more firmly. He slipped out of my grasp, but not before I reach for his face. The skin of his cheek burned under my fingers but nothing like the ache in my chest that was growing the longer he refused to acknowledge me. "Look at me."

"Why?" he snapped. Anger was no longer driving his words, it was something else entirely. Something full of pain. I recoiled at his words, dropping my hand and stepping back. "I'm sure you had a good laugh at my expense after seeing that didn't you." His voice edging into a tone full of worry.

"I didn't read... I would never—"

"Don't act like you don't know." He finally looked at me. Pain and anger clouding his vision, stormy blue and unrecognizable. "This was a mistake, this was all a mistake," he breathed out as he hung his head.

My heart clenched at his words as an aching pain pierced through my chest. I should've known better, this was how it always ended. I got pulled down into the bliss of a new relationship and my blinders went up. I saw nothing but the good, but I thought this was different. I thought he was different but as he continued to look at the floor the realization continued to set it.

The softer parts of me screamed for me to stay, that I only needed to wait out whatever this was and we would be fine. It wouldn't be the first time I'd begged someone to let me in their head or for them to tell me this was all some big misunderstanding.

An impasse staring me in the face, a chasm so large I feared I might be swallowed whole by it if I didn't act fast.

I could stay, put him first and hope this never happened again or I could walk away.

My heartbeats count the time that passed as I waited for him to say something, anything.

Only silence.

"Maybe I should go." My voice faltered on the words as I stepped back from him, internally begging for him to tell me to stay. But it never came.

The decision was easy. For once, I was going to put myself first.

FORTY-SEVEN

Abby

Peach margaritas and carnitas tacos should be a national treasure. Put them in a museum, take them on a tour of the nation, they're that good. The perfect elixir that could cure all, even broken hearts. If only it felt like they were working.

The words to describe the state I was in simply did not exist. One moment I was stuck in a well of melancholy the next moment I was floating closer into irritability territory. Neither was a place I wanted to stay in.

"So, tell me again what happened?" Carina asked as she rattled the ice at the bottom of her empty glass. Softened leather from my seat pulled at my skin as I slumped lower in the booth until my chin was in my chest. I swooped a chip off my plate and shoved it into my mouth. Anything to not talk about the disaster that was a few hours ago. I didn't want to talk about it, I didn't want to think about, I didn't want to acknowledge it. But their intent stares from the other side of the table told me I had no choice.

That's what I get I guess. When the roles are reversed I was just as pushy for information.

Heavy stares bore into me but I couldn't bring myself to look at them, instead I pushed the food around my plate, any appetite I had vanished. "I happened across some information that I wasn't supposed to, I swear I didn't go looking for it," I added quickly. "And he sort of freaked out." A short and sweet version was all I could muster up.

Carina watched me from across the booth as my sister leaned in to bump shoulders with me. Without thought I rested my head onto her, seeking any type of comfort she would spare.

"Well, what was it?" Carina questioned.

"I don't even know," I half shouted, causing the neighboring table to glance at us. "It was a letter, I stopped reading when I realized it was personal." I resumed pushing around my food and counting down the minutes until I could get out of here and into the comfort of my own bed. Tears flooded my waterline and I didn't want to be anywhere in public when they decided to spill over. "But there was also a ring," I muttered.

"A ring!" They exclaimed at the same time.

"Was he married before?" Lennon asked as Carina said, "Was it for you?"

"No, and no," I answered, shaking my head at the absurdity of it being for me.

A quick vision of Kaiser on one knee and me in a wedding gown flashed behind my eyes. As if someone pulled images from my wildest dreams and then whispered that I was foolish for even thinking them, causing my heart to ache. "I don't know what it was from."

Silence passed between us, Lennon was quiet, too quiet. My hands pricked, waiting for her to dole out some life changing big sister advice but so far nothing. She only sat beside me, chewing on her inner cheek, most likely thinking I was a fool.

Carina wasn't taking no for an answer and spoke up again. "You didn't read the letter though? I thought you could read fast, you're always flying through deposition reports when I give them to you to go through." We exchanged a look that forced a slow smile to creep across her face. "You did read it, didn't you?"

I groaned. "I didn't mean to and I stopped when I figured out what it was."

"And..."

She stared pointedly until I relented. "It was some sort of breakup letter."

"Oh, Abby," Lennon half chastised while Carina flashed a wicked smile. She lived for anything messy and this was two year old with their first ice cream cone messy. I was sure she was dying to ask exactly what I read.

"I just don't understand what the big deal was or why he got so mad. Everyone gets broken up with at some point, right and yeah it's shitty but why yell at me. What did I do?"

I wanted to be pissed off. If I was angry I wouldn't be on the verge of crying and wouldn't that be better? But I couldn't, for whatever reason I couldn't bring myself to be mad at him. So what did that make me? Naive? Gullible? Or was there some part of me trying to tell myself that this really was all a misunderstanding.

We all deserved grace in our lives. I could give him that, the benefit of the doubt, I'd give anything to make it so. Maybe he had a bad day, maybe the break up wasn't as far back as I thought and the hurt was still fresh. There could be a million reasons why he let me walk out of his house without a word.

Kaiser was the Winchester House of emotions. You open one door, thinking you'll find the way to what was going on in his head only to be met with a wall. Other doors lead you exactly to what he needs in order to open up. Every door was different and any door could push me further away from him. But I didn't want that.

Being empathic was not for the weak of heart, and if you're not careful it allowed for anyone to walk all over you, but I didn't think that was what this was with Kaiser. It could be the fact that I already knew I was head over heels in love with him but my gut was telling me whatever was going through his head didn't really have anything to do with me. I might have been a trigger or at least the box I stumbled on was, I simply became an easy target.

"Maybe you should just talk to him," Lennon finally chimed in.

Of course she would have an answer and it would be the most simple path. She was nothing if not level headed and straight to the point. It's what she did best.

Talk to him. I took a deep breath focusing on my plate as Carina and Lennon finished eating. I would go and talk to him, what would be the worst that could happen?

A waitress stopped by the table dropping off another round of drinks. Tomorrow I would talk to him, but tonight I was going to let my favorite elixir work its magic.

FORTY-EIGHT

Abby

TWO MARGARITAS WERE MY limit for a reason. Luckily I was only one drink past that, so I was fumbling around in that sweet spot where everything seemed funnier than it really was and it only took me three tries to get my key in the lock. If there's one thing I hated, it was the silence that drowned my home when I was the only one in it. If I had it my way, I would have a home full of life and noise. Someone that I could come home to and tell about my day, eat dinner with and fight about what show to watch, someone to slip into bed with and have them hold me through the night.

I shouldn't run to Kaiser, but I wanted to.

A soft glow of light from the small lamp on my kitchen counter guided my steps as I slipped off my purse and tossed it on the dining room table. Keeping crystals all over my house might not make sense to Kaiser or really anyone else but to me it did. And it wasn't random, I knew where they all were and why. When I moved back in I spent a weekend placing new ones in their spots. Nothing was out of order. I made sure of it.

So why was there a Moldavite stone sitting in the middle of my dining room table.

As much as I had read about crystals and had them strewn about my life there was still so much I didn't know. One of the first things I looked up when I was really starting to get into them was if there were bad crystals, because the last thing I needed was to bring more negative energy into my life. The answer varied from blog to blog but for the most part the answer was no, however the one stone that kept popping up was Moldavite.

It's a beautiful forest green stone from a meteorite crash in Southern Germany about fifteen million years ago and was said to bring an energy shift to the wearer. The further I delved into the research the more stories I found of people whose lives were turned upside down after they worked with the stone or wore it or had it simply in their possession. It was an easy decision for me to never want to come across it. I stuck with more surface level crystals. So I knew for a fact that this was not mine and I had no idea what it was doing on my table, let alone in my house.

The hairs on the back of neck pricked as I stood in a standoff with a rock.

It was quiet.

Too quiet.

It was incredible, what the body picked up on before you could actually see what was happening. It started in the air, it thickened as the seconds ticked by and settled onto my shoulders, weighing me down. My breaths began to come out in small pants, the opposite of what I needed. Not only was it harder to hear my surroundings but I might just hyperventilate myself and pass out before I figure out what was going on.

Terror laced itself through the seconds as I stood and watched that fucking rock but I couldn't move. My body wouldn't listen to my brain, I couldn't run like before, I was paralyzed to the ground. Time stretched as I strained my ears for anything out of place. It wasn't until I counted my thirtieth breath that a small creak sounded from down the hall. Soft footsteps followed and my skin broke out in a clammy sweat. Before I could even think I pulled out my phone and sent a single text. My thumb hit the number nine but before I could get to the one, before I could even blink, Liam slinked out of the dark hallway.

Why couldn't I scream?

Why couldn't I finishing dialing for help?

Why was he here?

"You fixed the house up nice." His voice deep and menacing. He leaned until his shoulder hit the wall next to him, crossing his arms and peering at me with wild, glassy eyes. "Did he help you?" He didn't even bother looking at me as he asked, he picked at his nails nonchalantly. Like I had asked him to come over and he would rather be doing anything but this.

My pulse thrummed, banging against every vein in my body. I shouldn't have ventured this far into my home, I should have ran. Why didn't I run?

My eyes flashed to the phone in my hands. "Ah, ah, ah," he teased. Two quick steps and he was in front of me, pulling the phone out of my grasp and then slipping it into his pocket. "I just need a few moments of your undivided attention."

All I hoped for was that my text went through, that they didn't call or text for more information, that one word would be enough.

Fear invaded the very essence of me. It constricted my throat and twisted around my gut and it's the only thing I could think of. Words vanished.

"You're special, Abby. I think you know that, God, I know I spent every second trying to make you understand but you could never get it through your head." He took a small step closer.

"Why are you here?" I choked on the question. Unable to get anything further out.

His laugh filled the entire house. "Why am I here?" he parroted. "You never knew how to ask the right questions."

The tears were forming. I couldn't let him see me cry, he always hated it when I cried.

"Why are you doing this?"

A few more steps and he backed me into a corner of my kitchen. The cold wall pressed up against my skin as I began to shake. "I'm not doing anything, it's you. First you abandon me, and I thought you would be smart enough to come crawling back to me but no. Not even a few weeks later I see you and him traipsing out of a store like I never mattered!" He screamed the last word, the whiskey on his breath enveloping me in a nauseating cloud.

My brain did backflips trying to figure out what he was even talking about. Kaiser and I only got together recently, I left Liam months ago. There was nobody in between him and Kaiser. "Have you been watching me?"

"Watching you, checking up on you, rearranging your house for you..." He said the words like a foreign language, rolling them about his mouth until he could digest him. "Yeah, I guess so. Here's the thing Abigail you are no one special, we both know this. But you were mine and then you decided you weren't." He took a step closer, eyes flicking to the window that led to the front yard. "And that wasn't your decision to make," he snarled.

Slowly it began to hit me, none of this was about me or us or our time together. There was never any real love in our relationship, instead it was a fabricated bond where he always had the upper hand and I was his to do whatever he wanted. Narcissists didn't feel the way an average person did, any emotions outside of their own barely even mattered. It was all about their appearance and what they wanted others around them to see. For a while I fit into his vision, but the moment I began to fight back was the moment his true colors began to shine through and leaving was never an option because it was never a part of his plan. "I don't belong to you, Liam."

One more step and he was all I could see, hovering over me until I had no choice but to cower beneath him. Eyes wild, still glancing to the window every few seconds. "You were so easy to control, so willing to be my puppet. You are mine and if I can't have you no one can." He snarled so low that I could feel the words sink into the depths of my bones.

His eyes flicked to the window once more, widening a fraction before turning back to me. A slow smile took over his face. "Right on time," he whispered and like lightning, his hand lashed out and locked onto my upper arm. I recoiled at the sudden intrusion, sending my head slamming into the wall behind me.

Liam was a lot of things but I was never truly scared of him. There were moments where the monster he kept hidden would peek out from behind the mask but he always reined it in before anything got out of hand.

But as he pressed closer, his restraint vanished, and I was horrified.

FORTY-NINE

Kaiser

Help

FIFTY

Kaiser

A SINGLE TEXT, FOUR simple letters, that was all it took for my heart to drop into my stomach. A second passed, that was it, one single second as I stared at my phone before I flew from my office chair, sending it rolling across the room and raced into the hallway toward the back door.

Kaity's voice shouted after me but I barely heard anything over the roar of blood rushing in my ears. My hands slammed against the emergency exit as I raced toward my truck. Gravel crunched and slipped under my boots as I reached the driver side door, flung it open and jumped in, all in one fluid motion. My truck roared to life, tires squealed under the weight of my foot on the gas pedal, sending loose pebbles flying. My only hope was that the old engine could keep up with the speed I was about to push it to.

Fairvale was small, and most of the time it could feel like everything was closing in on me but I think this was the first time I was ever grateful for that fact. Five minutes, that was all it took and my truck came speeding down her street. My eyes scanned every detail around me as I flew down the road, but nothing looked out of place. My truck tires hit the sidewalk and came to a screeching halt outside of her house.

Anything could be happening inside. All she texted was help. Help could mean anything. She broke something, she couldn't reach the top shelf, she fell, anything. The only thing I did know was that one simple word instilled a sense of fear in me that I never knew existed.

I thought I lost her after finding her in the garage with that God forsaken note. I did what I did best and shut down, pushed back at any opportunity to explain myself and instead made her feel like the best option was to leave entirely. I should have thrown it away years ago, decades really, the moment I first got it even. I should have tossed the ring the day I got the letter. I tried over the years, but something always made me hold back and now it finally came back to haunt me.

As soon as she left, every fiber of my being fought to go after her. My heart, the rational side of my brain, even my hand twitched to feel her, every single part of me except for one. That small voice that lived inside of my head, the one that told me I would never be good enough for her. A small voice that only grew louder over the years until all it did was yell that I did terrible things and because of that I didn't deserve anything good in this world.

The voice was sometimes so loud that I actually believed I'd be better off alone, so when she walked away, I let her. Even though it killed me to do it.

But right now all I knew was she called for me because she needed help, and I couldn't beg for forgiveness if something happened to her.

I wasn't a religious man, the closest I ever came to knowing God was the moment Abby walked into my life, flipping everything I knew on its head. She was the sole reason I believed, because if someone like her, as pure and full of light, could see past the stone wall I constructed and make me want to live, it couldn't be anything other than divine intervention.

So, please, God, universe, any supreme being that would listen to me—do people pray to crystals? Let me be overreacting.

Long, quick strides carried me up her walkway and I bolted toward her house as images of what might be happening inside flashed through my mind, fueling my urgency to get to her. My shoulder hit the door as I gripped the knob and knocked it open, sending it bouncing off the wall behind it. The sound of wood splintering echoed out as my head whipped around as I frantically looked for her.

But I didn't have to go far.

Crimson flooded my vision when I turned the corner and saw Abby backed into a corner as a man towered over her. My brain couldn't seem to process what was happening in front of me.

Who was he? Why was he here? Why did he look so familiar?

All normal questions someone would probably ask, but I didn't have time for any of that.

Relief washed over her features as our eyes connected. It was slight, her shoulders relaxed a fraction, her big blue eyes drifted closed in a slow blink as she took a deep breath.

It felt as if someone had reached into my chest, gripped my heart and squeezed. She was relieved that I came, almost as if she thought I wouldn't show up, and I hated that I ever made her feel like that. I hated that I wasn't here with her in the first place. But most of all I was filled with a white hot rage over the fact that this man, whoever the fuck he was, thought he had any right to come in to her home and get anywhere near her let alone put his hands on her.

He hadn't noticed me and that was all I needed.

A switch flipped in me, turning on a portion I long thought I had cut off. The side of me that made me ruthless overseas.

Four quick steps and I had the back of his shirt grasped in my hand. I pulled. Hard.

The stranger yelped at the intrusion and I used his surprise as an advantage. I kept his shirt in my hand, threads tearing as I drug him toward the door. His feet kicking wildly to stay upright. "Get the fuck off me," he yelled as we reached the threshold, as if he wasn't the intruder.

Another hard shove as he regained his footing, and he flew across the porch. Stumbling he hit the steps and fell backwards. His head landed against the concrete with a satisfying smack.

I should check on Abby, that's what a decent person would do.

But as that little voice had told me for the past twenty years, I was not a decent person

I would beg for forgiveness later.

His blonde hair flopped in front of his eyes as he scrambled backward, like a crab desperate to burrow into the sand as I stalked toward him. But I swore that for a second he smiled.

There's something vaguely familiar about him, but I didn't care, I continued forward. "Wait, wait, wait," he gasped out, pushing his hand up at me. Like that would do anything to slow me down.

My fingers curled around the collar of his shirt, dragging his torso up from the ground. My hand cocked back and slammed into his face. Pain sliced through my hand as skin tore from the bones.

"You don't want to do this." The words were a plea but nothing about his voice sounded like a man who didn't want to be hit again. There was a slight curve to his lip.

In the distance, sirens blared, and for a second, I thought the universe was merciful. Sending an ambulance for him before I had even begun. Blood dripped out of his nose and into his mouth. My fist raised again, and his smile only widened.

The sirens became louder.

"The bitch isn't—" I didn't let him finish.

Another satisfying crunch. And again. And again. And again.

My skin stung as it ripped open further. Sirens blared even louder and suddenly the night was washed in red and blue.

Abby was screaming, but her voice sounded a million miles away. I couldn't stop.

Maybe the universe was looking out for him. Good for him, he was going to need it.

More shouting joined Abby. Deeper voices. Two. Male. My vision was still red, growing darker by the second.

My hands became slick. The next hit slipped across his cheekbone. A pungent, coppery smell filled my senses.

I had lost all sense of what was happening and how this started. There was no time to dwell on any of it as I was ripped off of him only to have my face slammed into the concrete of the walkway. I groaned on impact.

My gaze flicked upwards as siren lights bounced off the silver shield badge pinned to the uniform of a cop. Pain wreaked havoc on my shoulder as my arms were yanked behind my back and cool metal was slapped around my wrists.

"He didn't do anything wrong." Abby frantically tried to bargain with the officer. "He was helping."

"I'm sorry, Ma'am, but your boyfriend can't just go around beating people up," A stern, no nonsense voice told her.

The concrete of her walkway scraped across my jaw as I maneuvered my head to find where she was still calling for my release.

"Liam is the one who broke into my home," she pleaded.

Fucking Liam. Of course.

I scanned the yard until my eyes locked on him. One of the other officers must have helped him up. His hand swiped under his nose, not like it made any difference. There was not an inch of skin that wasn't covered in blood.

As I stared at him, it dawned on me why he was so familiar. The fair. He was the guy with all the weird questions about Abby. I thought he was some random person with bad manners, but he'd been stalking her. And I never even saw it.

"Well what about him?" Her hand waved toward Liam. "Why isn't he in handcuffs?" Abby demanded.

He wouldn't get away with this. He couldn't, not this time. But handcuffed, face down with the smell of dirt filling my senses, it was hard to figure out how to get them to listen to her.

The officers stared back at her.

I may be cuffed and smelling pavement but she had never been more beautiful than she was at that moment. Her hair burned red as the lights bounced off it, standing tall, and demanding her questions be answered. And I had never been more in love.

"I'm sure he hasn't told you that he was only here because he broke into my house and waited for me to get home. If it wasn't for my boyfriend coming home he would have hurt me. He could have killed me." I think that was the first time she had ever called me that and I would do whatever it took to make sure it wasn't the last time.

The officer looked between Abby and I, then back over to Liam.

We all studied him from afar as his face contorted into what I was sure he hoped people perceived as innocent.

The officer looked down at me. "Is that true?"

I was beginning to think I was never going to get off of this ground.

"Do you think I just go around beating people up for fun. Tell me, what would you do if you came home to the love of your life cowering under a tyrant twice her size. He was in the house when I got there, his hands were on her. If you saw the look in her eyes, you wouldn't be asking me any questions either." My eyes never left her as I spoke.

That seemed to satisfy the officer, just enough for him to call over the other cop. "Hey, Sandavol, cuff him too and bring him to the station, we have questions."

I breathed my first sigh of relief at his words. I could handle a night in jail, as long as he was coming with me.

Fifty-One

Abby

Kaiser was not a man of many words, but there were times where he'd speak and it'd take my breath away. The first was when he told me that he would put me first if given the chance and the second was now as he proclaimed me the love of his life. It seemed different from simply telling someone 'I love you'. It was more profound in a way and he said it without hesitation. Like it's always been the truth and he was only reminding those around him.

If only I could stay in this moment, soak it in so I'd never forget. But that was impossible.

Instead, a chill settled in my bones. Red and blue whirled in the beacons of the police cruisers, swirling around and around like a macabre Law and Order episode.

I wish I was able to tell myself that I didn't know how we got here, but I couldn't. I had always known that there was a sinister part to Liam. I caught glimpses of it but I was so determined to see the good in him that I walked around with my own mask. One that kept me from seeing anything I didn't want to.

As they cuffed Liam, I took my first full breath of air and finally the mask that kept me in the dark was removed.

I might never forgive myself for the mess I made but this was a start.

He sputtered over his words, pulling his arms away from the officer who was walking him toward a cruiser. I almost even laughed as he fought back against the officers, screaming that they couldn't do this to him. That he was a lawyer, he knew his rights. The child-like tantrum he was in the midst of boiled over as he began screaming, and it was all directed at me. But I didn't cower, or shrink into myself. There were no tears and my heart didn't feel like it was breaking.

Instead a calmness flooded my systems, as if a dam broke. All at once the mask he had been wearing, for who knew how long, slid off and shattered. I wasn't alone anymore, everyone saw him for who he was. It was no longer a shameful secret I carried around like a heavy weight tied to my neck. It was no longer my burden.

He was a monster and everyone finally knew it.

Kaiser was hauled up off the ground. "Where are you taking him?" I panicked as they walked him toward the other cruiser.

"He still can't beat people bloody," the officer said remorsefully. "We'll take him down to the station to sort it all out."

My chest seized as I tried to reach for Kaiser. He looked back at me, head held high and only smiled. My favorite type of smile, where only the corner of his lips ticked upward, as if he had a secret that brought him joy.

"Don't worry, Dimples. I'll be home soon."

"Matty, we've known each other since we were, what, six? When our entire third grade class laughed at you while you cried during a book report, who stood up for you?" He rolled his eyes, actually rolled them so only the whites were seen for a fraction of a second and it was as if we were back in grade school.

Okay maybe that was the wrong example to use when I needed him to be on my side but it was true.

"Can't you bend the rules just this once?" I rapped my phone against the linoleum counter and asked for about the tenth time this morning. I even added in a *please* for good measure. We all knew you catch more flies with honey. I would even bat my eyelashes if I thought it would help.

After Kaiser was arrested, I followed the cruiser to the local station, but no amount of my badgering the front desk attendant got me information about what happened once a person was arrested. I sat in the waiting area until they told me it was too late and I would need to come back in the morning. I was just happy I only had to come back to this station and not all the way downtown to booking.

That seemed like a good sign to me.

Matty looked bored and was probably trying to figure out if I was breaking any laws just so he could put me behind bars to shut me up. "Abby, we may know each other but we're not friends." He half questioned.

Touché, but it was worth attempting to call in a favor I never had.

I squared my shoulders, channelling my best Carina. My eyes narrowed at him until he shifted uncomfortably before getting up from his desk. "Okay, let me see what I can do."

A smile broke across my face. "Thank you," I shouted at his back.

The wooden bench creaked under my weight as I sat down to wait for his answer. My knees shook violently as my pent up energy looked for a way out. The past twelve hours had been my version of Hell.

Kaiser stepped out of the back room fifteen minutes later. His steps quickened once he spotted me and before I could rise he was taking my hands in his and sat down next to me. My fingers traced the faint purple circles under his eyes. His brown flannel was crumpled and was missing a few buttons from the fight. Other than that he didn't have a scratch on him.

"I didn't know who else to ask," I said quietly. I adverted my gaze, unable to look at him any longer and suddenly felt ashamed over what happened.

"I am so fucking sorry I didn't get there sooner."

"I thought ..." my voice trembled, "I thought that maybe you were still mad. I thought I'd never get to tell you that I was sorry."

"If you call, I will always come for you. I didn't text you back or call, I just drove." He took my face in his hands and forced me to look at him. "Even if you don't call, I will always come for you. I will always be here for you," he promised again and I believed him. He placed a featherlight kiss against my trembling lips as a tear streaked down my face. "Ready to go home?"

FIFTY-TWO

Kaiser

WE WALKED INTO HER house hand in hand, the air thick with silence, neither one of us knowing where to start. My eyes burned from the lack of sleep. I had never been to jail before, there was nothing to compare it to but it was exactly how I imagined it would be. Not the worse thing in the world, since I knew I'd be out by morning but it was not somewhere I wanted to be again.

I pulled the chair out from her kitchen table and slid into the one next to her once she sat. All I wanted was to take her in my arms and soothe the tremble in her hands or reassure her over and over that none of this was her fault. But before I could my eyes snagged on another one of her rocks that sat on the table. It wasn't like any of the others I'd seen in her home. My arm reached out, I was inches away from picking it up when she yelled out.

"Don't touch that," she said frantically. The confusion must have been easy to read on my face. "It's Moldavite."

"I don't know what that is."

Her frown fractured into a small smile. "I know." Her chair scraped across the floor as she stood to quickly grab a bag and then carefully scooped the rock into it. "Crystals aren't inherently bad, most people would say there was no such thing but this guy is known to cause chaos."

My brows pinched together. "It's a rock though."

"So you've been telling me. Maybe it does nothing at all, maybe it's all in my head." Her laugh deepened.

"Or maybe they are things in this world that are beyond comprehension." I corrected her.

"Exactly."

I was limited when it came to knowing anything about love, I'd admit that, but the main trait had to be accepting of your partner's quirks. I'd never understand her fascination with them but I will always support it. But in order to do that I had some groveling to do.

"It was sitting on my table when I got home from dinner with Lennon and Carina. That's when I knew something was wrong." She tossed the bag up on the table and sat back in her seat. Her fingers plucked at each other as she avoided my gaze. "Liam hated the crystals, didn't like them in my home, didn't like my necklace, thought it was all made up and stupid. He always talked about finding the worst crystal to leave around me to ruin everything since I liked them so much."

"You were the first person that I thought of. I didn't know if you wanted to hear from me but I tried anyway because you are all I think about," she confessed.

I reached for her hands, stilling their movement. "What happened yesterday had nothing to do with you and everything to do with who I am and what I've done. What I had to do." I waited until she lifted her head, pools of ocean stared back at me and I knew I needed to tell her. If I didn't, I would die under the weight and I would lose her forever.

And that wasn't an option. I only wished it didn't make me feel like the world was being ripped out from under me.

"My first deployment, I was stationed in Afghanistan. I was…not excited, that's not the right word, but I felt a large sense of purpose when I got those orders. The one thing I wasn't looking forward to was leaving my fiancé, Ivy." I admitted.

"I thought you said you were never married?" she questioned.

"I wasn't," I scrambled to get out. "We were young, I loved her and I thought that's what you did, especially if you were facing your own mortality of being shipped off to a war zone." I pulled from her grasp, afraid that whatever was wrong in me would leech into her. But as she squeezed tighter it gave me strength to move on. "Woods and I were on a mission, it was supposed to be a quick in and out so only five of us were sent in. The house had been on surveillance for months, it was a known clandestine cell system, recruiting kids as young as ten." My voice cracked. I kept this story locked inside a dark part of me for twenty years. Breaking it out was harder than I thought it was going to be.

"When we dropped in, I remember thinking that I couldn't wait to get back home. I missed the trees. Everything there felt too open, and something wasn't sitting right in my stomach as we circled the building. But I gave the order anyway and when Rhodes kick the door in, clear off its hinges, they opened fired on us." I couldn't bring myself to look at her. "We had no choice but to return. I tried to get my squad out, I called for everyone to fall back and I don't know if they didn't hear me or if I was already too late, but Woods and I were the only two to come out with our lives."

I looked up at the ceiling before squeezing my eyes shut. Visions flashed in the dark. "I haven't been able sleep without seeing them, without knowing what this war has done to so many innocent people, what I have done and what my orders have cost."

There was a wall I built around the memory of that night. Each time I thought of it, a cracked formed making it weaker and weaker with each passing year and the second the last syllable left it burst wide open flooding me with every emotion I worked so hard to keep at bay. A gut wrenching sob tore through clenched teeth.

My brothers on that team left behind wives and children but I was still here and I hated that fact.

I didn't feel Abby arms until they were around me. Her face pushed into the crook of my neck, her fingers splayed across my back as panic and pain swept through me. Only Abby and the chair were keeping me upright.

"We didn't know anyone was going to be there, you have to believe me," I begged. "We didn't know and I would have never gave the call. Please believe me."

She held me tighter. "I know. I know."

Years of shame and guilt filled nearly every part of my body until they poured out from me in the only release I've never truly allowed myself. Tears cascaded down my face like an overfull dam that had been opened. Only for panic to swim between the remaining space because none of this could matter. My story, my apology, none of it might matter. I could still never be enough for her, she could never forgive me for letting her walk away.

We stayed there for moments, maybe hours as I cried and felt everything I had been bottling up for half my life.

Once it stopped, I reached into my back pocket and handed her the crumpled and torn letter that was once the cork to my feelings.

"Are you sure? You are allowed your privacy, Kaiser, you don't have to share everything for me to want to be there for you," she said.

"And that's why I'm sure."

Kaiser,

I'm hoping this letter will not come as a surprise, but I feel as if we had been both drifting apart and I have decided that I don't want to find my way back. There are things about you and what you have done that don't sit right with your soul or mine and I cannot be the one to help you. If I were a better person or a bigger person I could be that for you, I could love you through this but I can't and I don't know why.

Ivy

Her eyes roamed across the paper over and over, reading it more than once. "I don't understand," she finally said.

"After the mission went sideways, I was a wreck. It took a few days for me to even speak, Woods was on the verge of sending me to the medic to be shipped back home until I could get Ivy on a call. I thought it would help. I missed her more than anything and I thought if I could talk to her it would give me…" I said as I shook my head and ground the heel of my hands into my eyes. "I don't know what I was looking for in her, comfort maybe or just someone to talk to who I thought would love me no matter what but I was wrong. That was the last time I talked to her and not even a month later I got the letter."

"Oh, Kaiser," she whispered. I didn't want pity, I didn't want any of this. I didn't want to be a person who was seen as weak and vulnerable. She stood in front of me with these sad wide eyes and I couldn't help but think that I lost her.

"I saw her yesterday when I was out getting the part from my truck and you had called about where to find the nails. It had been twenty years, then suddenly there she was asking me to get a drink like nothing ever happened. Like it never mattered that she broke me. Like I never went to her in a time of need only for her to destroy every fragment of confidence had in myself that I was worthy of love."

Abby pulled back and looked at me, it was like a mirror. We were both wet eyed, and a crumbled exterior like she barely slept a wink since the day before. Then she really looked at me, her face softened and it took me a moment to realize but there wasn't pity in her eyes like I figured there would be. It was something else entirely.

"I need you to know how important you are to me, but it's more than that. When I'm around you, it's like... it's like I breathe in color. Everything is vibrant, the sky bluer, air cleaner. You make everything better. You make me better." The words tumbled out of my heart. Whatever happened after these next words might kill me but I had to say them. She deserved to know.

"You have to know by now that I love you," I said and it wasn't nauseating like I thought it would be. The thought of putting all my cards out on the table without even a hint at what she might be hiding in hers. Instead there was a calming effect that washed over me. I only knew that I couldn't wait any longer. If she decided that I wasn't someone she could love, or be with it would be okay. But I had to tell her how I felt, once and for all. "I can't go back to how it was being only your neighbor but I understand if you couldn't forgive me. The way I treated you was uncalled for and unnecessary but if you let me, I promise that it will never happen again and I will never let you leave without talking about the issue ever again."

She folded the letter carefully before handing it back, and it felt like she was slipping through my fingers like sand. She would be gone, but parts of her would stick to me, impossible to get rid of entirely.

The action was hard to decipher, was she handing it back so she could leave? Did she not understand or simply not care? For a moment I panicked. If she wanted to leave I wouldn't stop her but it wouldn't change anything. I loved her, I would love her for an eternity and still ask for more time. She could rip my heart from my chest and I would ask her what kind of box could I build for her to keep it in.

I was hers to keep, in every way, even if she wasn't mine.

Her ocean eyes glittered behind tears as they pinged between mine. "What about on days where feel I like I'm too much or days where I feel like I'm not enough?"

I wanted to scoff at the absurdity of her statement. "I could love you forever and it wouldn't be nearly enough time. I would spend a thousand lifetimes by your side or at your feet, however close you'd let me get. No part would be too small or too big, I would always want more of you. I want whatever you are willing to give me. I want everything you are and everything you will become, I just want you, Abby."

Her hand cupped my cheek. I exhaled and leaned into the warmth that I had become familiar with. Then ever so lightly, she leaned in, pressing her lips against mine. It was soft, there wasn't any urgency to the action, it was slow and achingly sweet. We moved in sync, her hand glided along my jaw until her fingers curled into the hairs at the base of my neck and then she pulled, hauling my chest into hers.

Every feeling that couldn't be put into words was poured into this one kiss. I wanted to get lost in her the way people found religion to be saved from the darkness. Abby was light, pure, un-filtered light that I would allow to guide me down whatever path she chose.

There are moments in life that you looked back on and realized they were life changing. This was one of those moments, no matter the outcome. I would never be the same. I was a better man because of her, and God, I hoped this wasn't the end. I hoped she wanted to keep me in her life.

She pulled back, breaking the spell her lips put me under with a smile. and after a moment of sitting with the weight of my words on our shoulders. "You love me?" She asked.

She stood at some point, her hair falling in soft waves around her as she looked down at me in my seat. "I do, more than anything."

"I've spent my life waiting to be loved, and then you came along and showed me that it wasn't love I was looking for. I wanted to be seen." Her fingers carded through my hair. "You see me, Kaiser, the good, the bad, the messy, can't bake, doesn't like to clean, is a little too into other worldly things, and you never batted an eye. You accepted every single part of me and made me feel like I was enough. I was never too much or not enough, you made me feel perfect when all I wanted to do was give up." She bent down, my hand still on her waist, our noses brushing. "And that's why I love you," she confessed and it felt like I'd woken up to a new life. A better life.

She squeaked as I pulled her into my lap. I slipped one arm under her knees, the other behind her back and dipped as I kissed her again.

I might never be able to convince myself I was good enough for her but for as long as I could keep her in my arms, I would do whatever it took to always be the man she needed. And that was enough.

FIFTY-THREE

Abby

For the longest time, I believed that love had to be loud. If it wasn't, how would you know it's there. If they yelled or were angry, that was fine, because if they could be that passionate about what I'd done wrong, then surely that meant they also loved me just as much as they wanted to control me.

Love needed to be shouted in order to be heard.

Love needed to hurt in order to be felt.

But it couldn't have been further from the truth.

In the month following the fight between Liam and Kaiser, it was the most peaceful I had felt in years. I no longer looked over my shoulder in fear that Liam was lurking around waiting for me. The tiny voices he instilled in my head that caused me to question everything I did and everything I loved about me had silenced for the most part. Even when they did rear their ugly head, they're quieter than they have been.

With the last flick of my wrist, I finished the final touches of my sister's birthday cake. I stepped back to look at my handiwork. Cocking my head to the side, I absentmindedly dragged my finger through the remaining frosting before popping it in my mouth. Kaiser took this exact moment to walk into the kitchen. I smiled around my finger before removing it and placing a quick kiss on his cheek.

"Is this going to be the one?"

"Yes, I finally know what it was missing. Lennon's going to love it." He handed me the pack of golden candles for the cake.

"What was missing?" he asked.

I paused with my hand over the sink as I tossed the spatula in to be washed later. "Wouldn't you like to know." He laughed his way out of the kitchen.

It was cinnamon.

It wasn't the prettiest, but I knew I nailed it this time. If not, I'd keep trying until I did. It was one of the last things on my list and to be honest I'd come to enjoy the process since.

Kaiser walked ahead of me as I balanced the cake on a platter and we both headed out to the backyard. Lennon only wanted something small for her birthday. She said the closer she got to forty, the less she felt like celebrating. It was Kaiser who suggested having everyone over for a BBQ, and I almost melted. An off key chorus of Happy Birthday rang out. Lennon threw her head back as she sat laughing in the patio chair looking around at all of us. Theo flanked her side, his hand clasped in hers and a look in his eyes that could only be described as love.

Carina was standing by the table next to Levi Decker. Lennon and I both were astounded when she let us know he was going to come with her for dinner. I knew there was something going on with them for a while, and after the incident at work, I thought for sure they would come out and let us know they were together, but Carina remained so secretive. And it was best to not pry. We'd get the full story from her one day but I was just glad she allowed at least one person close to her.

Once the last notes faded away and the slices were served, we sat on the deck of Kaiser's backyard until the sun sank below the tree horizons. It was more than anything I ever dreamed of, I had everyone I loved close.

The boys took the dishes inside leaving Carina, Lennon and I to ourselves for a moment. A phone chimed from where Lennon sat. Her brows scrunched inwards slightly while she stared at the screen, until her head perked up and caught my eyesight.

"It was mom, just wishing me a happy birthday," she said answering my unspoken question. She bit into her bottom lip before she tapped across the keyboard a few times. As she placed her phone back down on the table she said, to no one in particular. "Maybe next year, I'll be ready for her to come around."

There was no time to react before the door slid open and they all appeared again.

I looked out across the table and locked eyes with Kaiser. A small smile ghosted his lips and I knew we were thinking the same thing.

This life, these friends, meant everything, and it was just the beginning.

For far too long I swam in a sea of unforgiving waters, with waves that trapped me in a cycle that had me fighting to stay above water as my legs kicked wildly below the surface. I often wondered if the reason no one seemed to ask me if I needed help was because they never bothered looking below the surface. No one bothered to see me for everything that I was. I was so good at hiding my suffering that few people noticed and fewer tried to help as I slowly drowned in front of them.

Then came Liam and the life vest he threw me was weighted down with words of malice and feelings of never being enough. At its worst he held me below the surface with his own hands until the day I finally fought back and left. And for a while I thought that's all I would amount to—a woman who would never be good enough.

Someone who was destined to choke on water.

Until Kaiser.

He was like breaking the water's surface and sucking in that first breath of clean air.

There was no life vest from him, he jumped in and braved my hurricane at my side and when I was ready, he drained the water that had been weighing me down and coaxed me to my feet with endless love and words of comfort.

Kaiser taught me how to stand on my own, but that if I needed to, I could always lean on him.

There isn't enough time in this life for me to show him just how much I loved him, but I would spend whatever time we had together making sure he never doubted why I was here.

Because Kaiser felt like hope.
He felt like home.

Abby

ONE YEAR LATER

I WAS SEVEN THE first time I planned my wedding. My sister caught me making a veil out of toilet paper one day and instead of teasing me, she asked me what it would look like. With stars in my eyes, and no concept of a budget, I told her about midnight blue bridesmaid dresses on my friends and a mile long train of tulle as I walk down the aisle in a winter wonderland styled swanky hotel ballroom. But most importantly I'd have a husband who loved me and she would be by my side as my maid of honor.

My reflection moved side to side as the late June sun glinted off the white of my dress, through the window. My waist was cinched from the corset top before flowing out in a few less layers of tulle than I had once imagined. The comb of my veil was digging into my scalp, my toes pinched in my heels and I was becoming increasingly more and more agitated with every second that passed.

And for the life of me, I couldn't figure out why.

My wedding wasn't what I had planned when I was seven. It surpassed everything I ever imagined. It was as close to an average person could come to a fairytale from the moment he proposed and yet there was lead weight in the pit of my stomach.

The door creaked open and I flicked my gaze upwards toward the mirror. A smile spread across my face until I remembered he wasn't supposed to be here. My dress spun with me as I faced him while clutching the stems of my bouquet.

"Kaiser, what are you doing?" I whispered shouted and attempted to hide behind my flowers.

He clicked the door shut behind him and I registered him fully. His brown curls raked back just enough to give him a relaxed looked while in his tuxedo. My chest began to tighten as I watched his smile brighten the small dressing room I was waiting in as he crossed the room toward me.

He came to stop just inches away and stared. "I had to see you. I feel..." He didn't finish his sentence but the words formed in my mouth for him.

"Nervous?" I finished as I ran my hands down my dress until he caught it and pulled me in closer. "Are you nervous about marrying me?" The question spilled out without me thinking.

Years of being conditioned to expect the worse didn't just go away. I'd been better at accepting his affection but there were times where my insecurities still got the best of me.

He loved me, I knew this, but I needed to hear him say it.

"Nervous, yes, but not about marrying you. That will be the easiest part of today." He leaned his head in. "I just wish we could do it without all those eyes on us, that's what makes me nervous," he said with a small chuckle.

"You know I never needed all of this," I motioned around the room, but meant the wedding in general. "I would have been just as happy for a thirty minute ceremony at the courthouse. As long as I ended up your wife, that's all I wanted."

His fingers brushed the inside of my wrist in slow, steady motions. "You deserve to be loved loudly, publicly. I don't like being the center of attention but I do want everyone we love to know just how much I love you." He brought my hand up and placed a kiss to my palm. "I just needed to see you for just a second, that's all."

He smiled, kissed my cheek, then was gone.

When he asked me to marry him, it was simple and took me completely by surprise. I had been wandering aimlessly in the kitchen trying to put off cooking long enough to where we could order in. I was walking back into the living room when he asked. The words were simple. There was no fan fare or extreme display of affection and yet it was the most beautiful moment of my life and left me frozen in my tracks.

It was a normal Sunday night, and with four words, everything changed. It wasn't until I realized I hadn't answered that he got up and disappeared into the bedroom. By the time my mind registered his question, he returned. He stalked down the hall and dropped to one knee in the living room, a small black velvet box in his hands. He peered up at me with his blue eyes and I had never been more sure of anything in my entire life. The lid of the box tilted open and if I wasn't sure before, I quickly got there. Nestled into the cushion wasn't a simple diamond ring. Looking back at me from the box was a light pink, oval shaped stone, circled by small pearlescent circle stones and emerald cut diamonds around the bottom.

"I picked out the stones myself. Rose quartz in the center for unconditional love, moonstones for our new beginning, and because they represent stability and calmness which is what you are for me. And diamonds because you deserve them."

"How did you—"

"You remember that book you were reading in the bath, the week you stayed over?"

I nodded.

"I found it around the time I knew I was going to propose, I took it into the jewelry store on Main Street and I had this made. I knew it needed to be as unique as you and…"

I never let him finish his thought, and honestly I wasn't sure I even said word yes. All I knew was I felt chosen.

That was only six months ago, and in those months my sister, Carina, and I put together a wedding that seemed to live in the recess of my mind.

As if my thoughts could be heard the door opened again and they both walked in, my mother trailing behind them tentatively by a few steps. Our relationship had only gotten stronger since I confronted her. It's not perfect there are still times when my feelings for how Lennon and I were treated bubbled up to the surface but she continued to make an effort and that's what counted. She beamed at me from the doorway as Lennon fussed over my hair while tears filled her eyes.

Lennon's story with our mom was still being written, slowly but surely. Sometimes she joined us for lunches and other times she told me space was the what they needed. She might be doing it for me but there was a bridge being built and I, for one, couldn't wait for her to cross it. Their progress alone allowed for us all to be here, on my wedding day and I was overflowing with happiness.

"Is this everything you wanted?" my sister asked. I could no longer speak, but I nodded my head.

A knock at the door had all of our heads turning.

"We're ready for you," the wedding coordinator stated. Lennon and Carina both squealed and squeezed my hand.

My mom excused herself from the room with Kaiser's mom in tow to find him. A few minutes later the three of us were standing behind the closed doors that led into the venue which overlooked Wildflower Lake.

Music floated through the doors as my heart began to pound. The coordinator moved Carina into position to walk first but as she went to move Lennon I couldn't let her go. She looked back at me with eyebrows drawn inwards. The dusty blue of her dress bringing out the red of her pinned up hair. "What is it?"

"Will you walk with me?" I half whispered.

Her head tilted to the side.

"You are the most important person in my life, you raised me, I don't need to be given away, but I want you by my side until I reach him. Please."

She moved to myself and looped her arm in mine. "Of course, I told you if you called for me, I'd always come. I would do anything for you, Abigail."

The doors swung open and we watched Carina float down the aisle, her dark blue dress trailing behind her. Then the music changed, the guests rose from their seats and it was our turn. We slowly walked down the aisle as my hand grasped my sister's for support but all I saw was him.

The glass wall looked out over Wildflower Lake as the orange and pink sunset reflected off the water. Kaiser stood at the end of the aisle and all I could think was how freeing it was.

I had someone that encouraged me to be my authentic self and for that I would always be thankful.

My sister squeezed my arm and I began my walk to my forever.

Kaiser didn't let go of my hand since I placed it in his at the start of the ceremony. And for the first time since we met, he spent the entire day smiling. We were talking to the table that had a few of Kaiser's military friends when the coordinator came by to tell us it was time for our first dance. As we excused ourselves and walked toward the dance floor, he turned to me with a sheepish look on his face.

"You didn't think I forgot, did you?" he asked as he held out one of his hands for me to take as we approached the dance floor.

I placed my hand in his. "Forget what?"

"The last thing on your bucket list. Just follow me."

His other hand came up behind me to rest gently on my back as he pulled me in a bit closer. Then the music started and I was being spun around more gracefully than I ever thought he could move.

"Step back with your left foot, now to the side with your right." He was watching our feet as he slowed down.

"What are we doing?" I laugh.

"A waltz, obviously."

I almost stopped dancing altogether at his words. "You learned to waltz? For me?"

"I learned to waltz for you. A viennese waltz to be exact."

The urge was overwhelming, I stopped and threw both my arms around his neck and crushed his lips against mine. Our friends and family cheered around us and the sound of silverware clinking against glass filled the air as I lost myself in this moment.

We broke apart and I placed one hand back into his and the other on his shoulder. "Okay, I'm ready. Teach me to waltz, *Husband*."

It was choppy at first and I stepped on his toes roughly five times, but I always had been a fast learner. By the end of the music, he spun me one last time before pulling me in. We stood chest to chest while our guest clapped. My hand reached up to cup his face, before he kissed me.

"You'll have to make a new list now that you've done everything."

"That's okay, I'm sure there's a few more I can come up with." My head was already a running through a million ideas as we stood in the middle of the dance floor. "We have the rest of our lives, Mr. Price."

"We sure do, Mrs. Price."

I couldn't count how many times my knees had gone week over the names this man, my husband, has called me. Pretty girl, Dimples, even the simple use of my name would turn my bones to liquid, but nothing compared to finally feeling like I belonged to someone, that they belonged to me.

That we belonged together.

Kaiser

SOME TIME LATER

My son waddled across the hardwood floor, screeching into the arms of his mother as she walked through the door. Without missing a beat, Abby swooped down and gathered him in her arms before pressing her mouth to his neck, blowing obnoxiously loud raspberries. He squealed, then screamed again, and again as his chubby little arms wrapped around her.

The day he was born, a cosmic shift occurred somewhere deep inside my chest. I said before that falling in love with Abby started as a small tug at the base of my heart. I assumed it would be the same with Fredrick, that it would be a slow climb for me to be comfortable in my new role.

I was so wrong.

There was no metaphor for what it felt like to hold my child for the first time, only that I had never felt anything more right.

Nothing in the world changed and yet it was as if I had opened my eyes for the first time and everything was new. Indescribable colors exploded behind my eyes, and when I finally focused, my whole life changed. Then came our daughter, with dark blue eyes like her mother and soft brown curls like mine, and I was finally whole.

Without realizing it, I'd spent years of my life with pieces of myself missing and it wasn't until I met Abby that I even bothered to notice or care. I was an unfinished puzzle only to find out my missing pieces simply belonged to other people. That small tug I felt with Abby had to be the first missing piece sliding into place, Fredrick another, then Juliet slid the last piece and finally I was a complete picture.

And it was beautiful.

I grew up squished between bricks, with nowhere to turn and certainly no relief in sight. No matter how hard I fought. So by the time I turned twenty-five and my situation hadn't improved, I knew I was destined for a hard life. A life that broke you down little by little with no sympathy. I thought that's what I deserved, that a man like me wasn't worth anything more than what I had to fight tooth and nail for. I accepted that.

And then Abby came and every rough edge of my soul softened, and I was finally enough.

Over the years, she has treated me with more compassion than I deserved. She flung open the door and exposed the room I hid my feelings in and showed me that I could feel and still be worthy of love and affection. Even the nightmares had subsided. Abby swore it was the fluorite she kept under my pillow, but I knew it was all her.

Feelings didn't make me a weak man, they made me a stronger person.

She gave me the space to be anything I needed. I could be soft after spending a lifetime trapped between bricks.

It was everything.

She was everything.

Acknowledgements

Never wake up from this dream please.

A second book, I can hardly believe this is happening. When I released Anything For You I thought there was no way I could top it, that I had one story in me and that was it. I told myself this over and over, even as I began drafting and writing Everything You Are, especially when I scrapped this book to start over, **twice**. Turns out I was way off and I have quite a few stories in me and I owe it to you, the readers.

Making fictional characters fall in love is my favorite past time and I am forever grateful that there are people willing to give me and my stories a chance.

My amazing editor Ellie, I don't even want to think about where this book would be without you. Actually, I do know where it would be, still on my desktop riddled with spelling errors and the same he said, she said dialog tags. Your knowledge and help have made it so I could publish a story I am insanely proud of.

Lily, I couldn't have done any of this without you. I'd count the ways I love you, but there simply aren't enough numbers. Thank you for never hesitating anytime I asked for help. There's not a single sentence in this book that you haven't touched and I am lucky, blessed, hell at this point I'd call it divinely favored, to have you in my life.

While this story is a work of fiction it's is based on very real situations I found myself in when I was far too young. Nobody's words should define your worth, so if you read this story and parts feel a little too familiar please do not hesitate to ask for help.

National Domestic Violence Hotline
A confidential, toll-free hotline, text messaging, and online chat service that's available 24/7
Phone: (800) 799-7233
Text: START to 88788
Chat: Chat online at https://www.thehotline.org/get-help/

For all our service women and men, you have my heartfelt gratitude for the sacrifice you put forth to make it possible for us to live the lives we want. But that does not mean you should suffer in silence.

Veterans Crisis Line
A confidential, toll-free hotline, text messaging, and online chat service that's available 24/7
Phone: Dial 988 and press 1

Text: Text 838255

Chat: Chat online at veteranscrisisline.net/chat

This story was as much for my own healing as it is an open love letter to my husband. When I first started writing he continually asked if my stories were about him. My answer was always no.

Until now.

Richard, you have this uncanny ability to love me so effortlessly that I forget there was ever a time before you. That there was a time where I was forced to be someone I couldn't recognize and one I didn't even like. For almost fifteen years, you have dedicated your life to loving me regardless of everything this world sent to break me. You found me at my lowest when all I had to offer was a broken and tattered soul and instead of seeing me as damaged, you loved me enough to fill in cracks you didn't cause. You loved me through times where all I did was hate myself, reminded me that I am perfect the way I am. That no part of me will ever be too much or not enough for you. As always, I love you to the edge of the universe

My incredible family and friends, you never cease to amaze me with the amount of love and support you offer me. My dreams, these books would be nowhere, I would be nowhere, if not for all of you.

About the author

Brittney is a Northern California native who spends her nights crafting love stories. When she's not writing you can find her amongst friends deciding what game to play next, performing Taylor Swift songs to her unsuspecting husband, and binge watching period romance movies.

Instagram – @brittneylaurenwrites